SECURING SIDNEY

SEAL of Protection: Legacy, Book 2

SUSAN STOKER

CHAPTER ONE

Decker "Gumby" Kincade pulled into the veterinarian's office and couldn't help but smile as the woman who'd been following him as closely as she'd dared pulled into the space next to him. Her beat-up old Honda Accord had seen better days, but she didn't seem to notice or care that it was making a weird clanking noise.

By the time he had his truck door open, she was there.

"How'd she do? Is she okay? Was she crying?" The woman barked the questions at him, not giving Gumby time to answer the first before asking the second.

Sidney Hale was quite the contradiction. Her long black hair was in disarray from the fist fight he'd interrupted. She had a black eye forming, which just seemed to bring out the blue in her eyes even more. Her lip was swollen and still bleeding a little. The T-shirt she wore was torn and she had dirt on her jeans and hands.

But she obviously didn't care one whit about her own health; she had eyes only for the pathetic and hurt dog on the passenger-side seat of his truck.

Gumby shut the door and walked around the truck, Sidney right on his heels. "She did fine. Didn't hear a peep from her the entire way."

"Man, that's amazing. She's got to be hurting!" Sidney exclaimed. "I can't believe that asshole abused her like that. Are you sure this is a good vet? Maybe we should take her to the one I usually use."

Gumby ignored her as he opened the door and leaned in to gently pick up the bleeding and abused dog he'd named Hannah. Once again, the pit bull didn't try to bite him or otherwise show any aggression whatsoever. She *was* shaking though. "Easy, girl," Gumby murmured as he used his hip to shut the door of the truck.

As he walked toward the door, he looked at Sidney. "The vets here are great. Relax, Sidney."

She looked like she wanted to say something, but because they were at the doors, she rushed ahead to open them for him. He opened his mouth to tell the receptionist that he had an emergency, but Sidney beat him to it.

"We've got an injured dog here. We need to see a doctor immediately!"

The receptionist stood and gestured for them to follow her. Gumby was surprised when he felt Sidney's hand land on the small of his back, and she practically glued herself to his side as they entered the small treatment room.

"A technician will be here momentarily to get your information and triage your pet."

"Oh, but she's—"

"Thank you," Gumby said, interrupting Sidney.

When the lady had left, Sidney turned to him and frowned. "Why'd you cut me off?"

"The last thing I want is for them to think Hannah is a stray, or unwanted, because she's not."

Sidney opened her mouth to say something else, but a technician burst into the room before she could say a word.

"I heard we have an emergency. What's— Oh my!"

Gumby very gently placed Hannah on the raised table in the room and kept his hand on her head. "Yeah. It's bad."

"What happened?" the vet tech breathed.

"She was taken out of my yard," Gumby lied. "And we think the guy who took her was training her to be a bait dog or something for illegal dogfighting. He poured something caustic on her back, and it looks like she was dragged behind a car. Maybe he was trying to condition her and get her to run, but she couldn't keep up."

"Poor baby," the tech crooned, leaning over to pet Hannah.

The hackles on the back of the dog's neck rose and she growled low in her throat.

"Hannah," Gumby said in a low, hard tone. The dog immediately stopped and whimpered instead. "Sorry about that," he told the technician. "She's usually very docile, but we don't know what was done to her between when she was taken and when we got her back just now."

"Of course," the woman said. "It'll take her some time to trust again." She handed over a couple sheets of paper to Sidney. "I'll need you to fill those out and the doctor should be in here in a few minutes." She turned to Hannah. "Hang on, girl. We'll have you fixed up in a jiffy."

The second the woman left the room, Sidney turned to

Gumby and whisper-yelled, "Why'd you tell them she was stolen out of your yard? That was stupid."

Gumby ran his hand over Hannah's head and didn't miss the way the dog sighed in contentment and tried to crawl closer to him.

"What should I have said? That I just met the dog thirty minutes ago when you were in a fistfight with the asshole who had abused her? That you stole her from him? You think that would've gotten her treated any faster?" He went on before she could answer his rhetorical questions. "No. They would've wanted to know more details, and when we admitted that we know nothing about Hannah's history, they might've been reluctant to treat her at all. This way, she'll get the medical care she needs as soon as possible. Besides, I'm keeping her."

Gumby had been thinking about getting a dog for a while now. Ever since he'd almost died in Bahrain on his last mission. He'd always regretted not having one, and Hannah seemed to have been dropped in his lap. It was a sign—and Gumby was a big believer in them.

"We should go through the coordinator at the local rescue group I work with. I was going to bring her there. They get medical attention for the dogs that need it, and they do extensive background checks on potential adopters," Sidney told him.

"You do this a lot?" he asked.

"Do what?"

"Track down people you think are up to no good on social media? Then spy on them and, when they cross the line, take on men twice your size in order to rescue the animals they're abusing?"

Without blinking, Sidney said, "Yes."

It was Gumby's turn to be surprised. "Seriously?"

She nodded. "The animals are innocent. They didn't ask to be thrown into a pit to fight another dog. Or to be starved. Or to be chained up in a backyard for their entire lives. I'll take on whoever I have to in order to save a help-less, innocent animal."

"You ever gotten in trouble because of it?"

She grinned. "You mean do the low-life, abusive bastards turn me in? No. They're all too busy trying to protect themselves and stay under the radar of the cops to file complaints against *me*."

Gumby thought she looked a little too pleased with herself. But there was something in her eyes as she explained how she championed animals—guilt. And now he wanted to know why. Wanted to know her story.

His attention was diverted when the veterinarian entered the room. She was all business, and the next ten minutes were taken up with her examining poor Hannah and getting as much information as she could from Gumby...which wasn't much. He told her to do a full blood panel on Hannah, as he wasn't sure what had been done to her since she'd been taken. He wasn't proud of his lies, but if they helped get Hannah the care she needed and deserved, so be it.

The vet agreed that it looked like some sort of acid had been poured onto her back and that she'd been dragged. The dog had no toenails left and the pads of her feet had been worn off. It was the vet's opinion that her back looked worse than it probably was. She didn't think the hair would grow back, but she thought the wound should heal up pretty well.

When they went to take Hannah to the back to treat

her, however, the mild-mannered dog disappeared, and she began growling at the vet and her assistant.

Stepping back, the vet said, "Maybe you should come back with us. Just until we manage to get her sedated."

"Sedated?" Gumby asked.

"Yeah. Cleaning these wounds is gonna hurt, and I'd rather not harm her any more than I have to."

Gumby immediately nodded. "Right. Okay, we can come with you."

"I think just you," the vet said, giving her assistant a look Gumby couldn't interpret. "Your...friend can stay and fill out the paperwork."

"That okay, Sid?" Gumby asked, the nickname just coming out naturally.

Sidney nodded. "Of course."

"You think she'll let you pick her up again?" the vet asked.

"Only one way to see." Gumby leaned down and whispered to Hannah, "What do ya say? These nice people are gonna get you all fixed up. Let's not growl at them, okay?"

In response, Hannah lifted her head and licked Gumby's face with a loud slurp.

Everyone chuckled.

"Guess that means she's okay with it." And with that, Gumby once again picked up the large dog and followed the vet into the back area of the animal hospital.

Thirty minutes later, he went back out to the lobby and made a beeline for Sidney. Gumby was somewhat surprised she was still there. A part of him figured she'd bolt the second she was reassured the dog would be taken care of.

He couldn't help but feel a pang of...something...when

he saw her waiting for him. It had been a long time since he'd had anyone at his side when he'd had to deal with an emergency. Granted, he wouldn't even be dealing with this particular emergency if he hadn't found her fighting on the side of the road, but still.

"Hey," he said softly as he came up beside her and took a seat.

"Hey," she returned, and immediately handed over the clipboard with a piece of paper affixed to it. "I don't know your information."

Gumby stared down at the paper. She'd filled in the information she knew about Hannah, but the top part, where his address and phone number should go, was blank. He couldn't help but notice that her handwriting was beautiful. Neat and precise, nothing like his own.

As he turned his attention to completing the form, she said, "The vet tech asked if I was okay the second you were out of the room."

He looked at her. "What?"

"She wanted to know if I was safe, if I felt uneasy or threatened."

Gumby's fingers tightened on the pen he was holding. "She thought *I* hurt you?"

"Don't look so surprised," she said with a small laugh. "My lip is bleeding, my shirt is torn, and you're one hell of a big guy."

"I would *never* hurt you," Gumby said in a low, intense voice. He looked her in the eye. "I don't hurt women, children, or animals."

The smile left her face and she stared back at him just as intently. "But you do hurt men?"

He shrugged. "If they deserve it. Yes."

7

Surprised that she didn't ask for an in-depth explanation of what he meant, she only nodded and said, "I told her that we had to chase the guy who took Hannah. That I fell when I was running and busted my lip, and my shirt tore when we had to climb a fence. I don't think she bought it, but there wasn't much she could do if I said I was fine and that you hadn't hurt me."

Gumby brought his hand up to her face and gently ran his thumb over her bottom lip, where it had split in her earlier fight. "Are you really okay?"

"I'm okay," she whispered.

"Decker Kincade?" a loud voice asked from behind them, startling both Gumby and Sidney.

"Here," he said, turning to look at the receptionist who'd called his name.

"Just making sure you hadn't left," the woman said with a sheepish smile. "Take your time with those forms."

Gumby nodded and turned back to Sidney. "I'm about done here. I appreciate your help today."

"That's my line," she returned.

"You gonna give me your phone number so I can keep you updated on Hannah's recovery?" he asked.

She blinked, then retorted, "I think you have it backward. I think you should give me *your* number so I can keep *you* updated on her recovery."

"If you wanted my number, all you had to do was ask, Sid," Gumby teased.

She didn't smile. "I'm serious, Decker."

The grin slid off his face. "Hannah is mine," he told her quietly.

"That makes no sense," Sidney argued. "You can't tell me you had any intention of getting a dog before you found me. You can't make a decision like this at the drop of a hat."

"Come on," he said, standing, grabbing hold of her hand with one of his and pulling her to her feet.

"Decker! What are you—"

"Here are the forms," Gumby told the receptionist as he handed her the clipboard. "I still need to fill out my personal info, but I'll be right back to complete them." And with that, he towed Sidney out the doors and toward his truck.

Somewhat surprised when she didn't fight him, he stopped next to his truck. After he let go of her hand, Sidney crossed her arms over her chest and glared at him. Except, since she was only around five-two, it wasn't very effective if she was trying to intimidate him.

"I had every intention of getting a dog," he informed her, easily picking up where their conversation had stopped in the waiting area. "I own my own house, so I don't have to worry about any bullshit restrictions when it comes to what kind of dog I can have. I have a good job and I make plenty of money, so I can afford to feed her and make sure she stays healthy. I'm a good guy, Sidney. Why are you so opposed to me adopting her?"

He watched as the bravado slipped away and she sighed. Her arms dropped and her shoulders slumped. "I don't know you. I just met you a little bit ago. This isn't how adoptions work."

"Look at me." When her eyes met his, he said, "I'm gonna take good care of Hannah. She's gonna be spoiled rotten. I'll make a donation to the rescue group if that's what's bothering you."

"It's not the money," she protested. "We do background checks. Make sure adopters are the right fit for a pit bull."

"So do your background check," Gumby told her, confident she wouldn't find anything that would make her or anyone else at the rescue group feel like he wouldn't be a good dog parent.

"Really?" she asked.

"Really."

She gave him a skeptical look. "Most people don't like it when we tell them about the background check."

"I'm not most people," Gumby said, leaning toward Sidney as he said it.

Neither moved. Their faces were very close, and all he'd have to do is lean down a little bit more and he could take her lips with his own.

The thought was startling. He hadn't been interested in a woman in months. No, at least a year and a half...

Had it really been that long? Gumby tried to remember the last woman he'd gone out with...and couldn't.

But this battered, prickly, and confusing woman made him yearn for something he wasn't sure he could handle. With his job, he hadn't had the best luck when it came to women. His teammate, Rocco, might've found a woman who could deal with the fact he was a Navy SEAL, but it wasn't an easy thing. He was gone a lot, his job was dangerous, and he couldn't exactly tell a girlfriend or wife where he was going or even when he'd be back.

It would be hard enough to have a dog. A woman would complicate his life way more than a pet.

So why couldn't he stop thinking about how Sidney

Hale would taste? How easy it would be to lean down and cover her lips with his own? How she would look sitting in a chair on his back deck, watching the sunset over the ocean as they drank a glass of wine and watched Hannah frolicking in the sand nearby?

It was crazy.

But one thing Gumby had learned from being on the team was that he had to be flexible and go with the flow. Hell, it was one of the reasons he'd gotten his nickname. He'd always been that way. Never got ruffled with the curve balls life threw his way.

The team had also started calling him Gumby because one day, when they were in Survival, Evasion, Resistance, and Escape training, he'd been the only one of the six who'd been able to contort his limbs in order to break loose from his bindings.

"Now, will you please give me your number?" he asked.

"So you can let me know how Hannah's doing?" she asked.

"That too."

Her brow lifted.

"And so I can call you and ask you out."

She blinked. "Well, that's forward."

"Yup."

"Let me guess, women never turn you down and fall at your feet," she said, sounding exasperated.

"Actually," Gumby told her, stepping back, giving her space, "I haven't asked a woman out in longer than I can remember. I haven't been interested in anyone...until now."

"Why me?"

The second the question was out there, Gumby could tell Sidney wanted to take it back.

"Why you?" Gumby asked. "Because it's been a long time since a woman has impressed the hell out of me. I thought I was saving you from a beating, when in reality, you were doing just fine without me. The last thing I expected was for the fight to be over a dog. I'm fascinated by you. I want to know more."

"Oh."

She didn't say anything else, and Gumby frowned. Shit, she wasn't interested. He'd made a fool out of himself.

"Sorry," he said softly. "It's obviously been so long since I've done this that I'm losing my touch. I wasn't kidding about letting you do that background check though. I'm happy to do whatever adopters usually do so I can officially make Hannah mine."

Sidney put her hand on his forearm, and the skin-on-skin contact was oddly electrifying. She removed her hand almost as soon as she'd touched him, as if she felt the arc of connection between them just as he did. "I wouldn't mind if you called me," she said, then bit her lip. "I just… I'm not sure we're in the same league."

Gumby frowned again. "I don't think I want to know what you mean by that."

"I mean that you have your own house. That's impressive in California because real estate isn't cheap. And I live in a trailer that's seen better days. I don't have a college degree, and I only work for the trailer park on a part-time basis. You look like the kind of guy who has a perfect family, a perfect house, a kick-ass job, and you were probably voted most likely to succeed in your senior year of high school."

"Most likely to turn up dead before his twenty-first birthday, actually," Gumby told her.

It was Sidney's turn to frown.

"I don't give a shit where you live or that you haven't been to college. I know a lot of assholes who have a university degree who didn't learn a damn thing while they were there. I have never judged anyone by where they live, what job they do, or anything other than the kind of person they are. And from what I've seen in the time I've known you, I have nothing to fear from that quarter. If you just don't want to get to know me, fine, I'm not going to freak out or turn into some obsessed, scorned suiter. Just tell me. Don't make excuses."

Sidney stared at him a long moment before reaching behind her and taking out her phone. "Number?" she asked quietly.

Inwardly sighing in relief, Gumby gave it to her. He felt his phone vibrate in his own pocket, but didn't bother to take it out. "Thank you," he said. "I'll call you as soon as I hear from the vet later on today. She told me that Hannah would probably need to stay here for a bit, until the worst of her wounds heal. Then I can take her home."

"Okay."

"And, even though it might hurt my chances with you and your rescue organization, I have to admit that I don't know a hell of a lot about dogs. Will you help me?"

"You're really serious about keeping her?"

"Yes."

"Then I'll help you."

"Thank you." He turned to look back at the building before returning his gaze to hers. "Now I have to go in there and convince them I'm not beating you and that I'm perfectly harmless."

Sidney smiled. "I did see one or two employees peek out the window, probably making sure you weren't smacking me around out here."

Gumby's lips didn't even twitch. "Not funny."

Sidney rolled her eyes. "I need to get home and clean up anyway. I'm sure my boss has a list a mile long of things I need to work on this afternoon."

Gumby nodded and reached up toward her face. She didn't flinch away, not that she could go far with her back up against his truck. He gently brushed his thumb against the black mark forming under her eye. "Get some ice on that to try to stop some of the bruising."

"I will."

Forcing himself to step away from her, Gumby backed toward the building. "Drive safe."

"You too."

Then he turned and quickly strode for the doors to the veterinarian's office once more. With one hand on the door handle, he turned and watched as Sidney pulled out of the parking lot and merged into traffic.

Feeling as if his life had just made a one-eighty, Gumby couldn't stop himself from smiling as he made his way back inside to arrange payment and to make sure his information was on file for later.

Sidney might not think they were in the same league, and she'd be right. Gumby had a feeling she was so far above him it wasn't even funny. But he wasn't going to let her get away without a fight. It had been so long since he'd felt even the smallest desire to get to know a woman the way he wanted to know Sidney. She'd surprised and impressed him, and that was damn hard to do.

Just wait until he told his teammates that he'd gone from the quintessential bachelor to being a doggy dad—and maybe even being officially off the market—over his lunch break.

CHAPTER TWO

Later that afternoon, Sidney lay under a double-wide trailer as she messed with a leaky water pipe. She thought about everything that had gone down earlier, and it almost seemed as if it had happened to someone else.

She'd gotten very used to her life. It had a sameness that was, in many ways, comforting. Not very exciting, but comforting. How she'd ended up being a dog rescuer, she wasn't sure. It wasn't as if she'd planned it. But with her upbringing, she couldn't say she was that surprised.

"Hey, Sid! You under there?" a voice called out.

Smiling, Sidney said, "Yeah! Gimmie a second!" She finished tightening the connection and hoped that would fix the issue. If not, they'd have to replace the entire line, something she knew Jude would be pissed about.

Jude Camara was her boss and the owner of the trailer park. He was in his early sixties, but looked more like he was in his forties. He was big, buff, and tattooed. He'd given her a break when she'd first arrived in California, and Sidney owed him more than she could ever repay. Not in actual money, but because of all the help he'd given her over the years...including paying her to be the park's handy-woman. She'd learned everything she knew about plumbing, electricity, and basic home care from Jude.

Sidney crawled out from under the trailer and looked up at her neighbor. Nora was also thirty-two, but that's where the similarities between them ended. She was tall to Sidney's short. Had beautiful blonde hair to Sidney's dark. She was slender and proportional, and Sidney always felt dumpy and unsophisticated next to her. But Sidney also felt as if she had way more street smarts than Nora. The other woman was constantly jumping from one guy to the next, sure that each would be her ticket out of the trailer park.

Today, Nora was wearing a pair of jeans she looked like she'd been poured into, and a halter top that seemed as if it was one strong gust of wind away from exposing her boobs to the world. Her hair was extra teased and tall, and she'd done her makeup with a heavy hand.

"Hey, Nora," Sidney said as she stood and wiped dirt off her jeans. "What's up?"

"Jeez. What happened to your face?" Nora asked.

Sidney brushed off her concern. "Smacked it on the bottom of one of the trailers."

"Ouch. Anyway, I need your help."

Sidney wasn't surprised. Nora always needed help with something.

"I'm heading out to meet a guy I met on Tinder and was wondering if you'd be my wingman."

"Of course. You want me to text and if things aren't going well, you can pretend to have an emergency so you can leave?" Sidney asked.

Nora laughed. "Oh, no. Things are going to go well, I have no doubt about that."

"How do you know?"

Instead of answering, Nora pulled out her phone and clicked a few things before turning it so Sidney could see the picture she'd pulled up.

"That's how I know," Nora said with a smirk.

The guy on the screen was hot, there was no doubt. He was sitting on a Harley-Davidson and smirking. He wore a black muscle shirt that showed off his muscular and tattooed arms, but there was nothing about him that appealed to Sidney. It was as if the man was trying too hard. He was nothing like Decker.

That thought stopped Sidney in her tracks.

What in the world was she doing, comparing this guy to Decker? It was crazy. She'd just met the man today.

"He's good-looking," Sidney told her friend with a smile, trying to push thoughts of Decker Kincade to the back of her mind.

"Good-looking?" Nora asked in disbelief. "He's fucking *hot*. And I'm going to be in his bed this afternoon if it's the last thing I do."

Sidney chuckled and shook her head. Nora was nothing if not optimistic. "What do you need my help with then?"

"I told him that I had a roommate," Nora said. "I need you to call in about an hour and a half, and I'm going to pretend you told me we had a water pipe burst so I can't go home. I'll milk it so he'll feel sorry for me and let me stay at his place. Then I'll blow his...*mind*...so skillfully, he won't want me to leave anytime soon!"

Sidney didn't understand her friend's desire to sleep

with half the male population, but she didn't look down at her for it either. Nora definitely had the body to go with her sex drive. "You think he'll fall for it?"

"Oh, yeah," Nora said. "He's gonna take one look at this," she gestured to herself with one hand, "and fall over backward to get it."

"What does he do?" Sidney asked.

Nora shrugged. "No clue."

"Where's he from?"

Again Nora shrugged. "Here, I guess."

Sidney shook her head in exasperation. "Do you know anything about him at *all?*"

"I know he's got a Prince Albert and a big dick."

Sidney rolled her eyes. "I don't want to know how you know *that*, yet have no idea what he does for a living."

Nora smirked. "He sent me a picture, of course."

"Gross," Sidney said, wrinkling her nose.

"Oh, honey. We need to get you laid," Nora said sympathetically. "Because his Johnson definitely isn't gross. Not at all."

"I'm good, thanks," Sidney told her. "You have a condom?"

"A whole box, thanks, Mom," Nora said with a roll of her eyes.

"Good. And if you need me to rescue you because it turns out the picture he used on Tinder isn't really him, and he's actually an accountant who wears glasses, a pocket protector, and highwater pants, just call me. I'll go with the flow and say whatever you need me to in order to get you out of there."

"Sid, I don't care in the least if it's not him in the picture, as long as the picture he sent of his dick is the real thing. It's been a week and a half since I've gotten me some, and I'm due."

That was the other thing Sidney didn't understand. It had been three *years* since she'd slept with anyone and, frankly, her vibrator gave her three times the pleasure any man ever had. She didn't get the hype.

"Okay. You go and have fun. I'll call in a bit," Sidney told her.

"Thanks. You're a gem," Nora told her, then leaned forward and gave her an air kiss.

Sidney returned the gesture and watched as Nora strutted off. She had on a pair of four-inch heels and didn't seem fazed by the fact she was walking on uneven, rocky ground.

Looking down at herself, Sidney grimaced. She was covered in dirt from head to toe, and the one time she'd tried to walk in heels, she'd fallen flat on her face.

In many ways, she admired Nora. The woman didn't care that she used her body and face to get men to pay for shit. She didn't have a job, but she didn't need one, because men were constantly "loaning" her money. She wasn't a whore, didn't take money to sleep with men, but *because* she slept with them, they gave it to her. It was a thin line, but Sidney was the last person who would ever judge Nora.

She was kind, would happily share her last dollar if someone needed it, and always had a smile on her face. Yeah, Sidney liked her, and even envied her sometimes. She also had a great relationship with her family—something Sidney had never had.

Refusing to think about her family, knowing it would just lead her down a road she didn't want to travel, Sidney was about to grab her tool bag and head to the next job she had to get done when her phone vibrated in her pocket.

Pulling it out, she saw Decker's name on the screen.

Feeling suddenly giddy, she considered letting the call go to voicemail. But she was too curious about Hannah to do that.

"Hello?"

"Hey, Sidney. It's Decker."

"Hi."

"I wanted to call and let you know the doc called me back. Hannah's wounds looked worse than they were. She agreed with our assessment that she was dragged behind a car, which ripped out all her toenails and basically burned the pads off her feet. Those'll be wrapped up for a while so they can heal."

"And her back?"

"Her best guess is battery acid."

"God. People are such assholes," Sidney breathed.

"Yeah. Totally in agreement with you there. She cleaned her back and said the hair probably wouldn't grow back, but the damage wasn't as bad as it might've been if she hadn't gotten medical care so quickly. Apparently Hannah looks funny with half her back shaved, but she reassured me that the hair'll grow back quickly around the burn."

"Good. How long will they have to keep her?"

"She said probably only about a week or so. A lot depends on how she does once she wakes up."

"Right. I can call Faith, the lady who runs the pit bull rescue I've been working with, and she can pay for Hannah's treatment," Sidney told Decker.

"Nope. I got it. Just give me her number, and I'll call her and get the ball rolling on adopting Hannah."

Sidney bit her lip. "I haven't told her about Hannah yet."

Sidney was almost as surprised as Decker seemed to be, if his silence was any indication. Usually calling the president of the rescue group was the first thing she did after getting her hands on a pit bull. But for some reason, she hadn't this time. Some of it was because she'd once again broken the law in order to get Hannah out of that asshole's clutches.

But mostly it was because of Decker.

"You know I'm willing to do whatever's necessary in order to adopt her," Decker said after a moment.

"I know. But it seems as if it's just a lot of unnecessary red tape at this point. You want her. She likes you. Making you pay the adoption fee on top of what you're already paying the vet doesn't seem right."

"I feel kinda like a little kid whose mom just pushed him up on the diving board and told him to jump," Decker said with a laugh. "Will you help me figure out what I need to get for— Oh...shit."

"What?" Sidney asked, alarmed.

"My house. I'm in the middle of renovating it. There's shit everywhere. I can't bring a dog here."

"It can't be that bad," Sidney said. When Decker didn't respond, she winced. "*Is* it that bad?"

"I just...I live alone. And spend most of my time on my back deck. I haven't been in any hurry to get the house done. I bought it as a foreclosure and it needed a lot of work. Both inside and outside. But I got it for a steal. I figured I had boatloads of time."

"Do you want me to come over and take a look? I'm pretty handy."

The offer popped out before Sidney even thought about what she was saying. She bit her lip and closed her eyes. Shit, Decker was going to think she was totally coming on to him. He'd think she was easy, and probably take advantage.

"Seriously?"

Sidney opened her eyes and stared blankly at the side of the trailer she'd just been under. "Yeah."

"I'd love that." He sounded relieved.

"I'm sure a professional contractor would probably be a better bet," she told him honestly, trying to backtrack.

"I've got a contractor, but you're the dog expert. If you're serious, you can help me figure out what needs to be done immediately so Hannah will be safe here. Then I can call Max and get that done and work on the smaller shit when time permits."

"Okay."

"How about tomorrow?"

"Tomorrow?" Sidney asked in surprise.

"Yeah. I don't have a lot of time, not if Hannah is going to be released within the week," Decker told her.

"Right." Of course that's why he wanted her to come over so quickly.

"That, and I want to see you again," he added.

Swallowing hard, Sidney did her best to keep the butterflies in her stomach under control. It had been a long time since she'd felt this way about anything. Especially a man.

And Decker was one hell of a man. She'd noticed that he was good-looking; of course she had. But it wasn't until

Hannah had been taken to the back at the vet's that she'd really had time to reflect.

The T-shirt he'd had on pulled tight over his shoulders and biceps, showing off how buff he was. He had tattoos on his arms down to his wrists, all black, which was hot as hell. He also had a fairly full, neatly trimmed beard, which intrigued Sidney. She'd never dated a man with a beard before, and couldn't deny she was curious as to how it might feel to kiss him. Would the hair on his face be scratchy and annoying? Or would it be soft and tickle as his lips covered her own?

She closed her eyes and tried to get her mind back on track. She wasn't like Nora, didn't expect sex in return for doing him a favor, but she had a feeling a naked Decker would be absolutely beautiful—and almost overwhelming, next to her less-than-perfect figure.

"What time?" she asked, trying to get her mind out of the gutter.

"Whatever time is good for you," he returned immediately.

"Don't you have to work?" she asked, suddenly wondering what it was he did for a living. He'd certainly had time that afternoon to help her and take Hannah to the vet. He said he had a job, but maybe that was a lie? Maybe he *didn't* work. Maybe he was a trust-fund kid and lived off his parents' money...

"Yeah. But at the moment, my time is flexible. It's not always this way, but I might as well take advantage of it while I can."

She wanted to ask about his job, *so* bad, but decided it would sound rude. She'd ask tomorrow.

"Okay. How about two-ish? I need to help Jude out in the morning since I was gone most of today."

"Jude?" Decker asked.

Sidney thought she heard a note of jealousy in his tone, but that was crazy. "My boss."

"Hmmm."

"My sixty-three-year-old boss," she added, wanting to make sure he knew she wasn't in any way attracted to the other man.

"Right. I was that obvious, huh?" Decker said with a laugh. "Thank you for not playing games, Sid. Two sounds perfect. Do you want me to pick you up?"

"What? Why?"

"Because you're doing me a favor by coming to my place to help me. It's the least I could do."

"No. I'll meet you there," she said firmly. There was no way she was going to be trapped at his house without transportation. She'd just met the guy. She wasn't an idiot.

"You can trust me," Decker said, his voice having lowered. "I know how that sounded, but you have nothing to fear from me. To you, I'm harmless."

He didn't say he was harmless in general. Some wouldn't even note the distinction, but it was more than obvious to her.

"I'll come to you." The words sounded innocent in her head, but the second they came out of her lips, they seemed to have a deeper meaning.

"I'll text you my address," Decker said.

"Okay."

"Sidney?"

"Yeah?"

"Thank you."

"You're welcome."

"I'll see you tomorrow."

"Bye."

"Bye."

Sidney clicked off the phone and stared at it unseeingly. It wasn't until it vibrated in her hand that she shook herself out of the stupor she'd been in.

Looking down, she saw Decker had indeed texted his address. She brought it up on the map and inwardly groaned.

Of course he had a house right on the beach.

What was she doing? She hadn't been kidding when she'd said he was way out of her league. Someone like Nora could probably snare him in a second...but then she'd turn her back and walk away without a second glance, as well.

Decker Kincade didn't strike her as a ladies' man. He had a sincerity about him. A goodness.

And she should stay as far away from him as she could get.

She'd taint him. As sure as her name was Sidney Hale, she knew that without a doubt. She should go ahead and tell him who her brother was, get it over with.

But selfishly, she wanted a little more time to just be Sidney. To enjoy the strange connection she had with Decker...

Before he looked at her in horror and found a way to distance himself.

Sighing, Sidney shoved her phone back in her pocket and picked up her tool bag. She had shit to do, and thinking about the chocolate-brown eyes of Decker Kincade was not on the list.

CHAPTER THREE

Gumby paced.

Sidney was late. He wanted to call her, to reassure himself that she wasn't ghosting him. But he refrained. Traffic around Riverton was terrible. She was probably just stuck in it, and he didn't want to distract her by calling.

But he couldn't help the part of him that thought maybe he'd come on too strong. That she had absolutely no interest in him.

He didn't like feeling insecure. As a SEAL, he was always confident and optimistic. But Sidney had a way of making him feel as though he were a teenager hoping a girl would agree to hold his hand at lunch.

Running a hand through his hair, he paced. And worried.

Finally, around two forty-five, Gumby heard the distinctive rumbly engine of Sidney's Accord. He opened his front door and waited as she parked in his driveway and climbed out of her car.

When she was about four feet from him, she stopped,

looked up at him, and began to speak. Her words were rushed, as if she thought he would interrupt her.

"I'm so sorry I'm late. Jude asked me to stop over at old Mr. Cotter's trailer. He'd been complaining about low water pressure. He was right, he was barely getting a trickle out of his faucets. So I climbed under his trailer to see what the problem was and the second I touched the pipe leading into his trailer, it burst. I hadn't turned off the water yet because I was just doing some recon. I was soaked in an instant and, of course, the dirt I had been lying in immediately turned to mud. I had to scoot out, turn off the water, then go back under his house. The pipe was completely blocked by rust, which was what had caused the low water pressure, and also why it just disintegrated when I touched it. I swear it must've been as old as Mr. Cotter himself.

"I couldn't leave him without any water, so I had to get a new piece of pipe and patch it in as a temporary measure, but the entire line is probably going to have be replaced sooner rather than later. By the time I was done, it was already quarter to two and I had to go shower, because trust me, I looked exactly like the monster from that old campy movie, *Swamp Thing*, and then traffic sucked. I was going to call you and let you know I was running late, but I'd stupidly put my phone in my purse, which I threw in my backseat, and I didn't want to stop to grab it because that would only make me later. Are you mad?"

Gumby hadn't ever been *mad*. Worried. Upset. Unsure, yes. Mad, no. And by the time she'd finished her rambling explanation of why she'd been late, he was smiling. Of *course* she was late because she was helping someone else.

Even if it hadn't been her job, he had a feeling she'd never leave something half done.

Taking a step forward, Gumby didn't say anything. He simply pulled her into his embrace.

She stiffened at first, then slowly melted against him as if they'd hugged like this every day of their lives. Her cheek rested against his chest, and he could smell the fresh flowery scent of whatever shampoo she'd used wafting up from her hair. She felt even smaller against his body. It was hard to believe this slip of a woman had been physically duking it out the day before against the thug who'd been hurting Hannah.

Remembering the incident, and how she'd been injured, he pulled back and brought a hand up to her face. She hadn't tried to cover up her black eye with makeup, and he ran a thumb over the bruising on her face. "It hurt?" he asked.

She shook her head.

"Good. I'm not mad, Sid. I'm relieved that you're okay. That you weren't in a car accident on your way here and, more importantly, that you didn't decide I was a total creeper and there was no way you were you coming over to my house."

She chuckled and tried to step back, but Gumby didn't let go of her. If she'd insisted, he would've dropped his arms immediately, but the second she felt his grip not loosening, she relaxed into him once again. Her hands gripped his biceps and she looked up at him.

"I couldn't in good conscience let poor Hannah come to an unsafe house, now, could I?" she asked with a small smile.

Her answer was somewhat disappointing, considering

the direction *his* thoughts had wandered, but Gumby didn't let what he was feeling show on his face. "Right." He dropped his arms and took a step back, gesturing toward his door. "Ready for the grand tour?"

Sidney stopped him with a hand on his arm. "Decker, if I wasn't interested, I wouldn't be here."

He stopped and stared at her. He was pretty good at hiding his emotions. Had to be in his line of work. But Sidney had easily seen through him. It was disconcerting, but at the same time it was a relief. "I know I'm pushing," he told her. "And this isn't like me. But there's something about you that I can't resist."

"I'm nobody special," she said.

"And that right there is part of the reason why I'm so fascinated," Gumby told her. "You have no idea how special you are. Most women would've rescheduled the appointment with Mr. Cotter, but you didn't. And don't get me started on your compassion when it comes to dogs like Hannah."

Sidney shook her head. "Seriously, Decker. You don't even know me. Yeah, I like dogs, but that's not a reason to put me on a pedestal."

"It's more than that," he told her. "I can't put my finger on it, and I can't really explain it. But there's something that's drawing me to you like a moth to a flame."

"You're gonna get burned," Sidney told him.

Gumby knew she believed every word that was coming out of her mouth. Just as she had when she'd warned him yesterday that they weren't in the same league. He sensed she had some deep, dark secret...but he didn't care. Sidney Hale was a good person. He knew it with a sort of sixth sense.

He dealt with the worst of humanity on a fairly regular basis. He'd witnessed men strapping bombs onto their own flesh and blood and pushing the button to detonate those explosives in order to push their own agendas. He'd been lied to, spit on, looked down on, tortured, and shot by men and women who could probably blend right in here on the streets of Riverton if they tried hard enough.

But he'd looked into their eyes and seen the evil within.

One of the main things he saw when he looked into Sidney's eyes was pain.

Whatever demons she had may be locked down tight, but they didn't prevent her from helping out old men in her trailer park or helpless animals that couldn't fight for themselves.

"I've always been a bit of a risk taker," Gumby told her. He didn't reach for her, didn't brush the hair behind her ear as he wanted to. "The question is, am I the only one feeling the connection between us?"

She opened her mouth to answer, but he quickly talked over her, not wanting to chance hearing her say yes.

"Give me today," he pleaded. "Get to know me a bit more. If, after today, you don't feel the same pull toward me that I'm feeling toward you, I won't bother you again. I'm not looking for a pity date, Sidney. I'm too old for that shit. I want a woman who can't bear to be in the same room as I am without touching me, holding my hand, brushing her fingers against my arm. I want a woman who can stand up for herself when I'm not around, but isn't afraid to let me take charge when I am. I want a partner. Someone I can laugh with, but who I can also let go with, and have her take some of my burdens when I need to share.

"And I'm not saying you're that woman. But I *am* saying you're the first woman in a fuck of a long time to interest me even a little. But after today, if you only see us being friends, tell me. I won't freak out. Okay?"

She nodded.

Gumby knew he'd probably said too much, but he'd been honest. He didn't want to date someone just to get his rocks off. After almost dying in Bahrain, and then seeing how close his teammate, Rocco, had become with his girlfriend, Caite, he realized that he wanted what they had. Maybe Sidney wasn't that woman. But what if she was?

"Come on," he forced himself to say in a lighter tone. "I'll show you my house. But I warn you, it's a mess."

She smiled. "I'm sure it's not that bad."

Gumby winced as he opened the door for her. It was, but he'd let her see for herself.

Thirty minutes later, Gumby was staring at Sidney's ass as she knelt on his kitchen floor on her hands and knees, head hidden in the cabinet under his sink.

He'd wanted to impress her. Maybe convince her to sit out on his deck with him as they got to know each other better. But the second Sidney saw his kitchen—which was a disaster from the remodel that had been started but not finished because he'd been sent to Bahrain, and hadn't yet called the contractor back to complete the job—he'd lost her.

She'd demanded he tell her his vision for the space, and after he had, she'd started inspecting everything the contractor had done so far, telling him where she thought improvements could be made and what else needed to be done. She was currently inspecting the plumbing under his sink to see if the ice maker he'd wanted installed would be possible.

"Good news!" she called out, her words muffled by the cabinet. "I'm pretty sure it's doable!"

Gumby couldn't tear his eyes from her ass. He'd never really considered himself an ass man—or a tit man, for that matter. He just enjoyed women's bodies, period. They were all different. But mostly he just loved how they were softer than he was. He'd spent his entire life making sure his body was battle-ready, but he didn't want a woman who was hard like him. He wanted someone who was curvy and soft.

And Sidney certainly fit that bill. Looking at her ass as she shifted on her hands and knees in front of him made him revert back to a teenager looking at dirty magazines. He couldn't keep the fantasy of taking her that way from his mind.

She'd be on her hands and knees, just like she was now, on their bed. She'd look coyly behind her and shake her ass at him, urging him to hurry up and fuck her already. But he'd take his time. Drop to his knees behind her and eat her out that way. She'd fall to her elbows, tilting her hips up, giving him better access to her honey.

He was lost in his fantasy, even licking his lips, imagining he could taste her there, when she scooted out from under his sink, sat on her heels, and looked up at him. "Did you hear me?"

Blinking, Gumby realized his erection was practically in her face. She was at a perfect height to reach up and—

Shit.

Spinning around, Gumby rested his hands on the counter, trying to get his shit together.

"Yeah, I heard you. Great," he said quickly.

He heard her standing up. "Are you okay?"

"Of course. Are you thirsty?"

He felt her hand touch his back, and Gumby's fingers twitched with the need to spin around and haul Sidney into his arms. God, he hadn't been this horny in years. What was wrong with him? She was here to make sure his house was safe for Hannah. He was a pig for ogling her the way he'd been.

"What's wrong?" she asked. "I'm sorry I kinda lost it in here. This kitchen has such great potential, and I got carried away. We can look at the rest of the house now."

Gumby shook his head and didn't turn around. He felt every one of her fingers on his back as if she'd branded him. He both prayed she'd leave her hand there and hoped like hell she'd back away from him. "No, you're right. I was going the easy route, but I need to reevaluate, and the ideas you gave me are perfect."

"Decker?" she asked. "I feel as if I'm making you uncomfortable. Maybe I should go."

With that, he *did* spin around. So fast, she gasped and took a step away from him. She stumbled as she tripped over a stack of tile on the floor and would've fallen if he hadn't reached out and grabbed her around the waist.

He couldn't stop himself from hauling her close. He stared down at her for a long moment. Her black hair was in disarray around her shoulders, and the bruise on her face drew his attention. She had the most amazing blue eyes. They were like the ocean outside his back door right before it got too dark to see it...an amazing deep blue color that drew him in.

"You don't make me uncomfortable," he told her after a moment. He knew his erection was pressing against her belly, that she could feel it. She'd have to be completely clueless not to, and he knew she was anything but. "I like having you here in my space. A bit too much, if you know what I mean. I'm trying to be a gentleman and not freak you out, but I'm struggling."

"Oh," she said with a gasp, but didn't tear herself out of his arms. He hoped that was a good sign.

Taking a deep breath, and loving the way her flowery scent filled his senses, he let go of her and headed for the fridge. He took out a bottle of water and held it up. "Water?"

"Uh...yes please," she told him.

"Come on," he said. "I'll give you the rest of the tour and you can tell me what needs to be done immediately for Hannah. I have no idea if she's a chewer or not. I know I need to get an electrician over here to close up the sockets and shit."

Gumby forced himself to walk out of the kitchen. He heard her following. The next half hour was spent giving her a tour of his beach house and mentally cataloguing all the things she suggested. Basically, he was going to need to speed up the timetable on the renovation of his house. The last thing he wanted was for Hannah to get electrocuted because of stray wires, or to fall through the floorboards. He could shove a lot of the extra crap lying around into the guest room to deal with later, but after hearing Sidney's suggestions, he realized they were doable, and he could give Hannah a safe place to live.

When they were finished with the tour, he asked, "Want to sit outside on the deck?" He hoped like hell she'd say yes. Now that the tour was over, she could leave, but he wanted her to stay.

"Sure."

He held open the sliding glass door for her and gestured to the chair he usually sat in. She sat, and he settled himself in the not-as-comfortable chair next to her.

"This is amazing," Sidney said after a long moment of comfortable silence.

"It's why I bought the place. You should've seen it before I started fixing it up. It was a piece of shit. But I knew this view made the house."

"It does," she agreed.

Gumby took a sip of his water and stared out at the ocean. The property was tucked between rows of bigger, more expensive houses. Every house had a wooden walkway that led from its back deck down to the beach itself. There was about sixty yards of sand between the house and the ocean. They were located in a protected cove, so they never had any serious waves. At the moment, there were several families out on the sand, enjoying the late-afternoon sun.

"Is this a private beach?" Sidney asked.

"No. But it's hard to find and to get to," Gumby told her. "So it's rare that we get a lot of outsiders."

"Nice."

"Can you swim?"

She turned to him and smiled. "You could say that."

He crooked an eyebrow.

"I played water polo in high school."

"Ah. So not only can you swim, but you can beat the crap out of someone else in the process," Gumby teased.

Her smile grew. "Exactly. What about you? I'm assuming you swim since you own a house right on the beach."

It was that moment that Gumby realized how little he'd told Sidney about himself. "Yeah, Sid. I can swim."

She studied him, then asked, "Why do I sense there's more than you're saying?"

Deciding to just tell her and get it out of the way, Gumby said, "I'm a Navy SEAL."

Her eyes widened comically. "Seriously?"

"Yup."

"Well, shit."

That didn't sound good. "Does it bother you?" he asked.

She turned her head back to the beach and bit her lip.

"I love what I do," he told her quietly. "I work with the greatest group of men you'll ever meet. I'm sent on missions frequently, but it's rare that we're deployed for months at a time. This is my home base, and that makes me luckier than a lot of other military men and women. I know being with someone in the navy is tough, but I have a lot of role models who've proven that relationships can work." Gumby knew it was presumptuous of him to even be talking about a relationship with her at this point, but he couldn't stop the words from spilling out.

Sidney sighed and looked back over at him. "You're a good man."

He didn't answer, simply waited for her to continue. To get whatever it was that was going through her mind off her chest.

"Do you have family?" she asked.

"Yeah. My mom died about ten years ago, but my dad remarried a great woman. They live in Montana. I also have an older brother. He's married and lives in Illinois. I don't see him as often as I'd like to, but we're still good friends."

Sidney nodded as if she'd expected that answer.

"What about you?"

She took a deep breath, and then looked him dead in the eyes as she said, "My little brother is Brian James Hale."

Gumby's mouth fell open in shock at hearing the name.

"Yeah," Sidney said sadly. "I'm related to a serial killer."

CHAPTER FOUR

Sidney looked away from Decker, unable to stand the shock she saw on his face any longer. She'd been so excited —and nervous—to come to his house today. She was well aware that looking over his house to make sure it would be safe for Hannah was just an excuse. She felt the same connection that Decker mentioned. She wanted to get to know him better.

But she knew that getting to know him would mean telling him about her family. She refused to keep that part of her a secret from anyone she might want to date. The last thing she wanted was for him to find out later, when things were more serious, and dump her. It had already happened once.

So, after they'd toured his adorable house and sat on his porch, she'd known this was coming. She'd always found it was better to just be straight about her brother.

She heard his chair scrape along the deck and winced, assuming he was getting up to kick her out.

But to her shock, she felt him take hold of her hand.

Her head turned and she saw that he'd moved his chair closer to hers.

His brown eyes were focused on her face, and she couldn't look away. She held her breath, scared of what he was going to say.

"That has to be really tough."

Sidney blinked. People tended to react in one of two ways to hearing she was the sister of one of the most brutal serial killers the US had ever known. They either recoiled in horror, or they were almost *too* interested in hearing as many details as they could get out of her.

But no one—literally not one person—had ever reacted like Decker. Seeming to be more concerned about her than wanting to hear more about Brian.

She nodded, unable to speak if her life had depended on it.

"No wonder you're as amazing as you are."

Now *that* was a strange thing to say. Sidney was skeptical. "Why would you say that?"

"Because it's true," Decker said calmly. "I imagine growing up with him wasn't easy."

Sidney closed her eyes. He had no idea how "not easy" it had been.

The guilt that never went away threatened to overcome her. It had been a constant companion since she was a little girl. It didn't matter that she hadn't been the one to hurt others; it was there all the same.

Hating the way the guilt made her feel as if she were carrying around the world's biggest weight on her shoulders, Sidney tried to come up with a way to explain how she felt. How Brian's actions had scarred her for life. How, even if she were financially able to talk to a psychologist about her childhood and everything that had happened, she'd most likely *always* feel that guilt. Why she did stupid shit...

Like try to fight a man three times her size to save a dog like Hannah.

But Decker spoke before she could articulate any of her thoughts. "Men like Brian James Hale don't wake up one day and decide to start killing people. I imagine there's something wired wrong in their brains and, over many, many years, it festers and manifests itself a little at a time."

Sidney found herself nodding. She opened her eyes and stared at Decker. "It was hell," she whispered.

He scooted closer, and she had the urge to bury her face in his chest like a little kid. But she simply sat where she was, frozen. Both his hands gripped one of hers, and she held on to him as if he were a lifeline.

"I won't pretend to understand what you've been through, but I know one thing for certain—you're even stronger than I thought you were. Thank you for being honest with me."

She wasn't strong. She was so messed up inside, some days she wondered how she was able to function in normal, everyday life.

She pushed that aside. "Why aren't you freaking out? Why aren't you thanking me for looking over your house and kicking me out as fast as you can?"

"Are *you* a serial killer?" he asked evenly.

She shook her head.

"Then why would I kick you out? You aren't your brother, even if you carry some of the same DNA. You know more about renovating this house than I do. I'd be an idiot to kick you out when I need you. I don't know a hell of a lot about dogs and need your help there too. And besides all that, I *like* you. I'm attracted to you. I want to get to know you better. I want to watch you swim...I'll even race you." He grinned. "I want to find out what TV shows and books you like. I want to know what your favorite foods are, and if you prefer foam pillows or feather. Are you a bed hog or blanket stealer, are you a morning or night person?"

Sidney couldn't believe how he was reacting. It was like he didn't even care who her brother was.

Everyone cared.

"You aren't getting it. You have a loving family. You probably grew up without a care in the world. We come from very different worlds, Decker. I haven't talked to my parents since they decided to support my brother. I *still* don't understand how they could go to his trial and sit there day in and day out, hearing and seeing the evidence of what he'd done, and not disown him completely."

"He's their son," Decker said sympathetically. "I bet it was harder for them than you think."

"And I'm their daughter," she returned immediately. "They chose him over me."

"Explain."

Sidney was startled by the intensity of that one word. Without hesitation, she did as ordered. "I *told* them I was scared of Brian. Over and over, I tried to get them to understand something was wrong with him, but they didn't listen to me. Didn't care. After he'd been arrested, I told them I was going to testify against him. Tell the jury the things he'd done while growing up. They told me if I turned against my brother, that they'd never speak to me again. I did anyway. And they've completely disowned me."

Decker moved then. Got to his knees in front of her and put his hands on her face. Without thought, Sidney grabbed hold of his wrists. They stared into each other's eyes as he spoke.

"It's *their* loss," he said earnestly. "If they were too stupid to be thankful that their daughter was safe and unharmed, they don't deserve to have you in their lives. I don't know your history, but I'm assuming you moved out here to California without any support. You found a place to live, got a job, made friends, and are doing your damnedest to save animals who can't save themselves. That's fucking *amazing*."

Sidney couldn't do anything but stare at him and soak in his words. He didn't understand the motivation behind her need to rescue the animals, but at the moment, she didn't have the energy to explain it.

"Yeah, I had a good childhood. I admit it. But I don't give a shit that we had different upbringings. As far as I'm concerned, that makes us even more compatible, not less. We know what we want—me because I had it, and you because you didn't. You heard me say I was a SEAL, right?"

She nodded.

"I'm a mean son of a bitch," he told her. "I've killed people. Done it without remorse. I'll continue to do it. Some might say that makes me no better than your brother."

Sidney immediately shook her head. "It's not the same."

"I. Don't. Care. About. Your. Brother," he enunciated slowly. "No—that's a lie. I care about how he's hurt *you*. I

43

care about how he's shaped *your* life. And when you're ready to talk about it, I'm here. If you never want to talk about him, that's okay too. But please know that I'm serious when I say he has nothing to do with the two of us."

"People will talk," Sidney warned.

"Let them," Decker said immediately. "But if they dare say something to your face, I'm gonna shut that shit down."

Sidney couldn't stop the tears from forming.

"Don't cry," Decker pleaded. "Not over him." He wiped away the tears that fell down her cheeks.

"I'm not. I just...I don't understand why you're so adamant about protecting and supporting me."

"You will."

Sidney didn't understand his answer, either, but didn't get the chance to ask him to explain because the ringing of his doorbell sounded loudly from the house.

"Shit," Decker swore. He didn't make a move to get up.

"Are you going to get that?"

"No," he said.

But seconds later, the doorbell pealed again. This time, whoever was pushing the button was doing so impatiently and obnoxiously.

He sighed.

"I'm okay," Sidney told him.

"Don't move," he ordered as he climbed to his feet.

"I won't."

"I'll be right back. You want anything from the kitchen?"

"Are you gonna whip up a four-course meal in that disaster of a kitchen between now and when you come back from seeing what the person at your door wants?" she asked.

The smile that crossed his face was beautiful.

Sidney wasn't usually a morose person. She tried to look on the positive side of things, even when that was extremely difficult. She'd had her boohoo moment, but was ready to move on. Luckily, Decker seemed to understand.

"You have no idea what I'm capable of," he teased right back.

He leaned over, and Sidney stiffened in both anticipation and shock that he was going to kiss her. But instead of touching his lips to hers—as she was embarrassed to admit she was hoping for—his lips brushed her forehead, and then he stepped toward the sliding glass door and went into his house without another word.

Sidney swore she could feel her skin tingling where he'd kissed her. It was silly. But she couldn't deny that she liked Decker. A lot.

Seconds later, she heard a commotion in the house and looked through the glass door to see a group of five men standing in Decker's living room. They were all tall and bearded. They had a menacing air about them that didn't exactly give her warm fuzzies.

She could hear Decker arguing with them, but not exactly what was being said. It was obvious he wasn't happy with the men.

She stood and headed for the door, not sure what she was going to do to help him if things got ugly, but there was no chance in hell she was going to just sit on her ass outside.

As she opened the door, she heard the tail end of what was obviously a tense conversation.

"...not cool, guys."

"Come on, Gumby, we're curious."

"You've never, in all the time we've known you, talked about a woman with such enthusiasm."

"Yeah, and it's not like you were gonna introduce us anytime soon."

"Right, because I don't want you yahoos to scare her away," Decker said.

"We wouldn't— Oh...hi."

The man who was talking saw her before he could finish his sentence.

Decker immediately turned and walked over to her. He backed her up until they were once again outside on the deck. He slammed the sliding door shut and took her shoulders in his hands.

"Is everything okay? Do I need to call the cops?" she asked nervously.

Surprisingly, he chuckled. "I wish. But no. You have a choice."

Sidney leaned over and looked behind Decker into the house. All five men were staring at them, smiling, as if they were extremely amused about something. She supposed they were all good-looking in their own rights. The matching beards were an interesting touch. She'd gone from not thinking twice about men with beards to being surrounded by them.

Two of the men lifted their hands and waved at her.

She looked back up at Decker. "Yeah?"

"Those yahoos are my SEAL teammates. I told them about you and Hannah this morning at PT, and stupidly mentioned that you were coming over this afternoon to help me dog-proof my house. They've taken it upon themselves to come over to meet you."

She blinked in surprise. "Why?"

Decker sighed, and she swore she saw a sheen of pink appear on his cheekbones. "Because I might've told them a few too many times how amazing you were and how much I liked you."

"But you didn't even know me. Hell, you *still* don't know me!"

"I haven't talked about a woman in a very long time. So the mere fact that I was going on about you made them realize you're different. Important. Not to mention, Rocco and Ace know how much I've wanted to get a dog. And hearing how you were involved in me unofficially adopting Hannah, how you saved her, made them even more determined to meet you."

"Oh."

"So...your choice. I can distract them while you sneak around the side of the house and escape. Or the two of us can leave them here and go for a walk on the beach and hope they get bored and leave. *Or* we can go back in there and assuage their curiosity in the hopes that they'll leave sooner rather than later. But I have to warn you, if we go back in there, they'll probably want to chat like a bunch of women, and I'll most likely have to order something so they don't start standing in front of my fridge, gazing inside longingly in the hopes something will magically appear that they can eat."

She giggled, and Decker visibly relaxed.

"I know this isn't ideal," he said. "We were having a

pretty intense conversation and their interruption wasn't timely."

"It's okay. I was disgusting myself with how morose I was getting."

Decker's lips quirked upward, but he didn't quite smile. "You're always allowed to feel exactly how you feel," he told her seriously.

"Thanks. I think I'll take door number three."

"How'd I know you were going to choose that option?" he asked, more to himself than her. Then louder, he said, "If at any time they make you uncomfortable, just let me know and I'll kick them out."

"Okay."

"They're a little...um...rough around the edges," he warned.

Sidney smiled. "So am I."

"Seriously, if—"

She reached up and put her finger over his lips, stopping him from saying anything else. She shivered at the warmth of his skin on hers. "It's fine, Decker. Stop worrying. These are your friends. Your teammates. I'm not a delicate flower. I'm a handy-woman, for God's sake. I'm not going to faint in shock if they swear or something."

"It's a good thing," he muttered. "Okay. But before we go in there...I want to see you again."

She looked up at him in bemusement. Truth was that she wanted to see him again too. But she had a feeling he wanted to lock her agreement in now because he was worried what his friends were going to say. "Okay," she agreed.

"Yeah?" he asked.

"Yeah."

"I'm gonna hold you to that," he warned.

This insecure side of him was kind of cute. "And I'm gonna hold you to your holding to that."

He finally smiled. Without a word, he ran his hands from her shoulders down her upper arms to her hands. He squeezed them, then dropped one, but kept hold of her fingers with the other. He took a deep breath and slid open the door and led them both back inside his house to meet his friends.

CHAPTER FIVE

Gumby walked toward his friends, feeling nervous in a way he never felt when he was on a mission. He was the flexible one, the guy who went with the flow, but at the moment he was anxious as hell.

He wasn't concerned that anyone was going to hurt or upset Sidney. No way in hell would the men in front of him ever hurt a woman, especially not one their teammate was interested in. But the feeling of unease was there all the same, and it wasn't a welcome feeling. It was important to him that the guys like Sidney. They were a team. A unit. And Gumby knew as well as they all did that having a woman around who no one liked could hurt their closeness.

He hadn't been happy to see them at his door. It was too soon. He liked Sidney, and the last thing he wanted was for her to get freaked out by how close he and his friends were. Especially after learning about her brother.

That was a whole 'nother topic that he wanted to thoroughly research. He wanted to know what her childhood had been like, living with that psycho. He remembered only bits and pieces about Brian James Hale from the news, and now he needed to know everything about him...so he could find a way to make things better for Sidney.

But at the moment, he had to deal with his overexuberant friends.

"Sidney, I'd like you to meet the men on my team. Rocco, Ace, Bubba, Rex, and Phantom. I advise you to not take anything they say seriously."

She smiled up at him before turning to the others. "Hey."

"Fuck that," Bubba said, before taking a step forward and throwing his arms around Sidney.

Gumby tensed, but when Sidney didn't seem stressed about having a guy she didn't know hugging her, he tried to chill. He did keep his hand on the small of her back though, just in case he needed to pull her back and beat the shit out of one of his friends.

"We're kinda a hands-on group," Rex told her with a grin, pulling Bubba back with a tug on his shirt and enfolding Sidney in his own hug.

And so it went. Sidney hugged each one of his friends in greeting.

"So...you all have interesting names," she commented once Rocco had let her go.

"They're nicknames," Ace told her.

"And before you ask, we'd tell you what they mean, but then we'd have to kill you," Phantom said with a completely straight face.

Once again, Gumby tensed. Then was more relieved than he could say when Sidney laughed. Phantom had a

SUSAN STOKER

deadpan sense of humor. He was also the most standoffish one of the group.

"Right. Guess I'll have to mark 'be annoying until they break and tell me the meanings behind their nicknames' off my list," Sidney quipped.

Everyone chuckled, and for the first time since their arrival, Gumby completely relaxed.

"You guys had dinner yet?" Rex asked.

Sidney frowned and looked at her watch. "It's only like three-thirty."

"And?"

She smirked. "Let me guess. You're always hungry."

Rex patted his flat stomach as he said, "I burn a lot of calories. Need to keep myself fueled up."

Sidney rolled her eyes. Then looked sideways at Gumby before saying, "I should probably get going. You guys can hang out."

"No!" six male voices said at once.

Sidney blinked in surprise—then her lips twitched.

"Look. We see this asshole all the time," Rocco said, motioning to Gumby. "We came over to meet *you*. To get to know you."

"Oh, but...I'm really not that interesting," she protested.

"Guys..." Gumby warned.

"It's cool," Bubba said. "You're *more* than interesting. You're the first woman Gumby here has been attracted to for what seems like forever. Rocco got himself a chick, and Caite is awesome, so if Gumby likes you, we want to get to know you. So *we* can like you too."

Gumby shook his head and sighed. His friends meant

well, but they were idiots. Before he could say anything to try to salvage the situation, Ace spoke.

"We heard a lot about you this morning at PT. How smart you are. How you handle all the jobs at the trailer park you live in by yourself. That you've got beautiful long black hair and your eyes are the most amazing shade of blue." He grinned at Gumby at that. "We know you were single-handedly taking on a guy twice your size and didn't care about anything other than getting that dog help. So, of course we want to know more."

Gumby felt himself blushing. God, had he really said all that while they'd been working out that morning?

Sidney turned and studied him for a long moment. He refused to look away, even though he was embarrassed. He smiled sheepishly. "It's true. I might've bragged about you a bit to the guys."

"A bit?" He heard Phantom mutter under his breath.

Holding his gaze, she said, "I'm not familiar with this area. Are there any good pizza places?"

Whooping in delight, Rex pulled out his phone. "I got this. Anything you don't like on your pizza, sweetheart?"

Sidney still hadn't looked away from him. "No. I'm not picky. I'll eat whatever."

"Give me a second, guys," Gumby said, taking hold of Sidney's elbow and tugging her back out to the deck. He ignored the way his friends immediately started arguing about what kind of pizza to order.

When the sliding door shut behind them, Gumby put his hands on either side of Sidney's neck. His thumbs rested on her jaw as he leaned down. "Are you really okay with this?"

"Yeah."

"Because if you're not, I can kick their asses out, or we can leave them here and head to your place."

Sidney licked her lips, and Gumby couldn't help but stare at the way they glistened in the afternoon light. "You've known me one day, and you were saying all that stuff to your friends?"

Gumby nodded.

"Why?"

"Honestly?"

"Of course."

"Because even knowing you for only a couple hours, I knew you were different from anyone I've met before. And I couldn't stop thinking about you."

"I'm not sure how to feel about that."

"It's not a line, if that's what you're worried about. I'm not interested in a fling with you, Sidney."

"It's a good thing. I don't do one-night stands," she said quietly.

"Me either. I've enjoyed today."

"Me too."

"So we'll just go with the flow. Get to know more about each other. And as you might have noticed, my teammates are kinda a package deal."

She hadn't pulled out of his intimate embrace. Gumby could feel her hands resting on his chest, but didn't take his eyes from hers. His thumbs brushed lightly against the sides of her face as they talked.

"I think it's pretty awesome, actually. I wish I had friends like you do."

"Things between us work out, Sid, and you will. My friends are your friends. I think you'll like Caite too."

"She's with Rocco, right?"

"Yeah. She saved my life not too long ago."

Sidney frowned. "You mean, like figuratively, right?"

"No. Literally. Rocco, Ace, and I were in a situation overseas that we probably weren't going to make it out of alive, and in waltzed Caite."

"Holy shit."

"Yeah. She's got a core of steel, which is why I think you guys would get along."

"I wouldn't mind meeting her someday."

"Good. Now, you sure you're okay with hanging with my friends for a while? Whenever you want to go, don't be afraid to speak up."

"I'm sure."

"Okay. One more thing."

"What?"

Gumby leaned down and rubbed his nose gently against Sidney's. "This," he whispered, before his lips met hers.

Her fingers flexed on his chest, but she didn't push him away. He kept the kiss light, didn't try to deepen it, no matter how badly he wanted to taste her.

After he pulled back, she opened her eyes and grinned. "Marking your territory?" she asked with a small laugh.

He returned the smile. "Absolutely. I know those guys in there. If they think for a second there's a chance they can steal you away from me, they'll take it."

"I'm not interested in them," Sidney told him.

"But you're interested in me."

It came out as more of question than a statement, so Sidney replied, "Yes."

"Good. Come on. Let's get back in there before they decide to take on the rewiring of my kitchen themselves."

Her eyebrows shot up. "Would they do that?"

"In a heartbeat."

"*Can* they do that?" she clarified.

"Not without burning down the place," Gumby said with a chuckle.

Sidney turned and wrenched open the sliding glass door and stepped inside as she said, "Hands off, boys!"

All five turned guilty looks toward her from the kitchen.

"Step away from the electronics."

They held up their hands and smirked.

Sidney turned back to Gumby. "I'm assuming since you're a guy, and you're in the military, you've got some sort of shoot-em-up video game we can play to keep them out of trouble?"

"You assume right," he told her with a grin.

"You play?" Bubba asked.

"Guess you'll just have to find out," Sidney said.

"I want her on my team," Phantom declared.

"You don't even know if she's any good," Ace protested.

Phantom didn't take his eyes from her. "She's good," he predicted. "But any of you assholes who don't want to take the chance, you can be on the other team."

Within seconds, they'd broken up into two teams of three. Gumby didn't even care that he wasn't included. He was more than content to sit back and watch Sidney interact with his friends. He had no doubt that they'd like her. There was just something about her...something he knew the guys would pick up on.

A sort of vulnerability hidden beneath a bravado that was undeniably fascinating.

Three hours later, Gumby couldn't stop smiling. They'd

polished off half a dozen large pizzas, and his friends and Sidney had been playing *This is War* almost the entire time. As Phantom predicted, Sidney *was* kicking ass. They'd decided not fifteen minutes into the game to play against random people online instead of each other, which was probably a good decision. Sidney was a little bloodthirsty and ultra-competitive.

"Watch your six," Sidney warned.

"I see him," Rex told her.

"They're trying to sneak up on us from the left," Rocco warned.

"Fuck that," Sidney muttered.

His house might not be finished, but Gumby's living room was set up, if not completely done. The huge TV had six controllers attached and ready to go. It wasn't the first time the team had played the game together. In some respects, it improved their real-life missions. They practiced working together toward a common goal, even if was just a video game. The designer of the game was a genius. There were twists and turns and the scenarios were completely believable. Gumby had a hunch whoever it was, they had a military insider helping him or her.

He'd thought Sidney was cute before, but after watching her play with his friends for hours, he was even more enamored. And he knew the guys were just as enthralled. They'd come over to meet her, to make sure she was "good enough" for him...and he was pretty sure they'd come to the conclusion that she was *too* good.

"I'm taking a break," Rocco told the group. "Don't get us killed while I'm gone."

"You were slacking anyway," Ace mocked.

"Right? He was just standing around with his head up

his ass as we took out that last group of terrorists," Sidney teased.

Everyone laughed so hard, she had to reprimand them and tell them to keep their eyes on the screen.

Gumby followed Rocco to the kitchen. His friend grabbed a bottle of water from the fridge then leaned against the counter. The house was small, but it was easy for them to talk privately since Sidney was barking out orders left and right to the other guys.

"You're right," Rocco said softly. "She's pretty remarkable."

"You don't know the half of it," Gumby told his friend.

He lifted an eyebrow in question.

"You heard of Brian James Hale?"

"Who hasn't?" Rocco commented. "What about him?"

Gumby didn't feel bad telling his friend about the connection between the serial killer and Sidney. Partly because they shared everything, but also because it was more than obvious his friend liked and respected her.

"He's her younger brother."

Rocco's hand with the water bottle stopped halfway to his mouth, and he stared at Gumby in shock. "The fuck you say!"

Gumby nodded. "I don't have all the details, but I got the impression it wasn't good. She's estranged from her parents after they took his side over hers."

"He fucking killed over two dozen women," Rocco said in disgust. "That makes no sense."

"I know. She came out here to California without much money, no college degree, and has managed to land on her feet. And that's just the shit I've learned over the last day and a half."

Rocco nodded. "Well, she's not alone anymore."

"That's what I told her. Can I ask you something?" Gumby asked.

"Of course. What's up?"

Gumby looked into his living room. Sidney was hopping up and down in her seat, frantically fingering the control to the game and yelling at Bubba to kill whoever was shooting at her.

"How did you know that Caite was it for you?" he asked. "I mean, I know you were interested physically when you saw her in that elevator in Bahrain. But how did you know she wasn't just some chick you wanted to sleep with?"

Rocco put his drink down and faced Gumby. "I'm not sure I can explain it. Yeah, I was sexually attracted to Caite when I first saw her, but it was more than that. Her mannerisms, her shyness, the way she kept side-eyeing me but was too timid to actually talk to me. The way she didn't pitch a fit when the elevator got stuck, how she was polite to all of us in there, how she didn't hesitate when she had to climb out the top...it was just all of it. But one of the things that stood out the most was how I felt when I was with her. It's hard to explain."

"Hyperaware?" Gumby blurted.

Rocco looked surprised for a second, but then nodded slowly. "Yeah. That's as good a word as any. I worried about how hot it was outside, when she said she didn't like the heat. I worried about her boss, who was an asshole to her. I worried about the people on the base harassing her. The list goes on and on. Everything seemed to be about *her*. And I'm guessing it's too soon to have a discussion about sex..." He lifted an eyebrow in question.

Gumby nodded.

"Right, well, first off, it didn't matter to me when we made love for the first time. I would've waited as long as she needed to. In the past, sex was always in the back of my mind. How good would it be, how soon could I get it. But with Caite, that didn't matter. I just wanted to be near her. I would've waited years if that's what she needed.

"But, the second we got there, it was night-and-day different from any other woman. Hell, even kissing her was different. This is gonna sound lame but...you just *know* she's the one. I can't imagine ever kissing anyone else. And sleeping with them? No way in hell. She's the most important thing in my life. I'd do anything to keep her safe."

When Gumby didn't reply, Rocco asked, "Did that help? At all?"

"Yeah. I keep telling myself that I'm feeling things too soon. Or I'm feeling this way about her because it's been so long since I've been in any kind of relationship. That it's just the newness about it all. But then—"

His words were cut off by a whoop from the other room. They turned to see Sidney had leaped up from her seat and was doing a weird kind of victory dance. Shimmying her hips and pumping her arms in the air.

"Yeah, yeah," Bubba bitched. "Now sit down and help us get the hell back to the helicopter."

She giggled, but obediently sat. "Follow me, boys!" she crowed, then leaned forward to concentrate on the game once more.

"You were saying?" Rocco asked with a grin.

"But then she goes and does something like *that*, and I know the way I'm feeling about her isn't because I haven't dated anyone in a while. It's just her."

"Yup," Rocco agreed.

"What do I do if she doesn't feel the same way as me?" Gumby asked his friend.

"Don't give up on her," Rocco replied. "If she's meant to be yours, you have to work for it. Nothing good ever comes easy. You know that as well as I do. Obviously, if she doesn't feel the same way, you can't force her to, and you wouldn't want to be with her in that case anyway. But I have a feeling you're already in there. Move slow, get to know her and let her get to know you. Be honest with her. Communicate. If it's meant to be, then it'll work out."

"Thanks," Gumby told him. It was good to know he wasn't crazy. That the feelings he had for Sidney, even after knowing her such a short time, weren't absolutely off-the-wall insane.

Rocco slapped him on the back and grabbed his water bottle. He downed the rest and crumbled the plastic. "Now I need to go and make sure my team crosses the finish line," he said, throwing the empty water bottle into a recycle bin sitting next to the unfinished cabinets.

Gumby followed Rocco back to the other room and settled into his chair to watch his best friends conquer the video game world...all while following Sidney's every order.

Two hours later, Gumby stood on his front stoop with Sidney. The guys had left, after making Sidney promise to play with them again sometime soon. It was more than obvious they all liked her, and that the feeling was mutual.

He was feeling mellow and happy. His discussion with Rocco helped him not feel so stressed out about how much he liked the woman. He wanted to follow her home, make sure she got there safely, but even Gumby knew that would be a bit too much too soon. Though he couldn't help but think about a time in the future when she wouldn't leave. When they'd watch the sunset from his deck and walk hand-in-hand back into the house and to his bedroom. When he could fall asleep with her against his side and wake up to the same thing.

"I had a good time tonight," she told him, shoving her hands in her jean pockets.

"Me too."

"Sorry about taking over your game."

"Don't be," Gumby told her. "I loved watching you."

"I hate losing," she said sheepishly.

"You fit right in," he reassured her.

Sidney bit her lips. "I didn't do a whole lot of dog-proofing your house for you."

"It's okay."

"For what it's worth, I think you're mostly fine. You just need to make sure there aren't any boards with nails sticking up and that there's nothing Hannah can eat or drink that'll harm her. Having a dog isn't exactly like having a baby. You don't have to put protectors over all the plugs or anything. But with that said, you'll have to see if Hannah is the kind of dog who can open cabinet doors and if she's a counter-surfer."

"Counter-surfer?"

Sidney chuckled. "Yeah. She's a big dog. If she gets up on her hind legs to inspect what's on the counter...she could easily reach whatever's up there. And if it's food and she's hungry enough, she'll steal it. Counter-surf."

"Ah. Right. I'll watch for that. I still need to give you my info so that background check can be done on me," Gumby told her.

Sidney shook her head. "No. Don't. It's fine. I trust you."

Gumby couldn't help himself. He stepped into her personal space and leaned in close. "Do you?"

She nodded.

"But we just met yesterday. I could be a rapist luring you into letting your guard down."

"You're not," she said, but her voice wasn't exactly steady.

"But I could be," he insisted.

Sidney shook her head. "I wouldn't feel the way I do about you if you were."

Her words made the anxiety deep inside him settle. "Yeah?"

"Yeah."

"I still want to pay the adoption fee."

"Okay. But only because it'll help the rescue group."

"Text me the address and I'll send in a donation."

"I will."

"When can I see you again?" Gumby asked.

"I...I don't know."

"My friends liked you."

"And I liked them."

"Good. I'm sorry they interrupted today."

"It's fine. If I had friends as close as they seem to be, I would've done the same thing. They were just curious about me."

Gumby nodded. He couldn't resist touching her any longer. He brought a hand up and smoothed a lock of hair behind her ear. "It's really soft," he murmured.

Sidney bit her lip, but didn't respond.

Leaning down, Gumby nuzzled the side of her neck,

thrilled when she tilted her head, giving him more room. "And you smell so good."

"It's my lotion."

"I think it's just you," Gumby countered. He brushed his lips against the sensitive skin of her neck and loved the shiver that went through her body, which she tried to hide from him. Knowing he was pushing his luck, Gumby straightened. "I'll call soon."

"Okay. You'll let me know when Hannah is coming home?"

"Of course. Will you come with me when I pick her up?"

"Seriously?"

"Yeah."

"If I'm not working, then yes," she told him.

"I'll get with you and make sure whenever I pick her up works for your schedule."

"What are we doing?" she whispered.

"Getting to know each other," Gumby told her immediately.

"This is crazy."

"Not any crazier than using an app to meet someone," he countered.

She smiled. "True."

"Drive safe," Gumby implored.

"I always do."

"If you need anything, and I mean *anything*, you call me," Gumby ordered.

"I've lived on my own for a long time," she countered.

"I understand that. I know you're perfectly capable. Hell, you know more about household shit than I ever will. But I just want to make sure you understand that you're not alone anymore. You need someone to have your back while you check out an abused dog, you call me. You want to have a night out and not have to worry about anyone harassing you, you call me. You get bored and just want to talk to someone, you *call* me. Hear me?"

She stared up at him for a long moment before finally nodding.

"Good. I'm your friend, Sidney. As are all the other guys you met tonight. If I'm not around, you call one of them. If none of us are around, I'll make sure you have the number of my commander. It's important."

"Okay."

Gumby had the feeling she was agreeing with him simply to agree, but she'd figure it out sooner or later. She was now a part of his Navy SEAL family. And his family was there for each other no matter what.

He gestured toward her car with his chin. "Go on. Text me when you get home."

Sidney nodded and turned toward her car. Then she took a deep breath, spun back around toward him, and went up on her tiptoes. She grabbed his arms as she leaned in, and Gumby leaned down. Her kiss landed on the side of his mouth, and he didn't do anything to ruin the gesture.

She drew back, squeezed his arms, and stepped away. "Thanks for a great afternoon and evening."

"I had fun," Gumby said simply.

"Me too. I'll shoot you a note when I get home."

He nodded. "Bye."

"Bye."

She turned and jogged toward her car. Gumby stood on his porch for several minutes after her Accord disappeared from sight. He finally went back inside and stood at the edge of his living room, seeing his house in a whole new way. Everywhere he looked, he saw Sidney. Sitting on his couch. Standing in his kitchen. Hanging out on the back deck.

Today had changed him. He hadn't been sure exactly what he'd felt toward her before this evening.

But after seeing how easily she fit in with his teammates... Into his house. Into his life.

Gumby knew he'd found the woman he wanted to spend the rest of his days with.

Of course, there was no guarantee she wanted the same thing. He'd have to do whatever it took to make sure they were on the same page. As Rocco said, no matter how long it took, he'd be there while she made up her mind.

Sidney Hale might've had a hard life, but now that she'd met him, she'd find things were about to get much easier.

CHAPTER SIX

Sidney smiled when she looked down and saw the text she'd just received was from Decker. It had been a week since she'd seen him, been at his house, but that didn't mean they hadn't talked.

And Decker Kincade was a *talker*.

It was almost hard to believe.

He texted her all the time, but it was the phone calls that made her feel almost giddy. He'd called, like he said he would. And they'd talked for hours. Two nights ago, she'd looked at the clock and had been shocked to see that it was two-fifteen in the morning. She knew he had to get up at four-thirty to get to the naval base for PT. When she'd apologized, he'd said, "I'd forgo sleep any day of the week if it meant I got to talk to you."

It should've sounded cheesy. Like a line. But for some reason, it hadn't. He meant it.

Sidney had never come first in anyone's life. Ever. Brian was her parents' favorite. She was only three years older than her brother, but from the time she could remember,

Brian was always showered with more attention. He got more presents for his birthday and Christmas, her mom slaved over his Halloween costumes while she had to make do with what she could put together herself. Her parents' schedule revolved around Brian and his extracurricular activities, not hers.

And when she'd tried to tell them what Brian was doing in the shed in their backyard, they hadn't believed her. Had told her she was just jealous of her brother.

Pushing the memories of that shed out of her mind, Sidney read the text Decker had sent.

Decker: The vet says Hannah's ready to go home whenever I can come pick her up. What's your schedule look like?

Sidney immediately texted him back.

Sidney: I've got one more job to do this afternoon, then I'm free.

Decker: Awesome. I can pick you up around four? That will give us time to get to the vet before they close.

Sidney: I'll meet you there.

Decker: I can pick you up.

She sighed. One thing she'd learned about Decker through their phone calls was that he was stubborn. His protective instincts were huge. He'd told her a million times to be careful, to drive safe, and to watch out for herself over the last week.

Sidney: Deck, think about this. You aren't going to want to leave Hannah in your house to take me home. She's probably going to be in some pain, she'll be in a strange place, and if you leave her alone, she could get into trouble.

    Decker: She can come with me when I drive you home.

It seemed like he had an answer for everything.

Sidney: I'm perfectly fine driving home myself.

    Decker: Please?

She sighed.

Sidney: Fine.

    Decker: HURRAY!

Chuckling, Sidney rolled her eyes.

Decker: I'm gonna stop at the store to pick up some stuff for Hannah before I come and get you. Am I allowed to say I'm nervous about this? What if she doesn't like me anymore? I'm glad you're coming with me to get her.

．　．　．

She actually put a hand on her chest at his words. She really liked the fact that Decker was honest and forthcoming. It was refreshing. Oh, she knew there would be times she wouldn't appreciate it, like if he told her she looked fat in something she was wearing—not that he would, he wasn't that kind of guy. But still. Sidney quickly typed out a response.

Sidney: She's gonna like you. Why wouldn't she?

Decker: I don't know. I've just never had a dog before, even though I've wanted one. I promised myself if I lived through that shit in Bahrain that I'd get off my ass and make it happen, but now that it is, I'm scared to death.

Sidney: Stop panicking. Hannah chose *you*, Decker. Relax.

Decker: She did, didn't she?

Sidney: Yes. You have the list of things we talked about to get at the store, right?

Decker: Yeah. Sid?

Sidney: Right here, Deck.

Decker: Thanks.

Sidney: You're welcome. Now I have to go. Gotta change out the lock on someone's door because her stupid-ass boyfriend kicked it in last night.

Decker: You goin' over there with someone else?

Sidney: Relax. The guy's still in jail. It's fine.

Sidney: Decker?

Decker: For the record...I'm not happy.

．　．　．

Sidney couldn't help but smile. She knew perfectly well what he thought about some of the people who lived in her trailer park. But it wasn't as if she could help some but not others. And most of the time, during the day at least, most of the residents were either at work or sleeping off the night before. She felt perfectly safe working on the trailers during the day. It was only at night when she sometimes felt uneasy.

Sidney: It's fine. I'll see you at four.
    Decker: Yes, you will.
    Sidney: Later.
    Decker: Later.

As Sidney put her phone back in her pocket and headed for the trailer on the other side of the park from her own, she continued thinking about Decker. Being a Navy SEAL fit him perfectly. If she'd thought about it, she might've guessed that about him. She'd been fairly close to the base when she'd found Hannah, and he was built like she thought a Navy SEAL would be. Tall, muscular, and definitely menacing...when he needed to be.

His friends were fun. She'd been nervous at first, but playing the video game was a great way to break the ice. She was well aware that Decker had spent most of the afternoon simply watching her, but instead of making her uneasy, it had felt...good. She knew without a doubt that if any of his friends had gotten out of line, he would've taken care of it.

And while that was a good thing, it was also unsettling.

She'd never had a champion. Her brother had delighted in tormenting her, and never in a hundred years would he have stepped in if someone was bullying or otherwise threatening her.

Turning her thoughts away from her brother, Sidney decided to call Faith, the owner of the rescue group. It had been a while since she'd talked to her, and she needed to check in.

The older woman picked up after only one ring.

"Hi, Sidney, how are you?"

"I'm good. How are *you*?"

"Busy. We've been up to our eyeballs in abandoned animals. I swear I feel as if there's a memo that goes around to deadbeat dog owners that says to let their pets wander the streets on the same day."

Sidney chuckled. It wasn't really funny, but somehow Faith could lighten up even the worst situation. "I'm sorry I haven't been around much. It seems as if everything in the park has been breaking at the same time."

"I understand. I appreciate whatever you can do."

"Um…" Sidney hesitated to tell Faith about Hannah, because the other woman had warned her time and time again not to peruse Craigslist and Facebook Marketplace for animals. That it wasn't safe. And she knew her friend was right, knew she shouldn't be doing it…but she literally *couldn't* make herself stop.

Sidney was aware she might have a problem, that her behavior was a little self-destructive. But she convinced herself there were definitely worse things she could be doing. The dogs needed her help—and if she didn't help them, who would?

"What'd you do now?" Faith asked, interrupting Sidney's internal struggle.

"You know me," Sidney said, attempting to make her compulsion not seem like a big deal. "I couldn't help it! I accidentally saw a pit bull for sale and had to follow up. I swear I was just checking on the dog. He was abusing her, Faith, and I couldn't handle it anymore."

Faith sighed, but asked, "Did you get her?"

"Sort of."

"Explain," Faith ordered.

"I kind of got into a fistfight with the douchebag, but a guy saw us fighting and stopped to help. The asshole ran away, and the Good Samaritan helped me get the dog to a vet."

"How come I haven't heard about this before now?" Faith asked. "You know I need to be aware of this stuff as soon as possible so I can arrange funding. And the vet didn't call me with a new case. What's going on, Sidney?"

She sighed. "I know. The guy who stopped took Hannah to a vet near his house. And he wants to adopt her." She spoke even faster. "And before you yell at me some more, he's a good guy. I've been to his house, he really wants a pit bull, and Hannah totally adores him. He said he was going to send in a donation to the rescue, even though he doesn't have to."

The fact that Faith didn't say anything for a moment made Sidney nervous.

"Faith?"

"You like him," she said.

Sidney almost tripped over her feet as she continued toward the trailer where she had to replace the lock.

"No, I don't," she denied instinctively.

Faith didn't say anything again.

"Fine," Sidney huffed. "I do. But it has nothing to do with Hannah."

"You guys named the dog?"

"He did. Said she needed a nice feminine name. Are you mad?"

"No," Faith said immediately. "Well, not about the guy who wants to adopt her. That's the goal of the rescue, to find every single one of the dogs that make their way to us a home. I *am* upset that you continue to ignore my warnings not to chase after these assholes yourself. Honey, one of these days it's not going to go so well for you. What would you have done if this guy hadn't stopped?"

"I can handle myself," Sidney insisted.

"I don't doubt that. But dogfighting is big business. These guys make a lot of money. And if you get in the way of that, they won't hesitate to take you out. You *know* this. We've talked about it time and time again. You have to be more careful! You shouldn't be going after these guys on your own. Call me. Let me get my team to help. You know I've got the task force on the police department on speed dial. They're just as anxious as we are to end dog-fighting rings. They can move in within hours."

"Hannah didn't have hours," Sidney protested. "They'd dragged her behind a car or something, Faith. Her feet were bleeding and she had no toenails left. Not only that, but they'd poured battery acid on her back."

Faith sighed. Sidney relaxed a bit. She knew the older woman hated to hear about or see abused animals as much as Sidney did.

"Honey, if they could do that to a defenseless dog, what

do you think they'd do to someone who was trying to take their livelihood from them?"

Sidney didn't have a response for that. She'd called Faith because she wanted to hear a friendly voice, not to be lectured—despite knowing the woman was right.

Thoughts of her brother and the infamous shed came to her mind, but she pushed them back.

"No one else is there to care about the dogs," she said softly.

"I am," Faith rebutted immediately. "And everyone who works for me. You aren't the only one who can save them. But we can't do anything for the animals if we're dead."

Neither said anything, and Sidney stopped in front of the trailer she'd been heading toward.

Faith sighed. "Fine, I'll shut up for now. What's the latest on Hannah?"

"Decker is picking her up today. He's never had a dog, but had his mind made up that he wanted a pit bull when he did get one. Hannah is on the smaller side, all black. He said the wound on her back is healing up and eventually her toenails should grow back. He lives in a small house on a beach, and he's in the navy."

She heard Faith chuckle. "I asked about the dog, but it's nice to hear that your Decker seems to be a good guy with a house and a job."

Sidney mentally smacked herself in the forehead.

"Wait, did you say Decker?"

"Yeah, why?"

"Is his last name Kincade?"

"Yeah."

"That explains the amazingly generous donation that arrived earlier this week then. I was wondering."

"He said he was going to send in the adoption fee," Sidney told Faith.

"Yeah, well, I hope you aren't going around telling people it costs two thousand bucks to adopt an animal from us."

"What?"

"Yup. Received a check for two grand. It'll go a long way toward helping to pay for expenses this month."

"Holy crap," Sidney breathed. "I told him it was only a hundred and fifty dollars. He really sent two thousand?"

"Yup. I'm thinking I'm liking this Decker guy," Faith told her.

Yeah. The feeling was definitely mutual. But instead of thinking about how great Decker was, and how fast she was falling for him, she simply said, "I gotta go, Faith."

"Okay, honey. Let me know if you have any questions or problems with Hannah. I can call the vet if I need to and get updated on her case. But since she's not going through our official channels, I'm going to keep out of it as much as possible...unless either of you needs me. Make sure you give Decker my contact information. I'm happy to answer any questions he might have."

"Thanks, I'll let him know."

"It's been too long since I've seen you," Faith said. "Come by soon."

"I will."

"And bring your man along. Maybe Hannah too. I want to meet them."

"I'll talk to him," Sidney told her. She liked hearing Faith refer to Decker as "your man." That wasn't the first time she'd said it, and each time it felt more right. Which was crazy. They hadn't even known each other that long. But the feeling was still there.

"Be safe out there, Sid," Faith said. "I meant it when I told you not to take chances."

"I know. Later."

"Later."

Somewhat chastised, not sure if she felt better or worse after having talked to her friend, Sidney pushed the conversation to the back of her mind and headed for the front door of the trailer to get her job done.

CHAPTER SEVEN

Gumby pulled up in front of Sidney's trailer and turned off his truck engine. He hopped out and jogged to her door. The trailer park she lived in wasn't the worse he'd ever seen, though it also wasn't exactly posh either. But the trailers seemed to be well kept and the small grass spaces around them were, for the most part, mowed and clean.

He knocked on the door, nervous for some reason. He ran a hand over his hair, trying to calm down. Yeah, he was anxious to get to the vet's office and pick up Hannah, but he was also jittery because he was going to see Sidney again. They'd talked a lot over the last week, and every time he spoke with her, it was harder and harder to say goodbye. He hadn't felt so comfortable around a woman in...ever.

The last thing he wanted, however, was to be put in the friend zone. He didn't *think* he and Sidney were there, but he was nervous all the same.

The door opened, startling him. Gumby mentally

rolled his eyes. He couldn't remember the last time he'd been taken by surprise, he was usually always on alert.

"Hey!" she said, her blue eyes sparkling.

"Hi."

"You ready for this?" she asked as she turned and locked her door.

Gumby stared at her ass. She was wearing a pair of jeans, and the way they hugged her curves made his mouth water. The T-shirt she had on was molded to her upper body and the glimpse he'd gotten of her tits made him want to push her inside her house and forget all about dogs, veterinarians, and everything else.

She finished locking up and turned to him. "Decker?"

His eyes came up to hers, and he couldn't help himself. He stepped toward her, thrilled when she didn't back away from him, and curled a hand around the back of her neck.

"Deck?" she repeated.

He crowded into her personal space and could feel her hot breaths against his neck as she tilted her head back to stare at him.

"You look great," he managed.

Her brows came down. "I'm wearing a T-shirt and jeans," she said, telling him something he was well aware of.

"Yeah."

"Decker, I've been crawling underneath trailers all morning. I just jumped out of the shower like ten minutes ago."

He groaned. "Please stop talking about yourself in a shower."

Her frown turned to a grin. "Seriously?"

"Yeah."

"Why? Is it turning you on?" she teased.

Wrapping his free hand around her waist, he pulled her into him, hard and fast. She stumbled and let out an *oof* when she landed against him. The flowery scent he knew he'd always associate with her wafted up to his nostrils, and he inhaled deeply.

"Are you smelling me?" she asked.

"Yeah," he admitted without a trace of guile. "You smell delicious."

They stared at each other for a heartbeat, and Gumby could see her pulse hammering at the base of her throat. His fingers tightened on her nape, and he couldn't wait another second to taste her.

"Do I need to remind you that there are kids around here?" a female voice called out from behind them.

Gumby groaned.

Sidney giggled. She didn't try to pull out of his embrace, merely turned her head and said, "Like you care, Nora."

The woman standing there chuckled and leaned a hip against the front of his truck.

Reluctantly, Gumby let go of Sidney and stepped back. He glanced at the woman who'd interrupted them. She looked older than Sidney, but he knew that might be because of how she was dressed. She had on a mini skirt that would show off the woman's private parts if she dared to lean over. The heels on her feet had to be at least four inches and her blouse was basically a bikini top. She had blonde hair that was teased to within an inch of its life, surrounding the woman's made-up face like a big fluffy cloud. Gumby could also smell her perfume from all the way over where he was standing.

He shifted his hand to the back of Sidney's jeans and hooked a finger through her belt loop. It was obvious the women were friends, but he didn't want Sidney's fresh, clean, flowery scent to be overpowered by the other woman's perfume. There was no way he was going to let her go over and hug her friend. Nope. No way.

"Oh, I care, sugar. I care," Nora said. "Introduce me to your friend?"

Sidney looked up at Gumby and gave him a small smile. "Decker, this is Nora. And, Nora, this is Decker."

"Nice to meet you," Nora drawled, but didn't come toward him.

"Same," he said.

"Where you been hiding *him?*" Nora asked Sidney.

Decker grinned at the blush that turned Sidney's cheeks a light pink.

"I haven't been hiding him anywhere. We just met last week. Deck helped me with a situation with a dog."

Nora rolled her eyes. "You and those dogs."

The woman looked at Decker, and he could see the intelligence in her gaze. It was surprising—and he mentally berated himself for judging her based on how she was dressed. He knew more than most people not to judge a book by its cover.

"I hope you're getting our Sidney here to loosen up and have some fun," Nora said.

"I'm doing my best," he said.

"Good. Because she works too hard, and I haven't seen her with a man—or woman, for that matter—since I've known her."

Gumby liked that. It made him an asshole, but he couldn't help the satisfaction that coursed through him.

"Nora, shut up," Sidney said, taking a step toward her friend, but coming up short since Gumby still had hold of her jeans.

"Don't get your panties in a wad," Nora said. "All I'm sayin' is that you work too hard. You're always flitting around here doing whatever Jude tells you to. It's important to take some time for yourself...and I don't mean chasing mutts around. I've told you before and I'll tell you again, you need to get laid. Trust me, it'll cure what ails ya."

Gumby smiled when Sidney groaned. "Seriously, girl, shut it."

"What?" Nora asked not-so innocently. "Look, even though you've got questionable taste in clothing—I mean, who wears jeans on a date? Skirts allow for easy access...if you know what I mean. And you've got a smokin'-hot body. Curves in all the right places, a nice rack. And I'm thinking your man here knows his way around a woman's body and can definitely please you." She looked at Gumby. "Please tell me you *do* know your way around a woman's body."

He smiled again. Nora was certainly outspoken, but she seemed harmless enough. "It's been a while, but I haven't had any complaints."

Nora smiled huge. "See? A few hours with this hunk and your batteries will be recharged for sure."

"Kill me now," Sidney said, lowering her head and covering her eyes.

"Come to think about it...it's been a while since I've dated a man with a beard. And yours is nice and full. Bet it would feel awesome on sensitive inner thighs. Sid, if you're up for sharing, I'm always game for a threesome."

At that, Sidney's head came up and she narrowed her eyes at her friend. "Hands off, Nora. He's mine."

Nora smiled and held up said hands in capitulation. "I figured as much. Just wanted to see if you'd admit it. Have fun today. Don't do anything I wouldn't do."

"I'm not sure that's possible," Sidney mumbled.

Nora laughed. "True. I gotta go. I've got me a date." She winked.

"With the guy from last week?" Sidney asked.

Nora scoffed. "That asshole? No. He was married. I like me some cock, but I don't poach. I like my men unattached and hung like a horse." She eyed Gumby, her gaze lingering at his crotch. "You don't look like you have a problem in that area."

Sidney stepped in front of him. "Eyes to yourself, Nora. You know I love ya, but seriously?"

"Sorry, sorry, sorry!" Nora said. "Can't help it. You've got yourself a fine man there, Sid. You need any pointers, come see me tomorrow...but not too early. I have a feeling I'm gonna be *real* tired in the morning, if you know what I mean. I'll call you first thing."

"Be safe," Sidney called out as Nora started walking away.

"Always am!" the other woman called back as she expertly navigated the gravel driveway in her high heels and headed for a sleek convertible parked behind his truck.

When she got to the back of his vehicle, she pulled out her phone and took a picture of his license plate. She didn't look back at them afterward, simply got into her car and drove away. Gumby had been so focused on Sidney that he hadn't even heard the car pull up in the first place. He really was losing his edge.

"I think I'm embarrassed," Sidney said.

"Why?" Gumby asked.

She turned to look at him. "Seriously?"

He shrugged. "Yeah."

"Because my friend is basically a whore. I mean, she doesn't take money for sex, although she has no problem letting whatever guy of the week she's dating pay for everything from the hotel room to food and even clothes if she can get away with it. One guy she dated," Sidney put that last word in air quotes, "paid for her rent for an entire year, even though they'd stopped seeing each other after two months. Not only that, but she was pretty much eye-fucking you, she invited herself to have a threesome with us, told me I should be wearing a skirt so you could have easy access to my girly bits, and insinuated that I might be a lesbian!"

Because he wanted to touch her again, and he loved how she shivered under him when he put his hand on her nape, Gumby slid his hand behind her neck once more. "She sounds like she knows what she wants, and I like that she doesn't apologize for it. She's a good friend who's worried about you, she won't sleep with married men, and everything she said was with *your* well-being in mind."

Sidney stared up at him, obviously dubious.

"Am I wrong?" he asked.

She slowly shook her head. "Most people take one look at Nora and think she's a slut. That she's beneath them."

"She's not a slut," Gumby said. "She likes what she likes. I admire that. And she's smart. She was warning me not to treat you like shit and making sure I knew you had friends who had your back."

Sidney still looked skeptical. "No, she wasn't."

"Sid, she was. Telling you that she'd call you in the morning. Taking a picture of my license plate. Testing me to see if I'd jump at the chance for a threesome. She was doing everything she could to make me take the bait she was dangling—herself—to protect *you*. What would you have done if I'd agreed to her propositions?"

"Kneed you in the balls and shoved your ass off my doorstep."

"Exactly," he said.

She stared up at him as her friend's intentions sank in.

"For the record...I'm not into threesomes," he went on. "When I'm in bed with a woman, I'm completely focused on her. I'm not married, and I haven't compared the size of my dick to anyone else's since I was thirteen years old and in the middle school locker room, but I'm fairly sure you'll be satisfied. I agree with Nora that you've got killer curves, but disagree that these jeans you're wearing aren't sexy as all hell. I'll take you in jeans over a skirt any day of the week. Easy access isn't all it's cracked up to be. There's something to be said for anticipation."

"Wow," Sidney whispered as her eyes dilated and her breathing sped up.

Gumby ran his thumb over the side of her neck. "Have I thanked you for coming with me to get Hannah?"

"Yeah," she breathed.

They stood there gazing into each other's eyes for a heartbeat longer before Gumby couldn't hold back. He slowly bent toward her, satisfied when her head tilted back even farther and her eyes closed.

He brushed his lips against hers once. Then twice. On the third pass, her hand came up to his head and she tried to grab hold of his hair. It was too short for her to get much traction, but she pulled him closer to herself anyway and tilted her head. Her tongue came out and he opened for her.

Gumby couldn't help but tighten the hand around her nape as pleasure coursed through his body. He palmed her ass and pulled her flush against him, knowing she could feel his erection against her belly, and not caring.

How long they made out on her front stoop, he had no idea, but eventually their frantic kiss gentled until he pulled back a fraction of an inch.

Sidney was breathing hard, her tits brushed against his chest with every breath, and he could imagine how her erect nipples would feel against him if they were naked. His cock pulsed, and he knew if she put her hands on him, he'd probably blow in seconds.

Her eyes opened and Sidney blurted, "Your beard tickles."

He chuckled. "Yeah?"

She nodded. "But it's soft." She brought the hand that had been clutching the front of his shirt up as if to touch him, but hesitated at the last second.

"Go on. It's okay."

"I don't want to be rude."

"You can touch me anywhere, anytime, Sid," Gumby told her.

Her hand palmed his cheek, and he inhaled deeply when she stroked his beard.

"You like that?" she asked.

"Yeah," he told her honestly. He didn't like it, he *loved*

it. No one had ever caressed his beard. It was surprisingly intimate and sensual.

After a moment of her exploring his facial hair, she dropped her hand and smiled sheepishly at him. "Guess we should go."

"Yeah." As much as he liked kissing Sidney and having her hands on him, he knew they had to get to the veterinarian's office before they closed.

With one last caress of her nape, Gumby stepped away, hating the loss of her body heat against his. He grabbed hold of her hand and led her down the two stairs to his truck.

Sidney tried to compose herself on the way to the vet. She wasn't sure what had just happened. Nora had been...well... Nora. But now that Decker had pointed it out, she saw how protective the other woman had been. It was a good feeling. Nora wasn't exactly what someone would call a normal friend, but Sidney was closer to her than anyone else she'd met in California since she'd arrived.

They didn't hang out together. Didn't go out for drinks. But Nora was still a true friend.

And then there was Decker.

She hadn't planned that kiss, and she certainly hadn't meant to blurt out to Nora that he was hers, but both had felt right. Sidney didn't like the jealousy that had arisen in her when Nora propositioned Decker, or when she'd eye-fucked him.

And the comment about his beard was just out of line —but after kissing him and feeling the soft hair against her mouth and cheeks, she couldn't get what Nora had said out of her head. If it felt as good as it did while kissing him, having him between her legs would be fan-fucking-tastic.

Shifting in her seat and feeling her damp panties, Sidney knew she had to think of something else or she'd really embarrass herself. The last thing she needed was a wet spot on her jeans to announce to the world how badly she wanted the man sitting next to her.

Looking over at Decker, she saw the way he was white-knuckling the steering wheel and how tense his shoulders looked. There wasn't any traffic, so she assumed he wasn't nervous about driving.

"Relax, Decker."

He took a deep breath and let it out. "What if she doesn't remember me?"

"You've been visiting her this past week, right?"

"Yeah, I've been here a couple of times," he agreed.

"Then what are you worried about?"

He sighed again. "The vet told me that Hannah's been a bit aggressive in the last day or so. That she normally wouldn't recommend she go home this soon, but since she's 'not thriving' at the clinic—her words, not mine—that she thought it would be better for her to recuperate the rest of the time at home." He glanced over at her. "What if she can't get over what those assholes did to her?"

Sidney put her hand on Decker's thigh. He immediately reached for her hand and held on tight. "I honestly think dogs experience PTSD just like humans do. I think with lots of time and love, Hannah'll be fine."

He harrumphed, as if he didn't believe her.

"Decker, that dog worships the ground you walk on. If I hadn't seen it myself, I wouldn't have believed it. That's why I didn't protest you adopting her without going through the background check. From the second you came up on me and that asshole fighting, she couldn't take her eyes from you. She was hurting and scared out of her mind, but she let you pick her up. That doesn't happen very often. The dogs we rescue are typically very wary.

"Don't borrow trouble. If she has aggression issues, you can work with her. Show her that she can trust you. No dog's perfect. Maybe it's the cage at the vet's she doesn't like. Maybe it's the smell of the place. Maybe it's the other dogs. I just don't know. You'll have to learn her quirks as she learns yours."

Decker looked a bit more relaxed. "You're right."

"But, Deck, some dogs just can't be rehabilitated. You know that...right? They've been through too much. They've been treated horribly their entire lives and they can't trust."

He sighed. "Yeah. That's why I'm so worried."

Sidney squeezed his leg. "We'll just play it by ear."

She hadn't given much thought to what she was saying, but when he looked over at her and asked, "*We'll* just play it by ear?" she blushed.

"Figure of speech," she mumbled, trying to take her hand back.

He held on tighter. "I'm gonna hold you to that," Decker told her. "I have no idea what I'm doing. Obviously, if your reaction to all the shit I bought is any indication."

Sidney had to smile at that. She looked into the bed of the truck and shook her head at all the stuff he'd picked up at the store. It looked like he'd nearly bought out the place. Along with food and treats, he'd bought a bag full of toys, two fluffy dog beds, a bunch of leashes and collars, in addition to a ton of fleece blankets. There was a crate as well, although he'd told her he wasn't sure Hannah would like that, but he wanted to be prepared just in case.

"Hannah's one of the luckiest dogs I've ever met," Sidney said quietly. "She hit the doggy jackpot when you stopped to help us."

Decker nodded, but she could see that he was still nervous.

They pulled into the parking lot and Sidney hopped out, not waiting for Decker to come around and help her out. She grabbed his hand and he looked at her in silent thanks for a second before holding the door to the clinic open for her.

Within seconds, they were shown to an empty exam room to wait for the vet and Hannah.

Five minutes later, they heard a commotion behind the door that led to the back of the clinic. The door burst open and a vet tech backed into the room, practically dragging poor Hannah behind her.

The second the door shut, Decker went to his knees and reached for Hannah. The wound on her back looked much better than the last time Sidney had seen it. All four paws were wrapped in gauze, and the poor thing was trembling and growling low in her throat.

But the second she saw Decker, her entire demeanor changed. Her tail started wagging low and she got on her belly and crawled over to where he was kneeling on the floor.

"Come 'ere, girl."

Instead of just laying her head on his knees, Hannah literally crawled into his lap. Decker shifted and sat with his legs crossed, holding the fifty-pound pit bull close.

The vet tech stood above him, looking down in surprise.

Sidney put a hand on Decker's shoulder in support. Tears formed in her eyes at seeing Hannah so excited to see him. It looked like there was no place she'd rather be than right there in his lap.

The doctor came into the room—and stopped in her tracks when she saw her patient in Decker's lap.

"Wow," she exclaimed. "I knew Hannah liked you, but that's the most comfortable I've seen her since you brought her in."

"Has she been a lot of trouble?"

The vet tech laughed.

Even the doctor smiled. "Let's just say she's not that fond of being poked and prodded."

Sidney figured she was downplaying things. A lot.

The vet shook her head. "Seriously, that's amazing. I think we'll just leave her there with you while I show you her progress since the last time you were here."

And that's what they did. While Hannah stayed curled into a ball in Decker's lap, the doctor showed him how to clean the wound on her back, telling him not to worry if it still oozed a little blood and pus now and then, that it would help clean it out. Then she gently took one of Hannah's paws and unwrapped the bandage. The pad was actually regenerating already, and while the toenails had been worn down to nubs, the doctor said they would eventually grow back too.

Through it all, Hannah didn't growl or tense. Decker

kept up a steady stream of praise and calming words while petting her head and sides.

"Did you get her microchipped?" he asked when the vet had rebandaged Hannah's foot.

"Yes. You'll have to register it with the company. We'll give you the details when you check out. We also updated all her shots, as you requested. As you know, she was covered in fleas, and that's now cleared up. She does have heartworms, and we started her on the treatment for those."

"Will she die from that?" Decker asked, seeming to hold Hannah even closer, as if his arms alone could keep any chance of death from finding her.

"No. Dogs can die if the worms get bad enough, but it looks like we caught Hannah's case relatively early. She's got the deworming medicine, and we'll have to keep giving that to her, but eventually they should die out and she'll be okay. Just keep her calm, no strenuous activity for at least six weeks...not that she'll want to do much with those paws, anyway."

"I live on the beach," Decker said. "What about the sand, will that hurt her?"

"Keep her on the grass as much as possible for at least two weeks or so. After that, you can play it by ear. She'll let you know what she's ready for. If she does get sand on her paws, be sure to wash it off thoroughly. And no sand in that wound on her back. I don't know if she's a roller or not, but if so, you don't want the grains of sand being ground into her back."

Decker looked horrified. "No, I'll keep her out front in the grass," he said.

Sidney listened in amusement as Decker asked a

hundred and one questions of the doctor. Throughout it all, he stayed on the floor, his legs crossed, not moving an inch. She figured he had to be somewhat uncomfortable with Hannah's weight on him like it was, but he didn't even shift.

Finally, Decker seemed to run out of questions.

"You can always call if something comes up," the vet said gently. "I'm happy to answer any other questions you might have."

"I appreciate it," Decker said. "Sorry I took up so much of your time."

The doctor shook her head immediately. "I only wish everyone was as attentive to their pets as you are."

Hannah chose that moment to snore quite loudly, and they all chuckled. She'd rested her head on Decker's shoulder while he'd talked with the doctor and had obviously felt safe enough to fall asleep.

"Guess she's comfortable," Decker said sheepishly.

The doctor kneeled down in front of Decker once more and ran a hand over Hannah's head. "She hasn't gotten a lot of sleep while she's been here, but honestly, I haven't seen anything like this before."

"What?" Decker asked.

"She'd calm down when you came to visit, but each time you left, she was agitated and wary. She snapped at everyone, and we had to sedate her to clean her paws and her back. But with you here, she's as docile as a lamb. It's amazing."

"She probably just doesn't like the cage," Decker said.

The vet shook her head. "No. I don't think that's it. I mean, yeah, she's never going to be a fan of a crate, but I've seen this happen only a handful of times. And that's saying something, considering my line of work. You two are meant for each other. I don't know how to explain it really. Sometimes two souls just click...connect."

Decker turned his head and looked up at Sidney, and she swallowed hard. He couldn't be thinking that's what happened between them...could he?

Because that's what *she* was thinking. What were the odds that he'd be driving by at the exact moment she needed him?

She'd never really been overly interested in guys...until him. Now she already lived for his texts and phone calls, and when she'd opened her door to him today, everything inside her seemed to settle. She was always hyperaware of her surroundings and had a hard time settling down. But with him, she relaxed. Instinctively knew she didn't have to constantly scan the area, because he was there and would keep her safe.

Shrugging off the feeling, she smiled down at Decker. "She loves her doggy dad," she told him.

He smiled back, and the pride and love in his eyes for the dog in his lap was easy to see. God, Sidney knew she'd dream about that look tonight. About seeing it in his eyes when he was thinking about *her*.

"Help me up?" he asked.

Sidney nodded, not sure exactly how much help she'd be, but as it turned out, she mostly just needed to steady him as he unfolded himself from the floor and stood with Hannah still in his arms.

"She can walk," the vet said with a twinkle in her eye.

"I know. But she's tired. I'll carry her this time."

Decker strode out of the room with the pit bull in his arms.

Sidney started to follow him, but the doctor said softly, "Don't let him baby her too much. She needs to use those feet. I think it's harder for us to *watch* her try to walk than it is for her to actually do it."

"I won't."

"That's one lucky dog," she said, then nodded at Sidney and disappeared into the back of the office once more.

Sidney couldn't agree more.

Decker asked her to grab his wallet out of his back pocket, and she happily agreed, making sure to cop a feel as she removed it. He smirked, knowing she'd groped him a bit more than was necessary but not calling her on it.

It was fun to tease Decker, which was surprising. After learning he was a SEAL, she'd thought that maybe he'd be gruff and straight-laced, but that couldn't be further from the truth. If she hadn't seen him in "warrior" mode the day he'd chased off the asshole beating on her, she might not have even believed that he *was* a special forces operative.

Decker didn't blink at the bill, and Sidney was even more glad that it had been him who'd stopped to help. She knew Faith and the rescue group would've found the funds to help Hannah, but through Decker's generosity, they could now help another animal who needed it.

Before she knew it, Sidney was holding open the front door of his truck for Decker.

"You're sure you don't mind sitting in the back?" he asked for the third time.

"No, Deck. It's fine. Hannah would be crushed if she couldn't sit next to you."

He smiled sheepishly. The second he had Hannah settled in the seat, he pulled Sidney close. He wrapped his arms around her waist and buried his face in her neck. His beard brushed against her skin, and she shivered.

"Thank you again for coming with me."

"You're welcome."

He stood like that for a long moment, and just when Sidney was wondering what in the world he was doing, she felt one of his hands moving behind her. She turned her head and saw he was petting Hannah with one hand while his other was still holding her.

"Decker?"

"Yeah?"

"Are we gonna go?"

"In a second. I want her to know that you're with me. That you're important to me. That just because she's in the front seat doesn't mean she'll always get her way."

Sidney didn't know if she wanted to melt into a puddle at Decker's feet or snort and roll her eyes. She knew it wasn't that simple, especially with abused animals.

So she was shocked when Hannah lifted her nose and nuzzled at her back.

Decker turned her in his arms and stood behind her. Sidney reached out and ran a hand over Hannah's head. Decker twined his fingers with hers and ran them over the dog's side. Then he held their hands out for Hannah to sniff.

"See, girl? Sidney's with me. That means you can't growl at her or be mean. Besides, she's the one who saved you, not me. You should be loving on *her*, not me."

As if she understood, Hannah's tongue came out and licked at Sidney's fingers.

Delighted, and somehow not surprised, she laughed.

"You're gonna spoil her rotten," Sidney said, secretly

thrilled that Hannah seemed to like her. Maybe it was because she smelled like Decker. Maybe it was just because Decker was standing right there with her. But it didn't matter. Hannah was meant to be Decker's, just like he was meant to be her owner.

There were a lot of things Sidney was skeptical of. But fate was right there at the top of the list. She didn't believe that things were meant to be. Never had. Even with a brother who was evil down to his core, she still didn't think that his future had been set from the moment he was born. He'd been a happy kid. She could remember playing and laughing with Brian when they were little. She didn't know when he'd begun to change, but one day he was her happy-go-lucky little brother, and the next he was the scary little boy who gave her the creeps.

And even with all that had happened, she didn't believe life was predestined.

But standing there with Decker, being licked by a dog who by all rights should be a vicious, broken mess, she couldn't help thinking that Decker and Hannah were meant to find each other.

Turning in his arms, Sidney rested her head on his chest and hugged him to her.

"Not that I'm complaining, but what's this about?" he asked.

It was too hard to explain, so Sidney simply said, "I'm happy for you both."

"Me too," he said softly.

She felt him kiss the top of her head and she sighed in contentment. Then a second later, she let out a little screech when a cold, wet nose touched the skin at the back of her arm. Hannah had pushed up the sleeve of her shirt and was nudging her with her nose.

Laughing, Sidney pushed Decker back. "All right, all right. We're going." She looked up at the man she still had her arms around. "The princess wants to go home and see her new castle."

The smile on Decker's face was huge, and it made Sidney's breath stop. She'd seen him happy before, but right at that moment, he was *happy*. His white teeth gleamed in the afternoon sunlight and there were laugh lines alongside his eyes.

"Then by all means, let's get the princess home."

Sidney wanted to read more into his words, but she forced herself to let go of him and duck under his arm to open the back door of his pickup truck.

Home.

It had been a long time since she'd really felt like any place was home.

The house where she'd grown up had ceased to be a home the second Brian had made her dread opening the door. The trailer she lived in had never been a home, it was just a place for her to crash.

But thinking about Decker's house? Yeah, it was definitely a home...and it was more than dangerous for her to go down that line of thinking.

She strapped the seat belt on and sat back as Decker crooned nonsense to Hannah and drove them toward his beach house. Closing her eyes, Sidney lost herself in the sound of his voice.

CHAPTER EIGHT

It was dark outside, and Gumby knew he should take Sidney home, but the truth of the matter was that he didn't want to let her out of his sight. Today had been extremely emotional for him, and he was now feeling relaxed. Sidney was lying opposite him on his couch and Hannah was sprawled out on one of her two new dog beds, snoring. The vet had warned that he'd probably need to put the cone on Hannah so she couldn't lick her feet, but so far, every time she'd showed any interest in them, one word from him made her stop.

He'd ordered Chinese food for dinner and they'd turned on The Science Channel as they'd eaten. Neither was really watching the television, instead they'd talked. He told her stories about some of the missions he'd been on—without any top-secret details of course—and she'd talked about some of the dogs she'd rescued.

She told him how she'd gotten her job at the trailer park...she'd just moved in, and when one of the water pipes to her trailer had burst, she'd been in the middle of fixing it when the manager had happened upon her. He'd been impressed that she was able to take care of it herself and that was that. He had begged her to work for him. His last handyman had been lazy and preferred to sleep all day and party all night rather than actually work.

They'd talked more about Hannah and pit bulls in general. Sidney told him about Faith, the woman who ran the rescue group. Hours had passed before either realized, and it was obvious neither wanted to be the one to call an end to the night.

Gumby was slouched on one end of the couch as Sidney lay on her back with her toes stuffed under his thigh. He ran his hand up and down her shins rhythmically as they talked.

"The place looks great," she said after a beat.

"Thanks. Paid my contractor double to get the downstairs done."

She scowled at him. "You shouldn't have wasted the money. I would've helped you."

"I know. But trust me, there's still plenty of work to be done upstairs."

"I can help you with it, you know. I don't have any licenses or anything, but I know what I'm doing."

"Why don't you get them?"

"What? Licenses?"

"Yeah."

"Honestly?"

"Always."

"Money." She held up a hand to keep him from commenting. "I know, I know. If I invest in myself then I can make more money by hiring on with a contractor or something instead of doing the grunt work around the trailer park."

Gumby shrugged. "Then why don't you?"

"I never intended to stay here," she admitted, and his stomach clenched. "But then I met Jude and Nora and Faith. And one month led to another and after several years, I'm still here."

Gumby forced himself to relax. "What's holding you back? You could go to the community college and get a few certificates. I don't know anything about it, but don't they include the cost of the licensure tests as part of the class?"

Sidney shrugged.

"Talk to me, Sid," Gumby implored.

"I'm scared, okay?" she said defensively.

Gumby couldn't believe what he'd just heard. "What?"

"You heard me," she grumbled. "As a woman, the teacher would probably be extra hard on me. Besides, most contractors don't want a woman on their staff."

"You get shit a lot because of your gender?" he asked.

Sidney nodded. "I know it's hard to believe in today's day and age, but a lot of the tenants—male and female— don't like when I come to work on their shit because they claim I don't know what I'm doing. And in high school, the two times I took a shop kind of class, the teachers and my fellow students made it hell for me. I don't need that shit."

It didn't sound like she was scared, per se. Leery maybe, and Gumby couldn't blame her. He'd met some extraordinary women in the navy who probably would've made excellent SEALs, and even though the opportunity was now open for them to try out, he knew it was twice as hard for them as it was for men...and it was already pretty damn hard for *guys* to make it through all the training.

Leaning over, Gumby picked up his phone off the coffee table. He pressed a button and put the phone on speaker once it began to ring.

"Who are you—" Her words were cut off when someone answered.

"Hello?"

"Hi, Max, this is Gumby."

"Hey! How's it going? Anything wrong?"

"No, no, nothing like that. Everything's great. I appreciate you working so hard to get everything done. I brought Hannah home today, and she's currently snoring on the floor in front of me."

"Good, good. So what's up? You change your mind about me not starting on the upstairs right away?"

Gumby chuckled, but didn't take his gaze from Sidney. "No. I gotta sell a kidney as it is to pay for the work you've already done. But I do have a question for you."

Max chuckled on the other end of the line. "Shoot."

"What's your stance on having women work for you?"

There was a pause before the other man said, "You already know the answer to that."

"Humor me," Gumby told him.

"I hire anyone who's qualified to do the work. It's damn hard to find anyone, man or woman, who knows what they're doing these days. All I ask is that my employees show up on time and don't cut any corners. I want them to treat every job as if they're working on their grandma's house. Gender doesn't factor in. As you damn well know, since practically my entire crew was at your place over the last week."

Gumby *did* know that. He'd seen the guys joking and laughing with the females as they worked side by side to get his kitchen completed and finish up the rest of the first floor.

Sidney stared back at him, her face unreadable.

"Right."

"You got someone who needs a job?" Max asked.

"Needs? No. But she's of the opinion that contractors don't want to work with women."

"Fuck that. As long as she can handle the crude humor and cussing, she's more than welcome to work for me."

"I'll pass that along."

"You do that. And let me know when you're ready for us to start on your upstairs. I'm dying to get my hands on that master bathroom."

Gumby chuckled. His original plans had been to finish the master and his bathroom first, but making sure the entire first floor was safe for Hannah changed that. "You and me both," he told Max. "I'll call when I'm ready."

"Later."

"Later." Gumby clicked off the phone and put it back on the coffee table. Before Sidney could say anything, he squeezed her leg and said, "There's no way you can be scared of taking classes, Sid. The woman who has no problem tracking down animal abusers and confronting guys who operate dog-fighting rings can't be scared of a damn test. You heard Max, and I truly believe most reputable contractors don't give a shit what gender their employees are. They just want someone who is trustworthy and good at what they do. And from what I've seen, you're both. So...what's *really* up?"

Sidney sighed and looked at his ceiling. "I have dyslexia," she said quietly. "I suck at taking tests. I always run out of time, and I've failed way more than my share of the ones I've taken. I'm not smart enough to go to college, and with the kinds of tests I'd have to take to get my licenses, they might as well be written in Chinese."

Gumby's heart broke for her. But he was also pissed. "You have a learning disability, Sid. That doesn't make you stupid. Not in the least. And you can get accommodations so you have more time to take those tests if you need it. Didn't you have that in high school?"

She shrugged.

Gumby clenched his teeth. "Look at me, Sid." He waited until she met his gaze. "Please tell me your parents got you tested and made sure you had accommodations throughout school. Or that a teacher noticed you struggling and figured out the reason why."

She didn't say anything. Just stared back at him.

"Fuck," he swore. Then he dropped his hands from her legs and moved quickly until he was hovering over her. His knees rested on either side of her thighs, his hands by her shoulders.

She looked up at him in surprise, hands on his chest, eyes wide.

Gumby loved how her dark hair was spread over the decorative pillow on his couch. He wished it was the cream sheets he had on his bed, but he shook the thought away. He had a point to make and getting distracted by her lush body wasn't helping.

"Someday, I hope you'll tell me everything about your

childhood. I want to know every slight and every hurt you experienced so I can make it better for you. But, Sid, no matter what you think, you're smart, and I know you can pass those tests. I'm happy to go down to the local community college and help you get signed up. We'll make sure you get tested so you can get the accommodations you need. Needing more time to take a test doesn't make you less smart than anyone else, and I can guarantee Max wouldn't give a shit that you read slower than other people. All he cares about is if you can do your job."

When she didn't say anything, he leaned down until he was almost nose to nose with her. "Is this sinking in?"

Instead of answering his question, she said, "No one has ever stood up for me like you just did."

"Get used to it," Gumby told her.

She licked her lips, then moved. Her lips were on his, and she was demanding entrance to his mouth.

Opening, Gumby swallowed the moan she made as their tongues swirled and danced together. Her hands went to his waist and slipped under his shirt, making him inhale sharply. She kissed him almost desperately, and as much as Gumby was loving her touch, he needed to slow things down.

He fell to a hip and lifted Sidney up and over him, reversing their positions. He clamped her hips to his own, not caring that she'd feel how hard he was for her.

Her hair fell around their faces, tangling with his beard. Her hands stilled under his shirt, but Gumby could feel her fingers flexing against his belly. Reaching up, he shoved a hand into her hair and gently fisted it. Their kiss changed from desperate to intimate. She licked his lower lip, then the top. He followed suit, learning what she liked and what made her squirm with desire over him.

After another minute or so of kissing, she pulled her lips from his and pulled her hands out from under his shirt. She rested her head on his shoulder and sighed, her hot breath on his neck making his nipples go tight.

His hand relaxed in her hair, and he smoothed it over her scalp. Once. Twice. Having her against him felt so right. Nothing in his life had ever made him feel as relaxed and happy as having Sidney in his arms.

"I've been scared my entire life, Deck. I just try not to let it show."

"You don't have to be scared with me," he told her.

"I'm figuring that out."

Her words made him feel ten feet tall.

"Someday, I'll tell you how it all started."

"I'd like that." He didn't push her. Having her relaxed in his arms was enough for now.

Movement caught his attention, and Gumby glanced to his left and stifled a chuckle. "Don't look now, but we're being stared at."

Sidney turned her head, and he felt a laugh rumble up her chest, against his own. He'd never felt that with anyone else, and he immediately wanted to feel it again.

Hannah was no longer sleeping, but staring at the two of them on the couch as if she was trying to figure out what the two crazy humans were doing. When she saw them watching her, she pushed to her feet and gingerly walked over to the couch. Then she leaned in and began licking Sidney's face.

She screeched and giggled and tried to bring her hands

up to protect her face. Gumby began to laugh as well, and Hannah changed her attention from Sidney to him.

"Uncle, uncle!" he cried, and sat up with Sidney still clinging to him. When he swung his legs over the edge of the couch, Sidney stared at him for a long moment. They were as close as two people could be. Her legs spread over his thighs, their groins pressed together. Gumby refused to be embarrassed at how hard his dick was. He wanted her to know that he liked the feel of her against him. That he was attracted to her and wanted her.

"Thanks for a good day," she said after a moment.

"I think that's my line," he told her.

"Thanks for not looking down at Nora. She's a good friend...who just happens to like sex...a lot."

"I like sex a lot too," he told her with a grin. "But I'm a bit more selective than she seems to be."

"Me too," Sidney agreed.

Gumby glanced at his watch. "It's getting late."

Sidney nodded. "You gonna be okay with Hannah?"

He wanted to say no. Wanted to tell her that he needed her to stay the night just to be sure. But he knew she had to work in the morning, and so did he. The commander had warned them the day before that a mission was imminent, and he was going to have to be spending more time on the base getting ready. It wasn't an ideal time to get a dog, but between Caite agreeing to dog-sit when they left, and Sidney, Gumby felt as if he was covered.

"Yeah. I think we're good," he said, reaching a hand down to pet Hannah's head. She'd rested it on the couch next to Sidney's leg.

He stood, still holding Sidney, and she laughed and

gripped him even tighter. It was torture to walk with his erection, but he wouldn't've put her down for the world. Gumby carried her to the door, where he reluctantly removed his hands from her ass and she let her legs fall to the floor. Clasping his hands around her lower back, he held her to him for a beat.

"Wanna come over tomorrow night for dinner? And to check on Hannah?"

"Yes."

Gumby grinned. She hadn't even hesitated.

"But I'll meet you here this time. You don't have to come and pick me up."

"Scared of me talking to Nora again?" he teased.

"Damn straight."

"Text her when you get in tonight," he told her.

Sidney frowned. "Why?"

"So she knows I got you home safe and sound."

"But she's coming over tomorrow morning sometime."

Gumby nodded. "I know. But she was worried about you. Put her at ease and let her know I didn't kidnap you and dump your body in the ocean."

"Well, gosh, when you put it that way..." she teased. Then sobered. "You won't hurt me," she said with conviction.

"Damn straight I won't. But Nora doesn't know me from Adam."

"I'll text her."

"Good." He released her long enough to let her bend down and pick up her shoes, where she'd kicked them off when she'd arrived earlier. While she put them on, he laced up his own. Then he grabbed a leash and called to Hannah. "Wanna go for a ride, girl?"

With a happy, deep woof, the dog hobbled over to where they were standing by the door. Gumby leaned over and picked her up. "Get the door for us?" he asked Sidney.

She smiled and shook her head. "Rotten," she warned.

Without pause, he leaned over and touched his lips to hers. "There's nothing wrong with spoiling my girls." And with that, he headed out the door toward his truck.

CHAPTER NINE

The next week was a blur for Sidney. She sometimes met up with Nora in the morning to have coffee, which was a nice change in their relationship dynamic, as they previously didn't really hang out at all. She figured it was due to the other woman wanting to dig for details on her so-far nonexistent sex life with Decker, but since she liked Nora and she made her laugh, Sidney didn't even mind her nosiness. Then, after coffee, she did the jobs Jude had lined up for her. In the afternoons, she went over to Decker's house to hang with him and Hannah for the rest of the evening.

More often than not, she stayed later than she knew she probably should, especially since Decker had been looking more and more tired. Every time she told him she should go, he'd vehemently disagree, telling her that he'd rather spend more time with her and risk being a little tired.

Hannah was getting better by leaps and bounds. Her feet no longer needed to be wrapped and, while she still walked a little gingerly, she was showing more and more personality with each day that passed. Sidney hadn't heard her growl since the vet's office, and the dog seemed to be growing to love her just as much as Decker.

Today was one of the first days she'd had in a while with almost nothing to do. She'd completed an emergency repair on an air conditioner in one of the trailers, but other than that, she had nothing else on her list. Nora was hanging out at one of her boyfriends' houses and Decker was working at the base.

Sidney tried to remember what she used to do when she had free time, and was surprised to realize that most days, she'd stalked the Internet for abused dogs. Mostly Craigslist and sometimes Facebook Markets. That was how she'd found Hannah in the first place.

Feeling guilty that she'd let so much time go by without checking the ads, Sidney sat down at the small table in her trailer and pulled up Craigslist. She couldn't believe that she'd been so neglectful of the poor dogs who needed her. How had she let her obsession with Decker override what she considered to be her life's work?

She had to atone. Had to do whatever she could to help as many dogs as possible to make up for the ones she hadn't helped recently.

With a twinge, Sidney thought for probably the thousandth time about getting some professional help to deal with the feelings of guilt eating her alive since her teens. She knew she was obsessed with saving animals. Even knew why. But she couldn't make herself stop. She was far too willing to put herself, and sometimes even others, in potential danger if it meant saving a dog.

It was crazy. Hell, *she* was probably crazy...but the guilt wouldn't allow her to stop. And she couldn't really afford therapy, anyway.

Doing her best to shove those thoughts aside, Sidney continued to peruse the Internet.

It didn't take her long to find what she was looking for.

The same asshole who'd fought her for Hannah had put up a post saying he was looking for a pit bull for his daughter. He identified himself as Victor, and went on to say that it didn't matter if the dog was old or a puppy, he was desperate to get his sweet little girl whatever her heart desired.

It was all bullshit. Sidney was sure of it. She doubted he even *had* a daughter. It was more likely he wanted an older dog to serve as bait, and the younger ones he could train to be brutal fighters.

Her teeth clenched and her heart rate accelerated. There were a few comments on the guy's post, and she wondered if he'd already gotten more dogs for his nefarious activities.

There was only one way to find out.

She knew where he lived, of course; she'd stalked his house when he'd had Hannah. The thought that Victor might be treating another poor dog like he did Hannah made her physically sick.

She closed her laptop and headed for the door.

As she climbed into her car and drove out of the trailer park, she was surprised to realize that she didn't feel the rush or anticipation she usually did when she was on the trail of an abused dog. Yeah, she wanted to save another animal, but what happened last time was fresh on her mind. Decker wouldn't show up out of the clear blue to help her twice.

She tried to push down her misgivings. She could do this. *Had* done this at least a hundred times before. She couldn't let this guy torture an innocent animal.

She'd seen enough of that to last her a lifetime.

The area she was headed to wasn't the best part of town, but it wasn't the worst either. She had no idea why Victor's neighbors hadn't turned him in before now. Surely they'd seen Hannah in his backyard like she had. Did they just not want to get involved? Maybe afraid of Victor? Or were they truly all heartless?

She pulled over a couple houses down from Victor's place and sat there for a long moment. She was pissed at herself for even needing those few extra minutes. Two weeks ago, she wouldn't have hesitated.

But for some reason, everything was different now. She wasn't sure if it was her conversation with Faith or because she had more to lose. Things with Decker were going amazingly well. She really liked him, and honestly believed that he had true feelings for her too. She'd never been in such an intense relationship before...and they hadn't even done more than make out on his couch.

Sidney had a feeling that after they made love, that would be it. She was *already* half in love with Decker, and being intimate with him would push her over the edge.

She knew it. She also knew how he felt about her putting herself in danger. He hated it. *Loathed* it. He hadn't gone so far as to forbid her from doing exactly what she was doing right now, but she had a feeling if he knew where she was and what she was planning, he'd be furious.

That should've pissed her off. No one told her what she could and couldn't do. But instead, it made her feel cared for. Her parents had surely never given a rat's ass what she did. And after she'd testified for the prosecution in her brother's trial, they'd literally turned their backs on her. But she'd been alone even before that...for as long as she could remember.

Decker always insisted she text him when she got home. When he talked to her on the phone, he was genuinely interested in what she'd done since the last time he'd seen or talked to her. He was always keeping others from bumping into her when they went out, tried to take the outside seat when they ate in restaurants. He wasn't chauvinistic, but now that she was thinking about it, he did whatever he could to keep himself between her and whatever or whoever might cause her harm.

Deliberately pulling Hannah to the forefront of her mind, Sidney did her best to concentrate on why she was there. The animals. Victor wouldn't hesitate to kick, drag, and hurt another dog like he had Hannah. She figured he thought he was toughening them up for the ring or some such bullshit.

The dogs didn't ask to be abused. They didn't ask to be thrown into a pit with other dogs who'd been so brainwashed and battered that they fought whatever was put in there with them.

Her mind back to where it needed to be, on the dogs, Sidney climbed out of her car, pocketed her keys, and made her way toward Victor's house. She'd just do some recon. See if he had any other dogs in his backyard. She'd get the information she needed and pass it along to Faith, so she could get her network of cops and animal control officers to step in. She wouldn't get involved physically.

Happy with her plan, and thinking that maybe, just maybe, she was taking a small step toward getting over the guilt she'd held on to for so long, Sidney made her way stealthily toward the back of Victor's house and peeked through a small hole in the fence.

Gumby was tired. His nights with Sidney and the long days of reviewing the details of their next mission were catching up with him. Wanting to be with this woman had actually become more important than making sure his body was in peak condition. He knew it was dangerous, but he couldn't get enough of Sidney. The way she smelled, her laughter, her teasing...how she felt under his hands and lips when they made out.

He wanted to be inside her more than he wanted to breathe, but he was enjoying the push and pull of their relationship too much to rush things.

She was it for him. He knew that already, without a doubt. The woman he wanted to spend the rest of his life with. So he had to take things slow. Make sure she knew he wasn't with her simply for a roll in the hay. No. If he had his way, she'd eventually be Sidney Kincade. He'd need to get a bigger house to fit any children they might have, and the menagerie of animals he had no doubt they'd want. She had way too big a heart to be able to resist adopting animals. He could keep the beach house as a getaway and have a bigger house built in a subdivision with other families—

"What do you think, Gumby?" their commander asked.

Blinking, he focused on Storm North...and realized he'd completely missed what had just been discussed. "I'm sorry, Sir," he said a little sheepishly. "I missed that."

Their commander sighed, but he patiently repeated what he wanted Gumby's opinion on.

An hour later, Gumby headed out of the conference room with the rest of his team. He knew he had to apologize to the guys. He waited until they were all in the stairwell, then said, "Wait up a sec, guys."

Everyone stopped and waited for him to say what he needed to say.

"I want to apologize for not being completely present lately. It's inexcusable, and it won't happen again."

Rocco clapped a hand on his shoulder. "I get it."

Gumby knew out of all the guys, Rocco would. He had Caite now.

Phantom scowled. "This is what I was worried about with Rocco. Women always seem to fuck things up."

"We've had this conversation already," Rocco warned, turning to their teammate with his hands on his hips. "Just because I have a woman I love, doesn't mean I can't do my job too."

"Gumby only heard half of what we talked about in there," Phantom protested. "How the hell is he going to be able to do his job on this upcoming mission if he doesn't know half the shit we discussed?" He gestured back toward the conference room.

"I said I'm sorry," Gumby told Phantom and the rest of the team. "I know I fucked up, and I need to pull my head out of my ass."

"I hope the pussy's worth it," Phantom grumbled.

"Shut the fuck up," Gumby said, pissed now. He could admit that he'd screwed up, but he'd be damned if he sat around and let Phantom disparage Sidney.

"Not cool," Ace added.

"That was out of line," Bubba told Phantom.

His anger cooled a little at the support of his teammates. Gumby took a big breath and looked Phantom in the eye. "I know that you've been treated like shit by the women in your life—and I'm sorry for that. But Sidney is *not* them. Neither is Caite. I'm trying to do the right thing and apologize for not being one hundred percent dialed in. But I won't stand here and let you badmouth my woman. The last thing I want is for her to feel uncomfortable around any of you guys, but if you keep this up, I'll do whatever I can to keep her away from you. And *that* will hurt the dynamic of this team, which would suck.

"She's it for me, Phantom. I want to spend the rest of my life with her. But I also want her to look at all of you guys as her brothers. I want you to love her like a sister-in-law."

The others murmured their agreement, but Gumby only had eyes for Phantom. The man looked both pissed off and apologetic.

"In all the years we've known you, we haven't pressed for more details about your childhood. All we know is that it sucked and the women in your life made it that way. But you can't go on like this, man. Your bitterness is eating you up inside. Sidney's done nothing but be nice to you. You seemed to like her when you all showed up at my house to meet her. What's different now?"

The other man hesitated. Then said quietly, "I just don't want to see any of you get manipulated and treated like shit. The way my mother treated men."

Rex opened his mouth to reply, but Gumby held up a hand to stop him. "I love you, man. I know as guys, we aren't supposed to say that sort of shit, but fuck that. I love all of you. We've been through the worst kind of hell together. I've saved your lives and you've saved mine. And I'd expect you to speak up if some bitch is doing that shit to me. But Sidney isn't like that. I know it down to my bones. And...me loving Sidney isn't going to make me love you guys any less." He put his hand on Phantom's shoulder. "Give her a chance. It would kill me if you couldn't get along with her. I'm begging you, Phantom. Please."

He nodded once.

Relieved, Gumby dropped his hand. "And I'm going to do better at being present. I know I've been slacking, and it won't happen again."

"It's hard to figure out the balance between giving your woman what she needs and being able to give the SEALs one hundred percent too," Rocco said.

Gumby appreciated his insight. "I'm figuring that out."

"From what I observed, Sidney isn't the kind of woman who needs you by her side twenty-four seven. Just like Caite. She has a job, a life, outside of you."

"I know," Gumby said.

"And she kicks ass at *This is War*," Bubba threw in.

Everyone chuckled.

"True," Gumby said. "Anyway, I appreciate you cutting me some slack, but I'm good now. I get it, and you don't have to worry about me pulling my weight on this upcoming mission."

Everyone nodded and clapped him on the back as they headed down the stairs.

Gumby caught Phantom's arm. "Are we good?"

"We're good."

"I meant what I said," Gumby told him. "If you need an ear...I'm here."

Phantom nodded, but Gumby had a feeling his friend wouldn't be coming over to have a heart-to-heart anytime soon. He'd just have to deal with his demons in his own way and own time.

Gumby was headed to his car when his phone rang. Seeing it was Sidney, a smile formed on his face.

"Hey."

"I'm okay."

Gumby's heart rate immediately increased, and he stopped in his tracks. Right in the middle of the parking lot. "What?"

"I'm okay. I wanted to say that right off so you don't freak."

Too late for that. "What happened?"

"I kinda got into another...scrape...with that asshole dog guy."

"*What?*" Gumby couldn't get his mind to work.

"But I'm fine! I told you. I only have a few bruises and scrapes. But I managed to get another dog away from him."

Gumby felt sick. The black eye she'd gotten from that asshole the last time had finally healed, and now she'd gotten into *another* fight with him? "Where are you?" he bit out.

Sidney hesitated, and he knew he'd been too harsh, but he couldn't help it.

"I'm at Faith's."

"What's the address?"

"Decker, I'm fine," she said softly.

"What. Is. The. Address?" he asked again, enunciating each word clearly.

She gave it to him, then said, "I'm really okay, Decker."

"Don't go anywhere. I'll be there as soon as I can."

"I thought you had that meeting today?"

"I did. It's done. I was on my way home anyway."

"Oh." She paused. "Don't you want to know about the dog?" she asked.

Gumby started walking toward his truck, much more quickly now. "Honestly? No. I'm more concerned that my girlfriend put herself in danger again. That she's got bruises and scrapes from fighting with a fucking asshole who has no problem throwing acid on a defenseless animal." He took a deep breath, trying to get control over his emotions. Then he asked, "Did Faith put you up to this?"

She hesitated, and he knew what her answer was going to be before she said a word.

"No. I was sitting at home and realized I hadn't checked on the websites I usually look at in a while. Saw that Victor had posted, saying he was looking for more dogs. I wasn't going to do anything, I swear...but when I saw that poor puppy chained up in his backyard, crying, I couldn't just leave him there."

"You could've called the cops. Or Faith. Or me," Gumby told her.

When she didn't respond, he sighed. Feeling more and more tired, the two and three hours of sleep he was getting each night were finally catching up with him. He loved Sidney because of her compassion, even though right now, he hated it. "Okay. Stay put. I'll be there as soon as I can."

"You're mad," she said.

"Not mad," he countered. "Worried. Scared. And a little frustrated."

"I'm sorry."

"I'll see you soon."

"Okay. Drive safe."

"I will. Bye."

"Bye."

Taking a deep breath before he started his truck, trying to get his emotions under control, Gumby closed his eyes. Intellectually, he knew he couldn't be by Sidney's side every minute of the day, but he hated that she'd put herself in a position where she could've been seriously hurt. He had no doubt this Victor guy wouldn't have any problem taking out his frustrations on Sidney. He'd gotten his hands on her twice, and Gumby didn't want there to be a third.

But if Sidney didn't see how much danger she was putting herself in by going out and tracking down dog abusers by herself, he wasn't sure what he could do to keep her safe.

Shaking his head, Gumby pulled out of the parking lot and headed toward the address Sidney had given him.

———

Sidney bit her lip—and immediately regretted it. She'd forgotten that Victor had managed to get in a solid punch and split it. Her shoulder hurt from where he'd grabbed her arm and wrenched it upward in an attempt to get her to let go of the puppy, and her face hurt from where she'd scraped it on the fence while she was scrambling back over it, but she'd gotten the puppy away from him.

She'd felt on top of the world for being able to rescue the puppy, filled with adrenaline...until she'd gotten to Faith's house.

The older woman had taken one look at her and pressed her lips together as if she was disappointed.

It had hurt.

But after giving the puppy a much-needed bath and some food, and holding him as he slept in her arms, Sidney felt much better.

"He has a right to be pissed," Faith told her from the chair across from the sofa, where Sidney was currently sitting, holding the puppy.

"He's not the boss of me," Sidney said, and immediately felt like a surly teenager.

Faith just shook her head. "*I'm* pissed at you," she told Sidney. "I told you not to take such risks again."

"But..." Sidney gestured to the puppy in her lap. "I got him out."

"And if you'd called me, told me what was up, I could've contacted my sources and they would've been able to get him out *legally*."

"You know as well as I do that it wouldn't've been that simple. Animal control would've seen the dog house and bowl of water and would've had no reason to take him away. Victor does just enough to keep the law off him. He would've killed this puppy or raised him to be a fighter, and you know it."

"Be that as it may, you can't go around stealing

people's animals, Sidney," Faith reprimanded. "This rescue group isn't a vigilante operation. Word gets around that we're obtaining our animals illegally, we'll be shut down faster than you can say 'lawsuit.' I know you need to help dogs, Sid, I do, but you *can't* continue this way."

Sidney hated being scolded. Especially by a woman she looked up to and admired.

"I'm worried about you, Sidney. I've been in the rescue business a long time. I've seen a lot of shit. Met a lot of people who were passionate about what we do. But I think you know as well as I do that you're taking too many dangerous risks. You've *got* to back off."

"I...I know what I'm doing isn't healthy," Sidney admitted softly, burying her head into the clean fur of the puppy in her arms. "But I can't make myself stop."

"Then maybe you need to get some help with that," Faith said matter-of-factly.

"I'm afraid it's too late. I should've gotten it a long time ago, for lots of reasons."

"It's never too late," Faith told her gently. "Talking with someone, understanding why you feel the compulsion that you do to help the dogs, can go a long way toward making it easier to stop taking so many risks."

Sidney wasn't sure of that, but the more she thought about it, the more she wanted to try. She didn't want to jeopardize things with Decker. And she was tired of the guilt. Tired of feeling as if the safety of every abused animal was on her shoulders alone.

But the second the idea of getting help went through her mind, the very same guilt she was trying desperately to ignore came back full force.

Faith just didn't understand. But knowing she wouldn't be able to convince her right now, she simply nodded.

Faith sighed again, obviously not mollified by her less-than-believable capitulation.

Just then, a knock sounded at the door and Faith got to her feet. "Stay put," she told Sidney. "I'll let him in."

Sidney nodded again, not all that fired up to see Decker. She knew he was upset with her too, and she wasn't sure she could face him right now.

In seconds, he was kneeling on the couch in front of her. His hand went to her face and he palmed it. "Are you okay?" he whispered.

Even though she'd told him several times that she was all right, she told him what he needed to hear. "I'm good."

His eyes went to her lip, and he frowned. Then his gaze went down the rest of her body. She knew he couldn't see much because of the blanket she had in her lap and the puppy nestled there.

"Where else are you hurt?" he asked.

"Decker, I'm okay."

"Where else are you hurt?" he repeated. "You said you had scrapes and bruises."

"Her arm got wrenched," Faith cut in from behind them. "She told me her side was scraped from scrambling over the fence, and she's probably got more bruises under her clothes that she hasn't told me about."

Wanting to take his attention from her small aches and pains, Sidney held up the puppy. "Look. Isn't he cute?"

Decker's eyes landed on the puppy for a nanosecond before he was once more looking at her. "Yeah."

Stymied at his lack of reaction to the dog—or really,

more that her attempt to take his attention off of *her* had failed—she looked at his face…

And saw what she'd missed when he'd first entered. He looked wiped out. He had dark circles under his eyes and his brow was drawn down into what looked like a permanent frown.

"Are *you* okay? You look tired."

"I'm exhausted," he said immediately, not prevaricating.

Sidney felt guilty. She knew part of his tiredness was because she'd been over at his house until late every night for the past week. She knew he got up early every morning to work out, and that he and his teammates were preparing for some big mission. She hadn't asked too many questions because she knew he couldn't answer them, but now she regretted being so selfish. She'd wanted to spend time with him, and she knew he wanted the same. But she should've taken better care of him.

The thought startled her. He was a grown-ass man. She didn't need to "take care" of him…but the phrase wouldn't leave her mind. Instinctively, she knew he'd do whatever it took to make her happy, and she felt like shit that she hadn't seen how he'd been burning the candle at both ends.

Holding the dog to her chest with one hand, she held out the other. "Help me up," she told Decker.

He stood and did as she asked. As soon as she was standing, she walked to Faith and handed her the puppy. "I need to go," she told the older woman.

Looking surprised, Faith took the puppy from her.

Sidney knew she was acting out of character. Typically, she liked to spend hours making sure new dogs coming into the rescue were comfortable before turning over their care to anyone else. And here she was, only an hour after rescuing this little guy, abandoning him.

No, she wasn't abandoning him. She was letting Faith, who was perfectly able to take care of him, do just that. Sidney needed to take care of her man. He was at the end of his rope.

"Come on," she ordered, grabbing Decker's hand.

He pulled her to him and wrapped his arm around her waist instead. Sidney winced as his arm rubbed against the scrape on her side, but did her best to hide the slight discomfort from him.

Ever observant, he noticed anyway, and immediately changed the position of his arm before turning to Faith. "I'm sorry we didn't get a chance to talk. I'd like to get to know you better, as you're obviously important to Sidney."

Faith looked surprised again, but her face gentled. "I'm going to hold you to that. Since you're obviously important to Sidney, as well, I'd like to get to know you too."

Decker nodded.

Ignoring how happy she was that Faith seemed to like Decker and vice versa, she turned to him and said, "I'd say that I'll drive us both back to your house, but I know you need your truck in the morning. Are you okay to drive home?"

He gave her a look. "Of course."

She turned and waved at Faith and ushered them both out the door. After making sure the door was shut behind her, she turned in Decker's arms and looked up at him. "You're tired. And stressed. And me calling you and telling you what I did today isn't helping. I want to get you home, get some food in you, and let you get some sleep. I've been staying too late. I know that now, and I'm sorry. You need a full night's sleep, and I intend to make sure you get it."

"Sidney, I'm a SEAL. We're used to not getting much sleep," he told her.

"You said it yourself—you're exhausted. So, I'm gonna follow you home, get you settled, then leave you to get some much-needed rest. We can fight about what I did later."

"I don't want to fight with you," Decker said with a sigh. "I'm just worried sick about you and your need to rescue every dog, to the detriment of your own safety and health." He ran a thumb over her lip, barely touching her, but she felt the gentle caress down to her very soul.

"Are you really okay to drive?" she asked, trying to keep her composure.

"Yeah, Sid. I'm okay to drive."

"Good. I'll follow you then."

He sighed but nodded. "I'll let you feed me on one condition."

Sidney rolled her eyes. "What?"

"That you let me take care of you in return. I want to see your injuries. Let me make them better."

She stared into Decker's eyes, and realized he needed to see for himself that she was truly all right.

"Deal."

Leaning down, he brushed his lips over the uninjured side of her mouth. "Deal," he said quietly. Then he took her hand in his once more and led them down the stairs of Faith's house toward their vehicles.

It was an uneventful ride home. Decker met her at her car when she climbed out and took hold of her hand once more. He let them into the house and Hannah met them there. Her tail was wagging back and forth a million miles a minute. She greeted Decker first, then came over to Sidney to get some pets. She was extra interested in smelling her, most likely because of the puppy she'd been holding.

Decker let the dog outside to do her thing and afterward, Hannah eagerly pranced back inside. Happy that her human had returned, she padded over to her dog bed and collapsed.

Without a word, Decker led Sidney upstairs to the master bathroom and said, "Let me see."

Knowing she wasn't going to get any food down him and he wouldn't go to sleep before he'd seen to her wounds, she did as he asked. Lifting her shirt, she showed him the scrape on her side.

He didn't say a word, but frowned as he reached for a clean washcloth. He ran the water until it was warm and gently cleaned the abrasion. She had to unbutton her jeans for him to get to the scrape on her hip, but she had no worries that he'd act inappropriately. It was more than obvious he was more concerned about her health than anything sexual. When it came time for him to look at her arm, she guided it out of the shirt she was wearing. Sidney was still mostly covered, the material draped across her breasts, but she still felt naked in front of him.

Decker manipulated her arm, noting when she winced and when movement was uncomfortable. He brushed a kiss against the bruises in the shape of fingers on her upper arm, and helped get her hand back through the armhole.

"I don't think you need stitches on this lip," he said once she was dressed. "I'll go get you some ice packs, one for your lip and one for your shoulder. Do you want to change into something more comfortable? I've got a pair of sweats and a T-shirt you can borrow. They'll be big, but they might be more comfortable than what you've got on now, and they're clean."

Sidney closed her eyes for a second. He was always so caring. So gentle with her. He should be yelling. Telling her she was an idiot for what she'd done, but he was holding himself back and taking care of her.

"That'd be great," she said.

Nodding, Decker eyed her for a long moment before leaning forward and kissing her on the forehead. "I'll put something on the bed. Come out whenever you're ready." And with that, he turned and left the bathroom.

Sidney took a few minutes to get herself together. This was why she was so reluctant to leave each night. Why she had no problem talking to Decker until the wee hours of the morning. He had a way of making her feel special. As if there was no one but the two of them in the world, that he had nothing else better to do but sit and listen to her ramble on about nothing in particular.

Knowing he was waiting on her, Sidney forced herself to leave the bathroom and change into the things he'd left out for her. The gray T-shirt with the word NAVY across it was huge on her, as were the sweats. But they didn't rub against her side and she loved how they smelled like Decker. It was as if she were getting a nonstop, full-body hug.

Looking around his room, she saw that it was a disaster. There were boxes everywhere, and she was standing on particle board. Even the paint on the walls was peeling. The comparison of this room to the downstairs was almost shocking. Recalling the similar state of the bathroom she'd just been in—the lime-green counter, the godawful wallpaper on the walls, and the horrible bathtub/shower combo—she truly understood what Decker had done. Instead of making his own living space more comfortable and modern, he'd solely remodeled the areas Hannah spent the most time in.

She didn't know that many people who would've done the same thing. For a dog. Many people would probably tell him he was crazy. That Hannah was "just a dog." But he'd done it anyway.

Closing her eyes, Sidney realized at that very moment that she was head over heels for Decker.

It was crazy. She'd only met him a short time ago, but there it was. No one had made her feel as special and cared for. And now it was time for her to take care of him in return. She'd been a pretty shitty girlfriend. Were they even girlfriend/boyfriend? She didn't know. But it wasn't going to stop her from doing what she could to make sure Decker got what he needed...food and a good night's sleep.

When she got to the bottom of the stairs, she immediately saw Decker on the couch. There was a towel sitting on the coffee table in front of him, with two frozen bags of peas. Hannah was lying on the floor, her head on his feet, and Decker's head was resting on the back of the couch. His eyes were closed and he looked like he was asleep.

It was just more proof that he'd reached his breaking point. The Decker she'd gotten to know wouldn't have fallen asleep before he'd made sure she was taken care of and comfortable.

Tiptoeing to the kitchen, Sidney opened the refrigerator and peered inside. She saw he had what she needed to make him one of her favorite dishes...homemade mac and cheese. Crossing her fingers that he had pasta, she opened the pantry and smiled. Bingo.

Thirty minutes later, she was dishing up two bowls of creamy, gooey pasta when she heard Decker moving. She looked over and saw that he'd stood up and was headed her way.

"I'm sorry," he said, his eyes still looking glazed.

"Sit," she ordered, gesturing to the small table nearby with her head.

She was somewhat shocked when he did as ordered. She put a bowl of the mac and cheese in front of him, along with a bottle of water. She sat next to him and held her breath as he picked up a fork and speared a noodle and brought it to his mouth.

He closed his eyes and moaned, and Sidney grinned.

"Like it?"

"God, yes. Too much," he told her with a smile. He reached out, put his hand behind her neck and gently pulled her closer. He kissed her. It was a short, gentle meeting of lips rather than anything passionate, but Sidney still felt it all the way to her toes.

"Thank you," he said softly.

"You're welcome."

With one last glance at her lips, he let go of her neck and attacked his meal as if he hadn't eaten in days. After finishing the first bowl, he got up and served himself seconds before sitting down and eating that helping a little slower. When they were finished, Sidney carried the bowls to the sink and turned on the water.

"Leave 'em. I'll clean them tomorrow," he told her.

Sidney shook her head. "It won't take me long. I cleaned up the other dishes as I cooked."

He didn't protest, but didn't go and sit back down either. He stood in the kitchen, one hip against the counter, the bottle of water in his hand, and watched as she washed their dinner dishes. When she'd finished washing the bowls, he held out his hand. Sidney took it and he brought them back to the couch. They sat, and he leaned forward and grabbed the peas.

"They aren't quite frozen anymore, but they'll still do you some good," he told her before gently holding one to her face.

Sidney sucked in a breath at the chilly package against her warm skin, but didn't flinch away.

"Put this one under your shirt on your shoulder," he ordered, holding out the other package of peas wrapped in a small towel. She did as he asked, and then sighed in contentment when he pulled her into his side.

They sat like that a long time, until the peas became lukewarm. Knowing Decker was half asleep, Sidney didn't want to do anything to wake him all the way. She threw the peas and the towels on the coffee table and snuggled back against him. He surprised her by shifting around so he was lying flat on his back on the couch, and she was on top of him.

Sidney went to slide off, but he tightened his hold on her.

"I should go," she said softly.

"Stay," he countered.

"Decker, you're exhausted. You need to sleep."

"I need to hold you for a bit longer. You scared the shit out of me today, Sid."

How could she deny him that? Truth was, she'd been scared for herself for a while there. Victor had seemed way more pissed than he'd been the last time she'd fought him, and she didn't want to think about what he might've done to her if he'd managed to pull her back over the fence into his yard.

Relaxing into Decker, she let her body go limp.

"Thank you," he whispered.

"I'm only staying for a bit," she whispered back.

"Okay," he said.

Loving how he felt under her, how good his arms felt around her, Sidney closed her eyes. She was asleep in minutes.

***

On the other side of the city, Victor Kennedy was pissed.

Beyond pissed.

Not about the dog. Fuck the dog. He could get another hundred puppies if he wanted. But that the fucking do-gooder had gotten the best of him—*again*.

That shit wasn't going to happen a third time.

Ignoring the growls and barking going on in the fight behind him, he tried to think of a way to get his hands on the bitch. To show her that she'd messed with the wrong guy.

As the dogfight got more vicious, a delightful, horrible idea came to Victor.

He knew just what to do. She'd try again, there was no way she wouldn't. And he'd be ready for her. He'd make preparations before putting another ad on social media. That *had* to be how she'd known he'd obtained a new dog.

As he absently watched one pit bull in the ring tear the throat out of another, and keep biting and ripping flesh even after the other dog stopped moving, Victor smiled.

Yeah, the bitch would definitely rue the day she stole his dogs.

CHAPTER TEN

Gumby had woken up several times during the course of the night, probably because he'd fallen asleep so early. He hadn't been lying when he'd told Sidney he didn't need a lot of sleep. Of course, he needed more than he'd been getting, but ten hours in one night was a little bit overkill.

He'd loved waking up to find Sidney there with him. She was still lying on top of him, sleeping like the dead. He was obviously not the only one not getting enough sleep. For the first time in ages, he'd slept with a woman without having *slept* with her. He loved feeling Sidney's long, slow breaths against his neck and he loved the feel of her on top of him even more.

Not knowing her schedule, and knowing if he continued to lie there, his dick would get the wrong idea, Gumby slowly slid out from under her.

It was still dark outside, and he had to get to PT in about an hour, but he wasn't going to leave without letting her know.

Grumbling a bit, Sidney turned onto her side to try to

get comfortable. Grinning, Gumby covered her up with a blanket that was thrown over the back of the couch. When they'd been sharing body heat, the blanket hadn't been necessary, but now she needed the extra warmth. He tucked her in, loving how she sighed in contentment.

But seeing her split lip made him frown. He hated that she'd been injured again. Hated even more it had been because she'd been stealing another dog from the same asshole she'd been fighting when he'd met her.

He loved her big heart, loved that she had the compassion to save animals. But despised how she went about it. Her disregard for her own safety. There had to be something more behind it than he knew. Hopefully she'd feel safe enough, and trust him enough, to open up about whatever it was. He had a feeling until she could face her triggers head on, she wouldn't be able to get past them.

Kissing her forehead lightly, he stood and headed up the stairs to change. If he had his way, he'd stay home today. Hang with Sidney all day. But he and his fellow SEALs were preparing to head off to the Middle East, and currently finalizing preparations. Not to mention, Sidney had her own job to do.

He wanted to talk to her more about the rescue thing. Try to get across to her once more that what she was doing was extremely dangerous. That he had no problem with her wanting to rescue dogs and help abused animals, but stealing pit bulls from suspected dog fighters wasn't the best way to go about it.

But today wouldn't be that day. They both had things to do.

He was worried about her. He hated the bruises on her body, and he *really* hated seeing her blood. It was unacceptable, and Gumby wanted to lock her up for her own good.

But that would make her hate *him*—and that was unacceptable. He wasn't sure what the answer was yet. How she could continue to do what she loved and stay safe at the same time. But they'd figure it out. He hoped. He wasn't sure he could deal with any more phone calls like the one he'd gotten yesterday. The next time it might be a police officer calling. Or someone from the emergency room, saying that Sidney hadn't made it.

Gumby put on his PT clothes and packed a bag so he could shower and change on the base. He and the others were going to head right into meetings after working out so they could hopefully get off a bit early today. Rocco wanted to spend as much time with Caite as he could before they left, and the rest of them just wanted the break from thinking about what they were about to do overseas.

Tiptoeing down the stairs, he gestured to Hannah and she obediently got up off her bed and came toward him. He let her out to do her business and afterward, he brought her into the kitchen to take a look at her wounds. Her back was looking so much better. The oozing had stopped and all that was left was a pink, still-healing squiggly line down her back where the hair had been burned away. The skin was tender, but the vet assured him Hannah didn't really feel much pain there as the nerves had been burned by the acid.

Her paws were also doing better. The pads had actually peeled off, which had freaked Gumby out, but he had to believe the vet when she'd said it was a good thing. That the new pads underneath were growing back. Hannah wasn't limping quite as badly as she'd been when she'd first come home, and Gumby was satisfied that she'd heal completely.

He put some food in Hannah's bowl and refreshed her water. Watching as the happy-go-lucky dog wagged her tail as she ate, Gumby wondered for the thousandth time how someone could deliberately hurt an animal as sweet as Hannah

He sipped a cup of instant coffee as he waited for Hannah to finish her breakfast. The only light in the kitchen was coming from the bulb above the sink. He hadn't wanted to turn on any others so he wouldn't disturb Sidney. He couldn't see her from where he was standing, but he knew she was still asleep.

Gumby loved having her there. Loved waking up with her in his arms. It was hell to leave her just to go get dressed, but he didn't want to rush her into anything she wasn't ready for.

When Hannah finished her meal, she came over to him, tail still wagging a mile a minute. "Done, girl?" he asked quietly.

In response, her tail wagged faster and it totally looked like she was smiling up at him. "Take care of Sid today until she leaves, yeah?"

Hannah licked his hand then headed into the living area. Chugging the rest of his coffee, Gumby put his mug in the sink and followed his dog. When he rounded the couch, he blinked in surprise.

Hannah had gotten up on the couch, which was the first time he'd seen her do that, and curled herself into a ball in the crook of Sidney's knees.

Sid was on her side, still sleeping like the dead.

Gumby stood there a long moment, feeling emotional over the sight of his dog and his girl sleeping. It was something he wanted full time more than he could express. He'd always wanted a dog, but hadn't realized the satisfaction having one would give him. Hannah made him smile all the time, and it felt good to be able to give her a safe, happy home.

And Sidney. He wanted to give *her* a safe, happy home as well, but she wasn't a dog. She had her own mind and was doing just fine on her own without him. That was the rub—she didn't need him like Hannah did. But Gumby hoped like hell one day she'd decide she *wanted* him.

Deciding not to wake her up—how could he when she was sleeping so soundly—Gumby leaned over and kissed her on the temple. "Sleep well, Sid," he whispered, before standing up and heading for the kitchen once again.

Writing out a short note letting her know he would be working until around two and wanted to see her later if possible, Gumby propped it up next to his coffee maker. He hoped that she'd stay long enough to see it. Just to be safe, he decided to also text her after he got done with PT.

He got out a bottle of water and put it next to two painkillers on the counter as well. She would be sore after her latest bout with that asshole, Victor.

Knowing if he stayed much longer it would be even harder to leave, Gumby headed for the door.

With one last glance into his living room at the two females who meant the world to him, Gumby slipped out of the house and headed to work.

Sidney woke up completely refreshed. She couldn't remember the last time she'd slept so long and so hard. She'd woken up a few times in the night and realized that she was still at Decker's house, but had no desire to get up and go home.

For one, she was comfortable.

For two, she didn't want to wake Decker.

For three, she loved sleeping in his arms. He made the best pillow ever. Screw those commercials touting the "perfect pillow." Nothing could be as comfortable as Decker's chest.

She felt Hannah at her feet, her head heavy on her calves as she snored slightly. She knew Decker was gone; the house was quiet and the sunlight was just peeking in, letting her know it was past time for her to get up and get on with her day.

But she couldn't move just yet. The cushion under her head smelled like Decker. His dog was sleeping contentedly at her feet. And she'd just spent the night with the man she knew could break her if he decided he didn't want her around anymore.

She lay there for another few minutes before sighing deeply and sitting up. Hannah grumbled at the loss of her pillow, but scooted over and licked Sidney's hand before putting her head on her thigh.

Chuckling, Sidney petted her head and said, "Yeah, I know. Mornings suck. I'm with ya, girl."

Hannah's tail thumped against the cushion.

"Are you even allowed up here?"

Her tail thumped harder.

Laughing again, Sidney gave her one last pat before standing. She folded the blanket they'd used and draped it over the back of the couch. She visited the bathroom before heading into the kitchen.

The sight of the two small pills next to the bottle of water made her pause. It was silly really. It was just two ibuprofen. But having lived alone for as long as she had, and having taken care of herself for most of her life, the gesture was akin to him leaving her a pair of diamond earrings. That's how much it meant to her.

She swallowed the pills down, hoping they kicked in fast. Her lip was throbbing and her shoulder wasn't much better. She went to the coffeepot and found a note from Decker.

Morning, beautiful. I'm off to PT and then to a long day of meetings. But I'm getting off around two. Any chance I can talk you into coming over? :) I know you're busy, but it seems as if the more I'm around you, the more I want to see you. Hope you slept well. I know I did.

Xoxo
Decker

Sidney held the note to her chest and closed her eyes. "How did this happen?" she asked herself.

Feeling a nose nudge her leg, she opened her eyes and looked down at Hannah. The pit bull was staring up at her with a look so pathetic, Sidney could only laugh. "I have no doubt Deck already fed you."

When Hannah didn't stop with the puppy dog eyes, Sidney caved. She reached for the bowl with the dog treats in it and gave Hannah two. "You're gonna be five hundred pounds, dog," she told her as she trotted off after having gotten her way.

But how could she not spoil her when she'd been through such hell?

Thinking about Victor, and what he'd done to Hannah and probably countless other dogs, made her fists clench. Hearing paper crinkle, she immediately relaxed and straightened out the note Decker had written her.

She would save it forever. Silly and childish, maybe. But it was the first love note she'd ever received, and it was from Decker. It meant the world to her.

Knowing she had to get back to her trailer and see what Jude had planned for her today, Sidney found her shoes and got ready to leave. She let Hannah outside and watched as she sniffed all around Decker's front yard and finally did her thing. Once she got back inside, she went straight to her bed and lay down with a large sigh.

Sidney chuckled again. She loved how easily the dog could make her smile and laugh. It had been a long time since she'd felt so carefree. And it wasn't just Hannah, it was her owner too. Decker had done what no man had been able to do...made her feel comfortable being herself around him. She knew without a doubt that he would never purposely hurt her. He'd do whatever it took to keep her safe. Yeah, he was a bit too overprotective, but was that really a bad thing?

Closing the door behind her and turning the knob to make sure it was locked, Sidney made her way to her car. Her phone vibrated with an incoming text, and she looked down at it.

. . .

Decker: Just in case you didn't find the note I left you, I wanted to say good morning. I had to get to PT and work. I'm off around two and would love to see you this afternoon. Let me know.

Sidney immediately sent him a text back.

Sidney: It'll depend on what Jude has planned for me, but I'd love to see you too. By the way...your dog is spoiled rotten and if you aren't careful she's gonna weigh 500 lbs.

    Decker: Well, if someone wouldn't give her treats after she's already eaten, she wouldn't weigh 500 lbs.

Sidney found herself laughing out loud. Again. How Decker knew she'd caved and given Hannah treats, she had no idea. Deciding to be honest with him, she quickly typed out a response.

Sidney: I meant to leave after you fell asleep last night, but every time I woke up, I couldn't make myself get up and go.

    Decker: I'm glad. I loved having you with me. Next time we'll have to try it in a bed.

She blinked at that. The thought of sleeping next to Decker in bed made goose bumps spring up on her arms.

. . .

Decker: Too soon? Sorry. Let me know if you can get away this afternoon. I thought maybe we could go swimming together in my ocean.

Sidney: Your ocean?

Decker: It's right outside my back door, so yeah, my ocean. Lol

Sidney: I'd like that. I'll see what I can do.

Decker: Gotta go. The guys are giving me the evil eye.

Sidney: Tell them I said hello.

Decker: Will do. Have a good day. I'll be thinking about you.

Sidney: I'll text later and let you know if I'll be over.

Decker: Okay. Be safe today.

Sidney: Ltr.

Decker: Bye.

Sidney read over their texts and couldn't believe her luck. She seriously didn't deserve Decker, but she was going to go with the flow. She'd hold on to him for as long as possible...at least until he figured out that she wasn't worth his time or energy.

At three-thirty that afternoon, Gumby opened the door to Sidney. He'd had a long day, and they'd learned they'd be heading out on their mission the following morning. He'd known the time was approaching when they'd have to leave, but they'd all thought they'd have a few more days, maybe a week. But terrorists acting stupid didn't always stick to a convenient timetable.

Decker was more than relieved that Sidney had been able to come back over. He'd promised her a swim, and that's what he would give her...but in reality, all he wanted was to take her to his bed and spend the rest of the evening showing her how much she meant to him. He knew better than anyone that his safety wasn't guaranteed. He didn't want to regret not making love to Sidney, but honestly, he knew it wasn't the right time yet.

"Hi," she said when he opened the door.

"You didn't have to knock," he scolded gently. "You could've just come in."

She looked surprised. "I can't just walk into your house!"

"Why not? I knew you were coming, you texted right before you left. Not to mention I left you alone in here this morning. If I didn't trust you, I would've woken you up."

She shrugged. "It doesn't seem right."

Gumby put his hands on her shoulders. "Sid, you are welcome in my house day or night. I want you to feel as comfortable here as you are at your own place."

"No problem there," she muttered. "This place is a palace compared to my trailer."

He grinned and tugged her into his arms and stepped back just enough to be able to close the front door. "I haven't properly said hello yet," he said.

She glanced at him. "Yes, you did. When you opened the door."

"Nope," he countered, then lowered his head. He saw the second she recognized his intent, because her eyes closed and she went up on her tiptoes to meet him halfway.

When his mouth met hers, he was careful not to do anything that might hurt her split lip. His tongue caressed her lower lip and when she opened for him, he eased inside her mouth gently.

He wasn't sure who moaned. It could've been either or both of them. He could taste the cinnamon candy she'd eaten recently, and the combination of her own taste and the earthy spice was incredibly arousing. They made out for a long moment, and Gumby couldn't ever remember a kiss turning him on so much.

He pulled away and smiled down at her. "Hi."

"Hi," she replied immediately.

"How was your day?" he asked.

She shrugged. "It was a day. Had to do a bunch of stupid shit for stupid people who can't seem to get it through their brains that they can't flush half a roll of toilet paper down the commode, or that it's not smart to leave their oven on self-clean when they go out to do errands."

His eyebrow lifted.

"Yeah, they almost burned down the trailer. Luckily, they came home and realized the wooden cabinets around the stove were smoking and about to catch on fire. I had to take them out and measure to get new ones made."

Gumby was amazed at the stuff Sidney knew how to do. She wasn't just an expert on one thing, like plumbing, she knew how to do a bit of everything. That made her extremely valuable.

"Still want to go swimming?" he asked.

Sidney nodded and gestured to the bag she'd dropped inside the door when he'd pulled her inside. "Yeah, if you do. I brought my stuff."

Gumby couldn't wait to see her in a suit, but he managed to keep that to himself.

"Great. My contractor, Max, is coming over in about twenty minutes. He was being a pest and wanted to take another look at the upstairs, so I gave in. After I get rid of him, we can swim, then have dinner. Sound good?"

She nodded.

Gumby wasn't going to tell her that he'd begged Max to come over so he could introduce him to Sidney. He knew she'd be perfect for his business. She might not have confidence in herself, but he had confidence in her in spades. Maybe nothing would come of it, but at least it might give her some options.

Exactly twenty minutes later, the doorbell rang.

Gumby was startled when Hannah leaped off her bed growling and ran toward the door, barking her head off.

"Holy crap," Sidney said as she followed him to the door.

Gumby took hold of Hannah's collar. "Hannah. No!" But she didn't stop barking.

Sidney stepped up and opened the door. Talking over Hannah's barking, she greeted Max and he warily entered the house, keeping his eyes on the pit bull.

Gumby couldn't imagine what had gotten into Hannah. She was usually as docile as ever. He'd had people ring the doorbell before and she hadn't been this aggressive.

Then something occurred to him.

"Sidney, come stand behind me and Hannah, please."

She looked at him. "Why?"

"A hunch."

Without another word, she did as he asked—and almost immediately, Hannah calmed somewhat. She moved until she was in front of Sidney and sat down right on her feet.

"What the heck?" Sidney asked.

Gumby wanted to laugh, but managed not to.

"Nice-looking guard dog you have there," Max said.

"Sorry about that. This is the first time someone's come over when Sidney's been here."

"You think she did that because of me?" Sidney asked.

"I do. My guess is that she remembers how you fought with Victor, and she wants to make sure that doesn't happen again," Gumby said.

"That's a bit concerning," she said. "We can't have her scaring the crap out of people when they come to the door just because I'm here."

Gumby opened his mouth to disagree, but Max beat him to it. "Actually, I think it's a good thing. Anyone who hears her barking is gonna think twice about breaking in or doing anything that might hurt you."

Sidney squatted down next to Hannah and ran a hand over her head. "He's okay, Hannah," she crooned. "You don't have to rip his throat out, okay?"

Gumby bit back a laugh and saw Max doing the same thing...thank God. Many people wouldn't be as understanding as his contractor.

"Come here, Sid," Gumby said, holding out his arm.

Sidney stood and moved to him. He put his arm around her shoulders and said in a stern voice, "Hannah. Stay."

Remarkably, the dog stayed where she was while Gumby took Sidney over to Max. "Sid, I'd like you to meet my contractor, Max Wyner. Max, this is the woman I told you about, Sidney Hale. She's currently the handyman, or handywoman, for the Evergreen Trailer Park."

Max held out his hand. "It's good to meet you."

Sidney smiled. "Same."

"You as good as Decker claims?" Max asked.

Sidney looked surprised as she turned her attention to him. "You told him about me?"

Gumby nodded. "Yup."

She looked back to Max. "Probably not. He tends to exaggerate."

Max threw back his head and laughed. "I like her already," he told Gumby.

"Knew you would," Gumby replied.

Hannah whined, and Gumby looked down at her. "Okay, girl. If you're ready to behave yourself, you can come greet our visitor now."

He watched as Hannah lay down on her belly and crawled toward Max.

Sidney squatted down once more to reassure Hannah that Max wasn't going to hurt either of them. "See? He's nice. He's not going to hurt you or me."

Gumby was glad to see Max reach out and pet Hannah. If a dog as big and scary looking as Hannah greet him as she had, he wouldn't be too keen on petting her.

"What happened to her back?" he asked.

Before Gumby could answer, Sidney did. "Some asswipe decided to torture her by throwing acid on her back."

"Why?" Max asked incredulously.

Sidney shrugged. "Why does anyone do what they do? Because he's an ass. And probably because he was trying to toughen her up so she'd fight harder when he got her in a ring."

"Dogfighting?" Max asked. "God, anyone who condones that shit should be shot."

"Agreed," Sidney replied.

"Poor baby," Max told Hannah. "Well, you hit the jackpot here, didn't you?"

Gumby would've laughed at the way the big man baby-talked to his pit bull, but both Hannah and Sidney were eating it up, so he kept his mouth shut.

"If you're done spoiling my dog, you want to take another look at the upstairs?"

Max stood. "Sure thing."

"Go on up, we'll be there in a second," Gumby told him.

Max nodded and headed for the stairs.

When he was out of earshot, Gumby pulled Sidney into him once again. "We gotta be careful with Hannah."

She nodded.

"She's obviously very protective of you. If you're ever here alone and someone knocks on the door, you're gonna have to put her in the bathroom or something before you answer the door. Until we can get her into more training, we can't trust her."

"Okay. But I'm still not sure where this is coming from. I haven't even seen her all that much."

"Sidney, you've been over here almost every night for the last week or so. You've been around her almost as much as I have, since I'm gone during the day at work."

She looked a little surprised, but nodded. "You think she'd actually bite someone?"

"I doubt it," Gumby said immediately. "I think she's more bark than bite, but I'm not willing to take a chance."

"Me either."

"But I have to say, I'm kinda thrilled she's that protective over you. Eases my mind a bit."

Sidney just stared at him.

He smiled. "Not gonna ask why?"

She shook her head.

"Right. Well, I'll tell you anyway. I think it's because she somehow knows I feel protective over you. And it makes me feel better if I have to leave you two alone here, that she's willing to do whatever it takes to make sure you're safe."

He wasn't sure how Sidney would react to his statement—but he didn't expect impending tears.

"What? Sidney?"

She leaned forward and put her forehead on his chest and held on to his arms tighter. Gumby gave her a minute, enjoying having her close, even if he didn't like that she was upset for some reason.

"All my life I've been on my own. I never really felt safe. Ever. It feels good to know you worry about me."

Gumby kissed the top of her head. "I worry about you, Sid. Never doubt it."

"Thanks."

"Ready to go upstairs and see what Max has to say?"

She looked up then, and Gumby was glad to see that she hadn't actually shed any tears. "I can stay down here while you guys do your thing."

Gumby knew he had to tread carefully. He wanted her to tell Max exactly how *she* wanted the master bathroom to look, and the closet too. But he didn't want to freak her out. "I could use your suggestions," he said carefully.

She tilted her head at him. "Really?"

"Yeah. You know more about this stuff than me. I mean, if it was up to me, I'd probably just tell him to throw in the cheapest toilet and sink he can find and leave the tub and shower the way they are."

She looked horrified, and he inwardly grinned. He had her.

"I'll go up with you," she declared. "You obviously can't be trusted. Come on." And with that, she grabbed his hand and towed him toward the stairs, Hannah at their heels.

Thirty minutes later, Gumby was still listening as Sidney and Max talked shop. They'd toured the top floor and she'd immediately given Max her suggestions for the bathroom. By the time they were done, they'd decided to take down one of the walls, expand the master bedroom to make room for a larger closet, granite countertops for the bathroom, heated floors, a separate shower and tub, and two sinks. They'd even figured out that they could move the toilet to the other side of the room and, by using the space the current linen closet was taking up, enclose it behind a door.

They'd then finished designing the other bedroom, the linen closet in the hallway, as well as adding an additional bathroom and sink in the guest room.

Gumby just followed behind them, grinning.

By the time they'd made it back downstairs, he knew Sidney had sold herself to Max.

He held out his hand to her at the door. "You want a job, it's yours," he told her.

Sidney looked surprised. "What?"

"A job. I could use a foreman...er...woman...who knows what she's doing. You've got a good eye for design and you obviously know your shit."

"Oh, but..." She looked at Gumby, then back to Max. "I'm not looking for a job. And I don't have any licenses."

Max didn't seem fazed. He named a starting salary that made Sidney's eyes nearly bug out of her head.

"I'm sorry it's not more, but it's what I can do right now."

"No...it's...that's great." Sidney stumbled over her words.

"And don't worry about the licenses. We can work on you getting those after you're hired. I'd pay for them too. And if you need to take any classes to brush up on stuff before you took the tests, we'd cover those as well."

"I don't know what to say."

"You don't have to say anything right now. But get this guy to give me the green light to start sooner rather than later, would ya?" he teased.

"Give me a month or two," Gumby told him. "I gotta pay off the work you did down here first."

Max laughed and nodded. "It looks good."

"It does. Thank you."

"I'm gonna go." He pulled out a business card and handed it to Sidney. "Here's my card. Call me if you want that job. The offer's an open-ended one. I've been looking for months for the right person and haven't found anyone I think can do it."

"And you think I can after knowing me for what, half an hour?" Sidney asked.

Max got serious. "Yeah, Sidney, I do. I've been in this

business for a long time. I've had lots of men and women try to convince me they know what they're doing, but half the time it's all bullshit. You weren't even trying to sell yourself, and yet you still did. The job's yours if you want it."

"I...uh...thank you," she managed.

"You're welcome. Later, Decker."

"Later, Max. Thanks for coming over."

The older man nodded and headed for his truck parked behind Sidney's Accord.

She turned to him after he'd shut the door and jumped on him.

Surprised, Gumby caught her and laughed as his back hit the wall. Sidney wrapped her legs around him and tightened her arms around his neck. Hannah thought they were playing a game and barked as she jumped around the two of them.

Locking his hands under her ass, Gumby smiled at Sidney. "You happy?" he asked her.

"Happy? God, Decker, I'd make double working for him as I make working for Jude! I could probably even afford to move into a nice apartment or something. Happy doesn't even begin to describe what I'm feeling."

Gumby wanted to protest her moving anywhere but into his place, but kept his mouth shut.

"And he said he'd pay for me to take classes and get my licenses! It's almost too good to be true."

"Good things come to good people," Gumby said.

She rolled her eyes. "Whatever."

He couldn't help himself, his fingers flexed on her ass and he felt her tense briefly, then melt against him.

"Decker?"

"Yeah?"

"I think I want you."

He loved hearing the words, but needed more. "I'll wait until you're sure of it."

"I could be convinced," she said shyly.

"I don't want to have to convince you," he told her honestly. "I want you to *need* to make love to me down to the marrow of your bones. To feel like if you don't get me inside you in the next instant, you'll die."

She stared at him.

"Because that's how I feel about you. Every time I hear your voice, I want you more. When I see you, I want to throw you over my shoulder and take you up to my bed. When I touch you, I actually ache to make you mine."

"Decker..." Her voice trailed off.

"I'm not saying that to pressure you, Sid. I'm willing to wait as long as it takes. This is not a fling for me. Not a one-night stand or whatever you want to call it. I want to wake up with you in my arms every morning and fall asleep with you at my side as well. When you get there, let me know, and I'll do everything in my power to make you happier than you've ever been before. I'll bend over backward to give you everything you need and want."

"I'm already happier than I've ever been. But, Decker, there's a lot you don't know about me."

"There's a lot you don't know about me too, Sid. But there's nothing you can tell me that will change my mind. I know what I want, and that's you."

She stared at him, and Gumby instantly knew he'd freaked her out a little. Wanting to lighten the mood, he said, "You ready for me to kick your ass in a swim race?"

The furrow in her brow smoothed out as she smiled. "You think you can?"

"I *know* I can, baby. Question is, can you take it? I know how competitive you are."

"How about a wager?" she asked.

Gumby smiled. He was relieved she hadn't indicated she wanted down from his arms. He could hold her forever and die a happy man. He still had to tell her that he was leaving the next day for an unknown amount of time, but he wanted to live in the moment for now. He didn't want to do anything to ruin the good mood she was in. "What kind of wager?"

"If I win, you have to give me a thirty-minute back massage."

Gumby chuckled. As if that was really a punishment for losing. He'd kill to get his hands on her any way he could. "And if I win?"

"I'll give you one."

"Deal." Fuck yeah. He was a winner either way. Gumby had a feeling she felt the same, if the grin on her face was any indication. He slowly lowered her to the floor, her body caressing his the entire way. He knew he was hard—again—but did nothing to hide that fact from her.

"Go get changed. You can use the guest room or the bathroom down here. I'll meet you back here when you're ready."

She stayed in his arms, looking up at him for a long moment before saying, "I still think you're way too good for me, Decker, but I'm getting to the point where I don't really care."

"Good."

"Although I'm afraid that once you get to know me

better, you're going to wonder why you wasted so much time with me."

"Never, Sid. I know you aren't perfect, just as I'm not. I know exactly who you are here," he touched her temple with his finger, "and here," he placed his palm flat on her chest over her heart. "And I'm falling in love with you because of it."

She stared at him wide-eyed, but didn't say anything.

"Go put your suit on. And I hope to God you brought some sort of granny bathing suit, because if you have a bikini, I don't think my heart will be able to take it."

She smiled. "It's not a bikini."

He sighed in relief.

"But it's not a granny suit either."

"Shit."

She giggled. "Please tell *me* you wear a tight speedo."

He looked down at her in horror. "No way."

She pouted. "But I wanted to check out your ass."

Gumby shook his head and reached down and grabbed her bag. She took it when he handed it to her. "You're gonna be the death of me."

"As if you aren't going to be checking out *my* ass," she countered as she walked toward the stairs, Hannah at her side.

Gumby watched until he couldn't see her anymore, then reached down and adjusted his hard-as-nails cock. She wasn't wrong. He was totally planning on checking out her ass. And tits. And everything in between.

CHAPTER ELEVEN

Sidney treaded water in the ocean and stared at Decker. She hadn't laughed so hard in ages. The more time she spent with Decker, the more time she *wanted* to spend with him. He was like a drug...she needed more and more of him in order to be satisfied.

"Okay," Decker said. "We're gonna swim from here until we're even with that bright blue house down there." He pointed to a gaudy-colored house about five down from his own.

Sidney knew she wouldn't be able to beat him. He was a Navy SEAL, for God's sake, and it had been way too long since she'd gotten in the water. But the thought of being able to get her hands on him when he claimed his prize for having won would be worth trying. Not to mention the sight of him in his skin-tight bathing suit was well worth losing for.

He had extremely well-defined abs, and Sidney wanted to lick her way up them to make sure they were real. His thighs were muscular as hell and the knee-length, tight

Lycra clung to every curve, highlighting rather than hiding anything.

And the bulge between his legs was definitely drool worthy. Sidney hadn't thought she was a sex-starved maniac—not like Nora—but seeing Decker practically naked had nearly brought her to her knees. When he'd walked toward her in the house, she'd wanted to beg him to take her right then and there.

And the look in his eye when he saw her in her plain ol' black one-piece suit didn't do much to help her keep control of herself. His eyes had gone from her feet up her body to her boobs, then back down. The amount of heat emanating from him was enough to make her sweat. She'd never felt particularly sexy, and she was a little too fond of sugar to ever be called thin, but when Decker looked at her as if he was two seconds from ravishing her, she couldn't help but rethink her lifelong beliefs about her body.

"Hey, are you listening or still thinking about me in my suit?" Decker asked.

Sidney smiled. "You in your suit, of course."

He grinned back at her. "Fair enough, since I can't stop thinking about you either."

Just the sound of his deep voice turned her on. But she knew she had to do something, otherwise Decker would seriously kick her ass in this race.

She looked to her left and saw a small group of kids playing near the shore. Knowing what she was about to do was cheating, Sidney did it anyway.

"Oh my gosh," she said as she tried to look concerned. "Did one of those kids just yell for help?"

As she expected, Decker's smile died, and he looked

over to where she was pointing. He immediately started heading that way—and Sidney called out, "One-two-three-GO!" and took off swimming.

She didn't hear his response as she swam as fast as she could, but she couldn't stop smiling.

It wasn't too long before she saw Decker at her side when she turned her head to breathe. He'd caught up to her in seconds. She was a good swimmer, but he was obviously leagues better.

He swam right past her, and since she was completely wiped, she simply stopped where she was and tried to catch her breath while still laughing.

Decker realized she'd stopped not long after he passed her, and he swam back to where she was treading water. He snaked a hand around her waist and pulled her into him. Their legs kept bumping against each other, and eventually she stopped using her legs to keep her afloat. There was no need. Decker wouldn't let her sink. No way.

"You little cheater," he accused with a smile.

Unabashed, Sidney shrugged. "Hey, a girl's gotta do what a girl's gotta do."

"You do know that there's a penalty for cheaters, right?" he asked.

Trusting herself to him completely, Sidney hiked her legs up around his waist and put her arms around his shoulders. He was now completely holding her above the water, and she felt absolutely no concern whatsoever about his ability to do so. One of his hands felt huge against her back, and the other he used to tread water. "Yeah? What's that?"

"The wager is doubled. So now I get an hour-long massage instead of only thirty minutes."

Sidney rolled her eyes. "Whatever."

They stared at each other for a long moment. Even though they could hear others on the beach, it was as if they were the only two people in the world.

"I have no idea how I survived without you in my life," Decker said quietly.

"Ditto," Sidney returned immediately. "You make me happy, Decker. And I didn't even realize I wasn't all that happy until you came along."

He lowered his head and kissed her. It was a gentle kiss because her lip was still healing, but more intimate than anything they'd done before. They were plastered together from groin to chest, and since they were only wearing bathing suits, Sidney could feel every inch of Decker against her. Her nipples tightened and she knew she was soaking wet...and not because she was submerged in the ocean.

She could feel Decker's erection between them, and the urge to ride him long and hard struck her like a bolt of lightning. She moaned and tore her mouth from his. Staring into his eyes, she knew he felt the same way.

"I think I've had enough swimming," she told him softly.

"Right. Me too. Besides, Hannah's probably waiting for us to get home."

"Yeah." Sidney pounced on that excuse. In all reality, the dog was probably snoring on one of the extremely comfortable dog beds Decker had bought her, but Sidney was all about going back to his house.

Licking his lips, Decker leaned forward once more and gave her with a closed-mouthed kiss before slowly letting go, making sure she was good before gesturing with his hand back the way they'd come. "After you."

They swam back slowly to the beach in front of his house, and Sidney had to admit she was a bit disappointed when he wrapped one of the towels they'd left on the sand around his waist. Without a word, he grabbed hold of her hand and they walked back to his house.

Something had changed out there in the ocean. Sidney wasn't exactly sure what, but she felt closer to Decker as a result.

Forty-five minutes later, after they'd both showered, Decker was stretched out shirtless on the floor of his living room. He was wearing a pair of gray sweatpants that hung low on his hips. Hannah thought her human lounging on the floor was a fun new game, and it took a few minutes for her to understand that Decker wasn't lying there for her amusement. She lay down at his side, keeping her eyes on both him and Sidney.

Sidney was suddenly not as sure about this as she'd been earlier. The idea of giving Decker a back rub was one thing, but the reality was so much...more.

His back muscles rippled as he propped himself on one elbow and raised an eyebrow at her. "You reneging on our bet?"

She shook her head. "No. Just trying to figure out the best way to do this."

Decker reached out and grabbed her hand, pulling her toward him. "Straddle my thighs. Yeah...like that."

Perched on top of him, Sidney took a deep breath. God, he was built like a Mack truck. No wonder he could carry Hannah around as if she weighed nothing.

She leaned forward and tentatively put her hands on his back and pushed them upward.

He groaned.

Sidney stilled. "Decker?"

"Sorry. Keep going."

So she did. With every caress, she relaxed a little more. His arms were bent up and his head was resting on his hands and for the first time, she felt as if she could look her fill without feeling even a little awkward.

The dark tattoos on his arms blended in with his deep tan, enough that if she wasn't up close and personal like she was, she'd have a hard time even knowing they were there.

The jeans Sidney was wearing seemed way too tight, and she could feel she was already soaked between her legs. She was turned way the hell on and couldn't stop fantasizing about Decker.

As if he could read her mind, without warning, Decker spun and the next thing Sidney knew, he was looking up at her. His large hands were at her waist and she could feel his fingers on her bare skin, where her jeans met her shirt. She'd never felt so vulnerable and excited.

"It's only been fifteen minutes," she said softly.

"I can't take any more," Decker admitted. "I thought I could. I underestimated how good it would feel to have you straddling and touching me."

Sidney took a deep breath and his eyes went straight to her chest. She was wearing the jeans she'd had on earlier and a T-shirt, but she might as well have been naked for the impact his lustful gaze had on her body.

She looked down to try to avoid his intense stare, and came face-to-groin with the evidence of his arousal. She couldn't see him as clearly as she had when he was wearing the bathing suit, but it was more than obvious he was ready and able to move things along in the sex department.

"You are so beautiful," he said reverently.

Sidney moved her eyes away from his dick and up to his chest. She couldn't stop herself from running her hands up his belly to his nipples, then back down. "You're the beautiful one," she told him.

"Look at me," Decker ordered.

Taking a deep breath, Sidney did as he ordered. The heat she saw in his eyes was almost frightening. Without realizing it, she bit her lip and scooted back farther on his thighs.

Instantly, his hands came off her body and he put them under his head. "Easy, Sid."

"I just...I've never felt this way before. It's overwhelming."

He nodded. "I know. For me too." Then, moving slowly, he sat up, and Sidney went to her knees to give him room. He stood then reached down a hand to help her up. Once she was upright, he led them over to the couch and sat.

Without hesitation, Sidney sat and curled into him. One of Decker's arms went around her shoulders, and she rested her head on his chest. Her knees were bent up and his other arm went around them to hold her close.

They sat like that for five minutes or so before he spoke. "Don't ever be afraid of me."

Sidney shook her head. "I'm not."

"You were," he countered. "I never want to see you look like that again. At least not when it comes to me."

"I just…the look in your eyes was intense."

He nodded. "I'm kind of an intense guy," he told her. "I'm not sure I ever want you to see me when I'm in work mode. I get really focused and sort of have tunnel vision. But you never have to worry about me hurting you. Or rushing you into anything you aren't ready for."

"But that's the thing. I think I *am* ready," Sidney protested.

He shook his head, and she felt his beard brush against her forehead. "When you're sure, we'll see about moving our physical relationship along. Until then, we'll go at your pace."

"That's not fair," she protested, not sure why she was complaining. He was right, his intensity had scared her, but not in the way he thought. She knew he'd never hurt her. She glanced down at his lap and saw his erection was still just as big as it had been before. "You're hurting." Sidney gestured to his lap with her head.

Decker chuckled. "Sid, I've been this way for the last two weeks. This is nothing new. I can take care of it the same way I have since we met…by myself in the shower. Or lying in bed late at night after I've talked to you."

Sidney wasn't exactly shocked. She'd masturbated a few times after talking to him too. But she still felt bad.

Decker brought a hand up and put it under her chin. She lifted her head and looked him in the eye. They stared at each other for a moment before he leaned forward. Eagerly, she met him part way until they were kissing.

It started off slow and easy, but before too long, they were both straining toward each other. Sidney slanted her head and when Decker went to pull back, she put a hand on his head and held him in place.

The next few minutes, Sidney was lost in Decker. His fingers roamed, lighting a fire inside her wherever he touched. One hand snaked up the back of her shirt, touching her bare skin. Then it traveled down and he tucked it into the back of her jeans.

Even that small touch made her burn even more than before.

Wanting to be closer, Sidney straddled his lap and pressed herself against him without stopping their kiss. Her hands caressed his bare chest from top to bottom, even as she ground herself onto his cock.

For a second, she thought this was it. That they were going to make love right then and there on his couch. But when his hand slipped under the front of her shirt and cupped one of her breasts, she stiffened.

It was just for a second, but he felt it...and immediately removed his hand.

Sighing in frustration, Sidney pulled back and licked her kiss-swollen lips. Her brows furrowed as she stared at him. She wanted him. She *did*. But she had no idea why she kept pulling away every time he moved them a step closer to making love.

Without a word, he gathered her to him, and she relaxed against him, boneless. "Stop thinking so hard, Sid," he murmured, running a hand over her hair gently.

"I feel like I'm the biggest fucking tease," she murmured. "And I don't mean to be."

"Shhhh, you're not a tease. You just need to be sure. No matter my feelings, I know this is all happening fast. We don't have to be in a rush. There will only be one first time for us."

Sighing, she closed her eyes and took a moment to just

enjoy being with Decker. To appreciate the fact that he didn't expect her to jump into bed with him and seemed to genuinely be okay with them not doing more than making out on his couch.

Suddenly, he chuckled.

Lifting her head, Sidney said, "What?"

"Hannah."

She turned to look at the dog—and stifled a giggle.

Hannah was sitting next to the coffee table staring at them. When she saw them looking at her, her tail began to wag energetically.

"Nothing like having an audience," Decker quipped. "I kinda expected her to hold up a sign with a number judging us on our performance."

Sidney couldn't hold in her laughter anymore. She chuckled, then it turned into a full belly laugh. She laughed so hard her stomach hurt, and she had to climb off Decker in order to lean over and try to catch her breath. Of course, when she did that, Hannah came over and tried to lick her face.

"Oh my God," she said after she'd controlled herself. "I think I'm traumatized for life. Please tell me she won't be allowed in the bedroom when we do finally have sex."

She didn't give a thought to what she'd said until she realized Decker was no longer laughing. When she looked at him, he was smiling though. He had a tender look on his face...

And she suddenly had a flash forward to what he might look like at their wedding. Staring down at her with that exact same look on his face.

"No one sees your ass but me," he told her, still smiling.

The mood broken, Decker stood and held out a hand. "Help me find something to make for dinner?"

"Of course," she said, and let him pull her upright.

The next hour was spent happily cooking side by side with Decker and laughing. She'd never laughed so much in her life as she did with him. It was something new...and she liked it.

After they'd eaten dinner, Decker said, "We need to talk, Sid."

She froze. Oh, God. Had she read the day completely wrong? It couldn't be good when a guy said they had to talk...could it?

"Stop panicking," Decker said, obviously reading her thoughts...or her facial expression. "I'm not breaking up with you, I still want to see you, and you're stuck with me as long as you want to be. Okay?"

Sidney breathed out a sigh of relief. "Okay."

He went back to the couch and sat once again, and she took a seat next to him. She had no idea what in the world he wanted to talk about.

Gumby took a deep breath. Today had been amazing. One of the best days of his life...and he hated to have to tell her that he was leaving. He'd gotten very used to seeing Sidney almost every day, and the thought of having to go the next however many days without that sucked. He decided she was stressed enough and didn't drag it out.

"You know I'm a SEAL...well, tomorrow the team is headed out on a mission."

He watched as his words sank in. He knew it wasn't

whatever she'd expected him to say, but he was pleased when she didn't immediately protest or complain about him leaving.

"For how long?"

Pressing his lips together, Gumby said, "I don't know. It could be a few days, or it could be a couple weeks. It all depends on how soon we achieve our objective."

"And you can't tell me where you're going or what that objective is, can you?"

He shook his head. "Unfortunately, no. I know that sucks, and I'm sorry."

Sidney took a deep breath. "Actually, I think it's better. If I knew all the details, it would probably stress me out more."

God, he loved this woman. She was going to make an amazing SEAL wife. "Come here," he said, and she immediately burrowed into his side once again. "I need you to make me a promise."

She looked up at him warily. "What?"

"I need you to promise that you won't go off and check out Victor's house, or any other potential abused-dog situation, until I get home."

She didn't immediately agree, and his stomach clenched in worry. He hurried to make his case. "I get that you're an adult. That you've been rescuing dogs for a long time before I came into the picture. But it scares the shit out of me to think about you doing it by yourself. I love that you have a tender heart and want to help abused animals, but I'm not happy you put yourself in danger in the process. I'm not sure what's driving you to put yourself at risk like you do, but if you have the compulsion and you need to do it, I'll go with you. I'll have your back. All I'm asking is that you please don't do it when I'm gone. The thought of hearing about you being hurt while I can't get to you makes me physically ill."

"And if I said that I couldn't do that?" she asked.

Gumby sighed. "Then there'd be nothing I could do about it. I'd worry about you, which I'll do anyway, but even more so."

"What happens if you get hurt or, God forbid, die on this mission?"

"First of all, I'm not going to die. Believe that. But... what are you really asking?"

"We're dating. We aren't married, so I'm thinking the navy wouldn't notify me. Would I just never hear from you again? Would I drive by this house one day and see that it's for sale?"

Gumby shook his head vehemently. "No. Fuck no. My commander knows who you are because I've already given him your information. Not only that, but Caite, Rocco's girlfriend, knows about you too. Hell, just about everyone I work with knows who you are. If something happens to me, you'll be notified. All the guys have your number as well."

"So if you got hurt, they'd let me come to you? Be by your side?"

"Yeah, Sid. And I know without a doubt that I'd get better a hell of a lot faster if you were there with me."

She absorbed what he'd just told her, then said, "I won't go after any dogs while you're gone."

Gumby breathed out a long sigh of relief. "Thank you."

"But I can't give it up. You know that, right?"

He reluctantly nodded. "I do. I wish you'd do it safer

though. Can you tell me why? What drives you to put yourself in danger to rescue the dogs?"

For a second, he thought she was going to finally tell him, so he inwardly sighed in frustration when she just shrugged.

"I don't know."

"I won't push," he told her. "But I hope someday you'll feel safe enough and secure enough in my feelings for you that you'll let me in."

Sidney was obviously uncomfortable, and she changed the subject. "So everyone you work with knows about me? Including Caite?"

He nodded. "Yeah. Seems I can't keep my mouth shut about you."

"Think I figured that out when you brought Max here and got him to offer me a job."

"Hey, I didn't tell him to offer you anything. I just thought that you two would get along."

"Uh-huh," she said skeptically.

"I did! And I was right," he crowed.

"Any chance I'm going to meet Caite soon? I think I'd like to compare notes. You know, since she's dating a big bad Navy SEAL too."

Happy that she wanted to meet the other woman, Gumby nodded. "Hell yeah. I'll set it up as soon as we get back." He ran a hand over her hair and tucked a strand behind her ear. I'm going to leave you the numbers of all the guys, as well as my commander. Caite's too. You can call any of them if something goes wrong during my mission."

"Oh!" she said, sitting up straight. "Who's looking after Hannah? Do you need me to take her?"

Gumby winced. "About that."

"What?"

"I had already arranged it before we got close. And I could always switch things around, but Caite seemed excited to spend some time here at the house."

"So she's dog-sitting?"

"Yeah. There was an...incident...at the apartment complex a bit ago. Caite and a rear admiral's wife were in the wrong place at the wrong time and were held captive for a bit. Rocco is hesitant to leave her there by herself, and he asked if I minded if she stayed here. I jumped at the offer, because I wasn't sure where we would stand by the time I headed out on the mission. Caite loves the beach, and she and Rocco are looking at houses, but they haven't found anything yet."

Gumby knew he was rambling but couldn't make himself stop. The last thing he wanted to do was have Sidney think there was anything going on with him and Caite. And he hated to disappoint her.

"At the time, it was the perfect solution. She and Rocco came over the other morning and met Hannah, and she liked her...not the same way she likes you, but they got along." He took a deep breath. "Are you upset?"

She shook her head. "No, it's fine. I was going to offer to take Hannah to my trailer while you were gone, but she'll like being here at home better, I think. Moving her around too much this soon after she was rescued probably isn't a good thing."

"I'll make sure I introduce you and Caite as soon as we get back," Gumby told Sidney. "You'll like her, I think."

"Decker, I don't make friends easily. Some women are intimidated by me, probably because I don't give a shit what they think. And if I'm being honest, some women intimidate *me* too. Let me guess, Caite is probably super-smart, huh?"

"She's no smarter than you, Sid."

"Right. Bet she has a college degree?"

"Yeah. She has a job on the base. She's fluent in French and has been invaluable to NCIS."

"Jeez. The only other language I know is how to swear like a sailor when I smash my finger," Sidney joked. "And this is the woman who saved your life, right?"

Gumby leaned forward and took her face in his hands. "She's gonna love you," he said seriously. "From what Rocco says, Caite doesn't have that many friends either. I know you, Sid, and if I say you'll get along, you'll get along. I wouldn't push this so hard if I didn't think so."

Sidney nodded. He kissed her on the forehead then sat back, letting go of her, but wishing he could hold her to his chest forever.

"What about vet visits? Does Hannah have any follow-ups?"

"Not really. The vet said to come back in a few weeks as long as she was healing all right."

"I noticed that she was limping a bit today. How're her paws?"

Gumby loved how much she worried about his dog. "They're okay. Still tender, and the pads will take a while longer to grow back. Right now the new skin is pretty fragile, she still shouldn't be on the beach, and she's still got the heartworms, so staying inside and calm is on the agenda for while I'm gone."

"And Caite knows all this?"

"Yeah, she knows."

Sidney hesitated for a beat, then took a deep breath. "I'm gonna miss you," she said softly.

"Oh, Sid, I'm gonna miss you too," Gumby replied, and breathed out a long sigh of relief when Sidney burrowed into his arms once more.

"I might actually get a full night's sleep," she joked, then winced. "Sorry. That was rude when you probably won't be, since you'll be doing your mission thing."

"It's fine. And look at it this way...the less sleep I get, the faster this mission will be over." That wasn't quite true, but he'd say anything to make Sidney feel better. "Are you going to talk to Jude about the job with Max?"

"Yeah. I feel guilty though. Jude really helped me out when I first moved here. I was young and naïve about everything, and he even gave me a break on rent for at least two years while I figured out what I was going to do with my life."

"And in that time, I bet you helped him out for free, or almost free, didn't you?" Gumby guessed.

She shrugged. "Maybe."

"It's not like you're going to move out immediately," Gumby said. "I'm sure you can work something out with him. Like maybe you can keep working until he hires someone. Or you can work part time until the new person has the hang of things. Who knows...maybe the person Jude hires really needs a break...like you did when you got here."

"True," she said.

"So you'll talk to him?"

"Yeah." She snuggled in deeper. "I can't wait to get an apartment or something. I've lived in that old trailer for so long that an apartment will totally seem like a step up."

Gumby literally bit his tongue to keep from blurting out that he wanted her to move in with him. There would be time for that later. It wasn't as if she was going to go out and rent an apartment tomorrow. No, Sidney would be cautious with her money and want to save up a little nest egg before she took that step.

He had time to make her fall madly in love with him and agree to marry him and move in permanently.

Thinking about marriage didn't freak Gumby out as much as it might've a few months ago. Before he'd faced his own mortality in Bahrain, he hadn't really thought about settling down. He figured he had plenty of time for that. But now he knew differently. Life was short. Too short. And having met Sidney, he knew he wanted to get started on his life with her as soon as possible, so he didn't miss one minute of the time they could have together.

"What time do you leave tomorrow?"

"Early."

"I should go then."

Gumby hated to agree, but she was right. He had to get up at three in the morning to catch the transport out of the country, and he really did need to get some sleep before the shit hit the fan. There was never a guarantee of having any time to rest while on a mission. "I'll call the second I'm back," he told her.

Sidney nodded and sat up. "Be safe, hear me? I'm gonna be pissed if you come home with holes in you."

Gumby smiled. "Of course. I know we haven't talked about it much, but I work with some of the best guys in the navy. They have my back, and I have theirs. We've also been over and over this mission and have plans B, C, D, and E prepared, just in case, just like we do every time."

"That makes me feel better."

"Good." He stood, and took her in his arms when she joined him.

"I'm not good at long goodbyes," she informed him. "So I'm just gonna go."

He could tell she was holding back tears. And he hated this. It was the first time heading out on a mission didn't hold the appeal it had in the past.

He kissed her on the forehead, keeping his lips there for a long beat before stepping back. Gumby watched as she went over to Hannah and hugged her. The dog licked her face before Sidney could move out of reach. "Be good for Caite," Sidney said quietly before straightening and heading to the front door. She grabbed up her bag and opened the door.

She turned around when she was standing on his porch, and the tears on her face nearly did Gumby in.

"I'm proud of you," she said. "Kick some terrorist ass." Then she turned and walked quickly to her car. Within moments, all Gumby saw were her taillights headed down the street.

Hannah whimpered at his side.

"I know, girl. I already miss her too."

Then Gumby turned around, shut the door, and did his best to get his mind set for the upcoming mission.

CHAPTER TWELVE

Eight days.

That's how long it had been since Decker had left...not that Sidney was counting or anything.

She blew out a breath and rolled her eyes at herself. She was pathetic. She was an introvert. She *liked* being by herself. Had liked it until she'd met Decker and spent every evening for two weeks with him, either in person or on the phone.

She had a whole new respect for military spouses now. How in the hell did they do this all the time? And she didn't have children. Sidney couldn't imagine how hellish this would be if she had to be a single mother on top of everything else.

Looking at the clock, she saw it was five forty-two in the afternoon. She had nothing planned for the evening, and that sucked. She'd tried to keep busy over the last week. She'd had dinner with Nora a couple times, which was nice, had gone over and seen some new dogs Faith had received one night, and even told Jude she would be happy to work evenings, and he'd taken her up on her offer twice.

One night, she'd even gone so far as to go online and busy herself looking for posts from Victor.

And she'd found one. It was horrible. He'd made up some story about an older dog he'd supposedly had for years and years that he'd had to put down, and his little girl was devastated, and now he was looking for a puppy. That asshole didn't have a daughter. She'd bet every penny to her name on that. The low-life scum was just trying to find more dogs he could train to fight.

She'd wanted to go to his house and make sure he hadn't gotten his hands on any new dogs, but she'd promised Decker she wouldn't. The compulsion had been there though. And it had been strong. Fuck.

Fingers twitching, Sidney paced back and forth. She was thinking about the post she'd seen a few nights ago, and it was making her crazy. She had to think about something she could do that would take her mind off Victor, and what he might be doing to a poor defenseless dog, as well as Decker, and the danger he was most likely in.

She could binge watch something on TV. But she wasn't in the mood for anything.

She could read, but knew nothing would hold her attention, and a romance would probably make her sad right about now.

She couldn't go back online because if she did, she'd probably end up breaking her promise to Decker and going over to Victor's house.

Nora was out with one of her boyfriends.

Faith was busy.

And Jude had already told her that everything seemed calm for the night and he'd handle anything that came up.

"Damn it," she mumbled. How long were Decker's missions usually? She had no idea. Would he be gone a month? Two? She cursed. The least he could've done was given her a ballpark figure on how long she had to worry about him before he'd be back.

When her cell phone rang, Sidney practically leaped on it. Any distraction right now would be welcome.

Not recognizing the number on the screen, she answered cautiously. "Hello?"

"Sidney?"

"Yeah. It's me. Who's this?"

"Thank God! This is Caite. Caite McCallan. I don't know if Gumby told you about me or not, but I need help!"

The woman on the other end of the line sobbed, and Sidney tensed. Decker had told her he'd given Caite her number. But why the woman was calling was a mystery.

"Calm down, Caite. What's wrong?" Sidney asked.

Caite sobbed through her words and it was hard for Sidney to understand her.

"I got b-back to Gumby's house a little l-late today and when I w-walked in, there was b-blood everywhere!"

"What? Shit, slow down. Have you called 9-1-1?"

"No, it's not t-that."

Sidney was confused. "Not what?"

"It's H-Hannah! She's hurt, and I don't know what to d-do!" Caite wailed.

Every muscle in Sidney's body went tense. She was headed for the door before she even thought about it. "Hannah? What's wrong with her?"

"I don't know! She won't let me get near her. But there's b-blood everywhere! I swear to God it looks like a serial killer was in here chopping up his victims."

Sidney had no idea if Caite was being overdramatic or not because she didn't know her. But the thought of Hannah being hurt, in pain, was not acceptable.

Images from Sidney's childhood tried to overwhelm her, but she refused to think about anything but getting to Decker's house.

"I didn't know who else to call," Caite went on. The more she talked, the clearer her words became. Obviously simply having someone to talk to was helping to bring down her panic. "Gumby said if anything happened to call the vet. I tried, but they're closed. And I can't get Hannah to come to me to bring her to the emergency vet. He also said if I needed help with her, I could call *you*. So I'm calling you. What do I do?"

"First, calm down. I'm on my way."

"Thank God!" Caite breathed.

"Can you tell where the blood is coming from?" Sidney asked.

"No. It's everywhere though. I think it'll come up from the floors, but it's on the cabinets in the kitchen and all over her dog bed. Oh! And his couch. Oh my God, I think it's probably ruined!"

Sidney could tell Caite was panicking again. "It's just stuff, Caite. Decker won't care about it. Concentrate on Hannah. Is it coming from the wound on her back?"

She heard growling in the background and was somewhat surprised. She'd heard Hannah sound mean before, like the day she'd been over there when Max had come to the door, but she had no idea what the dog's deal was now.

"I don't think so. I mean, her fur is black, so it's hard to tell, but it looks like it's her paws or something."

As Sidney drove like a bat out of hell toward Decker's house, she nodded to herself. It was possible the pads of Hannah's feet had become irritated and started bleeding again. Although it had been a week since she'd seen the dog, and it seemed to her that they should be well on their way to being healed now.

"Oh, no!"

"What?" Sidney barked out.

"There's glass on the floor next to the couch! I put a vase of flowers there yesterday. Blake had them sent to me at work. I think Hannah must've knocked them over and the vase broke."

That would explain it. Hannah's paws were still delicate and healing, a piece of glass could've easily cut the pad of her foot, and those tended to bleed like crazy. And if she walked around the room, of course it would spread the blood everywhere.

Feeling a little calmer now that she knew Hannah probably wasn't bleeding out or anything, Sidney took a deep breath. "Okay, Caite, you're probably right. Can you clean up the glass so she doesn't step in it again?"

"Oh, yeah. Of course. Are you still coming?"

"Yes. I'm about halfway there now."

"Thank you! I'm worried about Hannah. She's never acted like this with me before. I haven't had any trouble with her the entire time I've been here. She's lying on her bed and growling."

"At you?" Sidney asked. "Or just growling."

"Oh, um... Now that you mention it, I think she's just growling in general."

"Right. It's probably because her foot hurts and she doesn't understand why. Just clean up the vase and don't go near her. We'll see how she is when I get there."

"Okay. Sidney?"

"Yeah?"

"Thank you again. I didn't know what to do. I know you and Gumby just started dating and we haven't met, but I appreciate you coming over."

"I only met Rocco once, but I liked him. And trust me, I definitely don't like everyone I meet. I'm glad you called me. I've missed Hannah."

There was silence on the other end of the line before Caite said, "Oh, shit, you probably wanted to dog-sit her, didn't you? I'm such an idiot! I should've thought about that. I just went along with it when Blake asked if I wouldn't mind. I know he did it to get me out of the apartment while he was gone. *Shit!* I should've thought this through. I'm so sorry."

"It's fine," Sidney said, liking the other woman more and more.

"No, it's not," Caite countered. "Blake was being overprotective, which most of the time I don't mind, but this had to be upsetting for you. I swear that I don't have a thing for Gumby. I mean, I like him—what's not to like—but I don't *like* him, if you know what I mean."

Sidney chuckled. "I do."

"I swear it didn't even cross my mind—because I'm an idiot—that Gumby might've wanted *you* to stay here instead of me. He was probably just being nice. Because he *is* nice."

"Seriously, it's okay," Sidney said when Caite took a breath. She had a feeling the other woman would just keep apologizing over and over if given the chance. "I've been busy, and it's good for Hannah to get used to other people."

"Well, when Blake and Gumby get home, I'm gonna make sure they know they're idiots," Caite huffed.

Sidney couldn't help but laugh. It was a release of tension more than anything, but Caite *was* amusing.

"Are you almost here?" Caite asked. "I threw away the glass, but I'm really worried about Hannah."

"I'm about three minutes away," Sidney told her. "Has she moved yet?"

"No. She's just sitting on her bed, licking one of her paws and giving me the evil eye."

"The evil eye?" Sidney asked. "Is that even possible?"

"Yes and yes," Caite said. "Now that I'm not freaking out, and I can tell she's not actually growling at *me*, she's actually kinda pathetic and I feel really bad for her."

"Just give her some room and I'll be there in a second."

"I'm going to the door to meet you."

"Okay. I'm hanging up. I'll see you soon."

"Great. Thanks."

"Bye."

"Bye."

Sidney clicked off her Bluetooth and concentrated on getting to Decker's house. When she pulled into the driveway behind what had to be Caite's car moments later, she saw a petite woman standing in the doorway of Decker's house. She had on a pair of khaki pants and a light blue blouse. She looked to be a little taller than Sidney, but not by much. She had brown hair that was mussed, as if she'd run her hands through it in agitation.

But what made Sidney happy was the fact she looked so...normal.

She knew she was being irrational, but if she'd driven up and Caite looked like a freaking runway model, she wouldn't have been happy. It was bad enough knowing Decker had a kind of special relationship with her because she'd literally saved his life. It would've been too much if she'd looked like she came off the pages of a beauty magazine.

Not to say that Caite wasn't pretty, she was, but it was more in a "girl next door" kind of way than a "wow is she beautiful" way.

Shaking her head at how ridiculous she was being, Sidney turned off her car, climbed out, stuck her phone in her pocket, and walked quickly up to where Caite was waiting for her.

Without hesitation, Caite threw her arms around Sidney and hugged her. Hard.

Startled, Sidney returned the embrace.

"Thank you so much for coming!" Caite said.

"Of course."

"Come on," Caite told her, stepping back. "Gumby told me how much Hannah loves you. Hopefully seeing you will make her stop growling."

The second Sidney stepped into Decker's house, she stopped in her tracks. Looking around wide-eyed, she couldn't believe what she was seeing.

"Told you," Caite mumbled.

"Holy shit. I thought for sure you were exaggerating."

"Unfortunately, I wasn't."

"I see that," Sidney said. The house was exactly as Caite had described. There was literally blood everywhere.

On the walls. On the floor. She saw there were even foot-prints on the door when it closed behind her. But instead of thinking about how long it would take to clean the house, she could only think about poor Hannah.

She followed Caite into the living area and saw Hannah right where Caite had said she was. Lying on her dog bed in the corner, licking one of her paws. She was so engrossed in what she was doing, she hadn't even noticed or cared that Caite had opened the door.

"Hannah, girl, what did you do to yourself?" Sidney asked quietly.

The dog's head came up at the sound of her voice, and a whimper replaced the growl deep in her throat. Hannah leaped to her feet and charged at Sidney. Caite gasped and took a step backward, but Sidney went to her knees on the floor and held out her arms.

Hannah's head careened into Sidney's chest, nearly knocking her backward off her knees onto the floor. She went ahead and sat on her ass anyway, figuring it was prob-ably safer. The whimpers increased, and Hannah's tail wagged a million miles an hour. "Hey, baby. Are you okay?" Sidney crooned.

Hannah did her best to crawl onto Sidney's lap and buried her snout under her arm. Her butt was still on the floor, but her upper body was pinning Sidney down.

Bemused, Sidney looked up at Caite.

The other woman was staring down at them, and when she saw Sidney looking at her, she smiled. "Guess she missed you, huh? Definitely having words with my man and Gumby when they get home."

Sidney looked back down at the fifty-plus pounds of dog in her lap and ran her hand down Hannah's back. The wound there looked really good. Better than it had earlier. The angry red had turned into a lighter pink, indicating that it was healing. It even looked like some of the hair on the outer edges of the wound might be growing back. She knew it wouldn't ever completely cover the scar, but the sight of it was encouraging.

"You gonna let me look at your foot, baby?" Sidney asked.

Hannah didn't remove her head from her lap, but her tail wagged faster.

"What do you need?" Caite asked.

"Paper towels. Maybe a warm wet rag? I don't know what else until I can get a look at where she cut herself."

"I'm so sorry," Caite said. "I should've moved the flowers to the counter this morning before I left for work."

"It's not your fault," Sidney said immediately. "Dogs are curious. Besides, it's obvious she has good taste. I'm assuming the flowers are toast?"

Caite chuckled. "Yeah, trampled, and I think she even ate some."

"Sucks. I don't think I've ever received flowers from a guy before."

"Really? Never?"

"Nope"

"Blake manages to have them delivered for me every time he's gone. It's a small way to show me that he's thinking about me even when he's not here."

That was the sweetest thing Sidney had ever heard. "You're lucky," she said.

"Believe me, I know. I'll be right back," Caite told her, and turned to head into the kitchen.

Sidney leaned over Hannah and said softly, "I missed you, baby. Have you been good? Besides the whole flower thing today, I mean." Hannah didn't answer in words, but she did wiggle in closer. "I'm gonna need to see your paw, girl. I know you don't want me to, but if there's still glass in there, I gotta get it out. You aren't going to bite me, are you?"

The fact of the matter was that Sidney wasn't sure *what* the dog was going to do when she started treating her cut pad. She knew better than most that injured animals sometimes lashed out when they were hurting. Hannah knew her, and seemed to love her, but pain sometimes overruled everything else.

Caite came back and put the things she'd asked for on the floor next to her. "Can I help?" she asked.

"Let's play it by ear," Sidney said. "The last thing I want is for you to get bitten if she decides she doesn't like what I'm doing to her."

"What about *you* getting bitten?" Caite asked.

Sidney shrugged. "Won't be the first time."

Caite frowned, but didn't respond.

Shifting so the bulk of Hannah's body was across her lap, Sidney carefully bent one of Hannah's front legs back, the one she'd been licking. The dog whimpered, but didn't otherwise move or growl.

"That's it, girl, just let me help you. I'll get you fixed right up," Sidney murmured. She took the wet washrag and gently swiped it across the dog's paw. "Ah, yeah, you really did a number on yourself, didn't you? Caite?"

"Yeah?" The other woman kept her voice low and even, which Sidney appreciated.

"Do you think you can find me a pair of needle-nosed

pliers or something? I'm gonna need something other than my fingers to dig this piece of glass out of her pad."

"Um...sure, but...what do they look like?"

Sidney looked up in surprise. "What...needle-nosed pliers?"

Caite blushed. "Yeah. I know, I know, I should know. But I'm hopeless with that sort of thing. I get confused about the difference between a Phillips head and a flat-head screwdriver too."

"Seriously? I mean, a flat-head screwdriver literally describes what it is in the name."

"I know, but if someone asks for a Phillips head, I still get confused and I'm not sure which they want. Go ahead and laugh. I'm used to it. Blake makes fun of me all the time."

Sidney couldn't have stopped the laughter from escaping if her life depended on it. Finally, she got herself under control. "Sorry. I work with tools all day, every day, so it just surprises me when I hear shit like that. I think I saw a toolbox in the front closet when Decker was giving me a tour. If you bring it over here, I'll point out what I need."

"Okay. Deal!" Caite said happily as she moved to the closet.

In moments, she was back with the battered red tool-box. Just as Sidney hoped, Decker had a pair of needle-nosed pliers right on top. "Those. The thing with the blue handle and the long spike things that look like a really long snout."

Caite beamed. "See? You know how to ask for things in a way I understand."

Still chuckling, Sidney took the pliers from her when

she held them out. Then she got serious. "Okay, step back. I'm gonna do this nice and fast so Hannah doesn't have time to freak out."

"So *Hannah* doesn't have time to freak out?" Caite asked perceptively.

"Yup. That's my story and I'm sticking to it," Sidney told her. "Here goes." She wiped away the blood that had welled up while she'd been talking. The piece of glass wasn't huge, but it wasn't small either. She clasped it, and winced when Hannah whimpered. "I know, baby, but once this is out, you'll feel a whole lot better, promise."

Then she quickly and firmly pulled the piece of glass out of the dog's foot. Hannah whimpered some more, but didn't snap at her or make any threatening moves whatsoever.

Breathing out a sigh of relief, Sidney held out the pliers with the piece of glass still grasped in the nose. "Can you take this?" she asked Caite.

"God, my heart is beating a million miles an hour," Caite said as she took the tool from Sidney.

"Mine too," Sidney said with a smile. "And Hannah's."

While Caite headed into the kitchen, Sidney covered Hannah's pad with the wet cloth and held it firmly in place. The pad would continue to bleed, but hopefully with direct pressure it would stop sooner rather than later.

Taking a look around her, Sidney winced. There was a lot to clean up. She had no idea what in the world Hannah had been doing to get blood absolutely everywhere, but there was no way she could leave Caite to deal with this all on her own.

Forty minutes later, Hannah was back on her bed—stripped of the comfy outer cover, which was in the washer

—watching as Sidney and Caite scrubbed the walls and floors.

Caite had changed into a pair of sweatpants and a T-shirt, and Sidney had nabbed one of Decker's T-shirts from his dresser. It was way too big, but she tied it in a knot at her waist and figured since it was only her and Caite, her fashion faux pas would be forgiven.

"Seriously, how in the world did blood get up here on the countertop?" Caite muttered as she worked in the kitchen.

"Same way it got under the couch," Sidney commiserated.

The two women talked about nothing and everything as they cleaned, until Sidney sat back on her heels and said, "You know what would make this better?"

"Um...finding someone else to do it for us?" Caite replied.

Sidney laughed. "Yes, definitely that, but I was thinking alcohol."

Caite stopped wiping the cabinets and looked over at her. "It *is* Friday night, and I don't have to work tomorrow."

They grinned at each other and put down their cleaning supplies and starting raiding Decker's kitchen. They came up with a bottle of rum and Kool-Aid. It wasn't exactly highbrow, but neither cared.

An hour later, with the house mostly clean, Caite sat on one end of the couch, and Sidney snuggled with Hannah on the other. Luckily, the bleeding had stopped completely, but Sidney kept a washcloth wrapped around it, just in case.

"I don't think the blood is ever going to come out of these cushions," Sidney lamented.

"Then Gumby will just have to buy a new couch!" Caite exclaimed a little too exuberantly.

The bottle of rum was almost gone. Between the two of them, and with a whole lot of Kool-Aid, they'd about polished it off. It had been a while since Sidney had gotten drunk, but tonight had definitely called for it.

Caite was just as drunk as Sidney, but she seemed to be a happy drunk, whereas Sidney always got super-emotional. Not crazy, like starting fights, just weepy.

"How did Rocco manage to send you flowers when he's on a mission?" Sidney asked the other woman. She'd been thinking about it ever since Caite figured out how Hannah had gotten hurt.

"He sets it up ahead of time. Sometimes they come the day after he leaves, and other times they come a week later. I think he does it so they're always a surprise. I mean, I'm always pretty sure they're coming, but I don't know *when*."

"That's so sweet," Sidney told her, resting her head on the back of the sofa.

"I know. And looking at him, you'd never guess he was so romantic."

"What's up with the beards?" Sidney asked.

Caite giggled. "Right? I mean, I'm all for a hot guy with a beard, but to have every single one of the guys on the team with one is kinda crazy." She leaned forward and winked. "But now that I'm sleeping with a bearded hottie, I can definitively say that I'm pro-beard in bed."

Sidney smiled politely.

"Oh my God, seriously?"

"What?" Sidney asked, looking around in bewilderment.

"You haven't slept with Gumby yet?"

Sidney knew she was blushing, but couldn't help it. She took another drink of the homemade "trash-can punch" they'd concocted. "This really does taste like straight-up Kool-Aid."

"Stop trying to change the subject," Caite scolded, shaking her finger at Sidney. "I thought for sure you guys were doing the nasty."

"We haven't known each other that long," Sidney defended.

"Girl, whatever you're waiting on, stop it."

"I just...I don't sleep around, and I keep thinking Decker is too good to be true."

Caite shook her head fiercely. "No, he's not. I thought the same thing about Blake. But these guys...they're... amazing. That's a crappy word for what I'm trying to say, but my brain isn't working too well right now. They're honorable, sweet, and completely badass. If Gumby likes you, you don't have to worry about him cheating or being a dick."

Sidney raised an eyebrow. "All men can be dicks."

Caite waved off her words. "Oh, I'm not saying he won't fuck up. He will. All guys do. They can't help it. It's ingrained in their DNA. What I mean is that if you decide to be with him, *really* be with him, he'll make sure you know how special you are."

"Is that what Rocco does with you?"

"Um, *yes*. Flowers?"

Sidney nodded. Caite did have a point.

"And the beard thing? *Totally* hot. Especially when he goes down on you."

Sidney knew she was beet red.

Caite rolled her eyes. "Tell me you haven't thought about it."

Sidney shrugged. "I've thought about it."

The other woman grinned huge and nodded. "As I said...mind-blowing."

"Can I ask something else?"

"Of course. I think after cleaning up what looked like a murder scene, we're like, best friends now or something. I wouldn't be surprised if we wake up in a jail cell tomorrow morning, wondering what the hell we did the night before." She laughed at her own joke, and Sidney couldn't help but smile at her.

"Decker said you saved his life?"

Caite rolled her eyes. "Those guys are way too focused on that."

"So it's true?" Sidney asked.

Caite shrugged. "I guess. I mean, I'm sure they would've figured out a way out of that hole they were in before the bad guys came along and shot them if I hadn't shown up."

Sidney's eyes nearly bugged out of her head. "*What?*"

"Yeah. It was in Bahrain. They were only supposed to be checking things out. Nothing bad was supposed to happen, but they were ambushed and thrown down into this cellar. I heard the bad guys talking about going back and shooting them, and I couldn't let that happen. Blake had asked me out on a date, and it had been forever since I'd been on one, and I *wanted* that date, damn it! So I went into the city, found them, and opened the hatch where they were kept. That's all I did. They're making it into way more than it was. Did you know that Gumby saved *my* life?"

Sidney's mind was spinning. Intellectually, she knew Decker was a Navy SEAL, but hearing all this, she was getting a whole new picture of the man he truly was. And it was both scary and hot as hell. "No."

"Yeah, I can't swim. Well, I can float. Sort of. A bad guy decided he wanted to kill me because of shit that went down in Bahrain, and to get away from him, I stupidly went into the ocean. Gumby and this other SEAL guy, Cookie, showed up out of nowhere and towed me to shore."

"Seriously?"

"Yup. Totally saved my life."

"No, I mean, you seriously can't swim?" Sidney wasn't surprised Decker had gone into the ocean after Caite. He was a really good swimmer.

"Well, I'm better now. Blake is teaching me. Let me guess, you're probably an Olympian or something, right?"

Sidney laughed. "No."

"Whew."

"But I was all-state on my water polo team in high school."

"Bitch," Caite said. But she said it with a smile on her face, so Sidney simply giggled.

After a moment, she said, "I like you."

"I like you too," Caite returned.

"I wasn't sure I was going to," Sidney admitted. "I mean, the guy I like was excited to tell me that you saved his life and how much he admired you. Then he asked you to dog-sit Hannah instead of me, which, I'll admit, kinda hurt. I was prepared to be polite to you, but I genuinely like you."

"Oh my God!" Caite exclaimed. "I felt the same way. Well, not about dog-sitting Hannah, because I didn't know that he didn't ask you. When Blake said he'd come over here and met you, and how nice you were, I was kinda jealous. I know Blake would never cheat, but I kinda didn't like that you were encroaching on 'my' guys. I mean, I'm not dating them, it's not like some sort of reverse harem or anything, but I kinda started thinking about the team as mine, you know? But you were the only person I could think to call, and you came right away, and were so worried about poor Hannah..." Her voice trailed off.

Sidney ran a hand over Hannah's head and heard the dog sigh in contentment. Then she said, "I don't make friends easily. But I'd like to think we're friends now?" She felt tears in the back of her eyes, and she did everything possible to keep them from falling. If she cried, Caite would think she was a complete dork. Damn alcohol, making her weepy!

"Yes! We're totally friends. You're so cool, and I can't believe you don't have a million friends already. You're way cooler than I am. I mean, I majored in French in college. Who *does* that?"

"Well, I didn't even *go* to college," Sidney admitted.

"Then you saved a ton of money. Go you!" Caite said with a smile.

It was hard to believe Caite was as genuine as she was, but judging by the way she smiled at her, Sidney knew it was true.

"How do you deal with Rocco being gone?" Sidney

blurted. "We don't have any idea where they went or how long they'll be away."

"It sucks," Caite said with a frown. "I won't lie. But I have to trust that they know what they're doing. They always go over and over the missions before they leave. Blake told me that they have a ton of backup plans just in case something goes wrong."

"Decker mentioned that too," Sidney admitted.

"I just have to believe that he'll come home safe and sound. But even if he gets hurt, I'd never leave him," Caite said fiercely. "I've heard so many stories of women leaving their men while they're laid up in the hospital."

"They do not?!" Sidney said, shocked.

Caite nodded. "Yup. But I don't care what happens, I'll never leave Blake. Ever. He's stuck with me."

Sidney couldn't even think about something happening to Decker. It hurt her heart.

It was at that moment when she knew exactly *how* badly she'd fallen for the Navy SEAL.

"It helps to talk about it with someone," Caite said. "Blake introduced me to a group of SEALs he's worked with, and their wives, and I have to tell you, I was super jealous of how close they all were."

"How come you didn't call one of *them* tonight?" Sidney asked, genuinely curious.

Caite shrugged. "They were all really nice, and I know Blake wants me to call them if I ever need anything, but I don't know...they're all so...established. They've been with their men for years, have kids, and are very close with each other. I kinda feel like an outsider. Not because of anything they've said or done, but just because Blake isn't a part of the team their men are on. Does that make sense?" she asked.

"Surprisingly, yes," Sidney reassured her. She held up her cup. "To new friends!"

"To new friends," Caite echoed, holding up her own cup.

"You can call me anytime."

"And you can call me," Caite returned.

They smiled at each other.

The room was spinning, and Sidney knew she'd definitely drank enough. She leaned forward, ignoring the way Hannah grumbled at being jostled, and put her cup on the coffee table. She grabbed a blanket from the back of the couch and covered both her and Hannah.

"You think Decker is gonna be mad I raided his closet?" she asked Caite.

"What else were you supposed to wear?" the other woman asked, shrugging. "If he was here, I bet he'd be totally eye-fucking you. Guys like it when their women wear their clothes."

"What's up with that?" Sidney asked. "That's weird."

Caite shrugged. "No clue. But I have to admit that I love wearing Blake's T-shirts. Especially when he's gone. They smell like him and make me feel less lonely."

Just like that, the tears were back in Sidney's eyes. "Yeah," she agreed.

"You're staying the night, right?" Caite asked, her words slurring.

"Uh-huh...if that's okay."

"Of course it is. No way I'd let you drive anyway. I should probably go back to my apartment tomorrow and let you dog-sit Hannah until the guys get back."

"No way. Decker asked you."

"But I got Hannah hurt," Caite said sadly.

"No, you didn't. She's a curious dog. That's a good thing. It shows she's getting more brave, and after what happened to her with that jerk, that's a good thing."

"She's lucky you found her."

Earlier, Sidney had explained the circumstances behind Decker getting Hannah in the first place. "There're so many other dogs like her out there," Sidney said with a sniffle. "In fact, the asshole who hurt her probably has more dogs right now."

"Seriously?"

"Yeah. I looked online and saw that he's been posting more messages on social media, asking if anyone has any dogs they don't want anymore."

"What an asshole!"

"Yup. But I promised Decker I wouldn't confront him while he was gone on his mission."

"That sucks."

"Yeah."

"Sidney?"

"Yeah?"

"If I forget anything we talked about tomorrow, you'll remind me, right?"

Sidney chuckled. "Yeah, Caite. I'll remind you."

"You won't pretend that you don't know me?" She grinned.

"Nope. We cleaned up a crime scene together. Like you said, that means we're best friends forever now," Sidney joked.

"Good. I'm gonna close my eyes now."

"Night, Caite. Thanks for calling me."

"Night. Thanks for coming over."

Sidney closed her eyes, feeling more comfortable than she'd been in a long time. With a heavy, warm dog in her lap, alcohol coursing through her bloodstream, a new awareness of her feelings for Decker, and a new best friend, how could she be anything but?

CHAPTER THIRTEEN

Gumby put the key into the lock on his door and held it open for Rocco. He had no idea why Sidney was at his house, but he was more than thrilled she was. When he'd driven down his street, he'd been surprised to see her car in his driveway. He was instantly a little worried, yet happy he'd get to see her sooner than he'd planned.

It was one in the morning, and he'd been traveling and in wrap-up meetings for almost twenty hours. He was exhausted, and his plan had been to get a few hours' sleep, then text Sidney and let her know he was home.

But suddenly, his exhaustion seemed to disappear as if by magic. He couldn't wait to see Sidney. To hold her.

The mission had gone off without a hitch. They'd met up with a team of Delta Force operatives stationed out of Texas and had tracked down one of the mostly highly sought-after terrorists in Afghanistan. The intel on where he'd been hiding out had been correct and, after several days of surveillance, the two teams had made their move and taken him out.

One down, way too many to go, Gumby thought to himself as he closed the door behind him and Rocco. There was a light on in the kitchen that was bright enough to illuminate the small living area of the house.

Rocco stood at the end of the couch, silent and not moving. Gumby came up beside him—and blinked in confusion at what he saw.

Sidney was on the floor with her head resting on Hannah's dog bed. She was curled into a little ball and had one arm around his dog, as if she was snuggling her. Hannah's tail was wagging furiously, but she didn't get up to come greet him...probably because Sidney was wrapped around her so tightly.

Caite was asleep on the sofa. She was on her back, one arm thrown over her head, mouth open and breathing very deeply. The coffee table had a mostly empty bottle of rum and two empty glasses with red stuff on the bottom. A roll of paper towels and a washcloth concluded the odd scene.

"What in the world?" Gumby said softly as Rocco went to sit beside his girlfriend. Gumby stood over Sidney, not sure how to go about moving her. He hated to wake her, but he was going to have to. There was no way he could loosen her grip on his dog without disturbing her.

"Oh my God!" Caite said loudly after Rocco had woken her up. "You're back!"

"I'm back," he agreed.

Gumby ignored the lovers' reunion and turned his attention back to Sidney. He squatted down and put one hand on her shoulder, giving Hannah a pet with the other.

"Sidney?" he called gently. When she didn't move, he jostled her a bit harder. "Wake up, Sid. I'm home."

Her eyes popped open as if she'd been awake the whole time—and immediately filled with tears.

Alarmed, he put his hand on her face. "Sid?"

"You came back," she said softly.

"Of course I came back. I'm happy to see you and glad you're here, but why are you on the floor?"

Instead of answering, Sidney sat up and threw her arms around his neck, holding on for dear life. Gumby's eyes met Rocco's, and they shared a look of amused confusion. He picked Sidney up off the floor and carried her over to the big chair next to the sofa. He sat on the edge and simply waited her out.

Hannah stood, stretched, then limped over to where he was sitting with Sidney. Frowning, Gumby tilted his head and tried to assess the dog.

"You okay?" Rocco asked Caite.

"Yeah. I'm good," she said, sounding very awake for having been practically passed out a minute earlier.

"Why was Sidney sleeping on the floor?" Rocco asked.

"I called her. Hannah was hurt, and she came over and helped. We had some drinks, cleaned up the crime scene, raided Gumby's drawers, and now we're best friends."

"She's trashed," Rocco said, turning to smirk at Gumby.

"Crime scene?" he questioned.

But Caite had buried her face into Rocco's chest, and Rocco merely shrugged, as much in the dark as to what the women had been up to as Gumby.

"Sid?" he asked, leaning back to look at her face. She gave him a watery smile. "Everything good here?"

"Uh-huh."

He needed more. "You came over because Hannah was hurt?" he prompted.

Sidney nodded and put her head on his shoulder. She was cuddled into him as if he were the world's best pillow. He couldn't deny it made him feel ten feet tall, but he still needed answers.

"She cut the pad of her foot. Decker?"

"Yeah?"

"I hope you don't ever have the CSI people come over and inspect the place."

The comment was so out of left field, Gumby could only think to ask, "Why?"

"Because if they use that luminal stuff, this place is gonna light up like a Christmas tree."

"*What?*"

"There was blood everywhere. I mean, *everywhere*. Hannah managed to cover almost every inch of the floor with her blood, and it was on the cabinets and stuff too. I took some pictures because I knew you wouldn't believe how bad it was. Anyway, if you're ever investigated, they're gonna find you guilty because it'll look like a massacre took place in here. Trust me...I know how that stuff works. Since me and Caite cleaned it up, it'll look like a bunch of smears and stuff when they look at it under the special light."

That explained the crime scene comment from Caite. But that had been a lot of info, and Gumby didn't like what Sidney was inferring. Not that he would ever be investigated...but that she knew what smeared blood looked like under the chemicals in luminal.

He looked around the room and saw what he'd missed earlier, because he'd had eyes only for Sidney. There were paw prints in what he assumed was blood on his couch, and he saw a few small spots on the tile floor that also looked like blood. There was a mop propped up in the corner over by the kitchen, and a bucket sat on the counter by the sink.

He could only imagine what the place had looked like *before* the women had cleaned.

"Deck?" Sidney mumbled.

"Yeah?"

"You're much more comfortable than the couch. I fell asleep there, but Hannah got restless, so we moved to the floor. I'm glad you're home."

"Me too, sweetheart. Me too."

"How drunk are you?" Gumby heard Rocco asking Caite.

She giggled. "On a scale of one to ten, I'd say probably around a seven and a half."

"You want to stay?" Gumby asked his friend.

Rocco looked like he was considering it, then finally shook his head. "Nah, I'm gonna get Caite home. She might be hurting tomorrow, and I know she'd prefer to be in her own bed."

Gumby nodded. He didn't blame him—and was secretly a little relieved. He loved Rocco and adored Caite, but having Sidney to himself in the morning definitely appealed. "I'll come out and move Sidney's car so you can drive Caite's back."

"'Preciate it," Rocco said. "I'll come back tomorrow afternoon and grab her stuff...if it's okay to leave it in the guest room overnight."

"Of course," Gumby told his friend. Then he stood, keeping his arms around Sidney until he was sure she could stand on her own. "Why don't you go upstairs and climb into bed?"

"Your bed?" she asked.

His stomach clenched with how right those words sounded on her lips. "Yeah."

Sidney nodded, but instead of walking over to the stairs, she headed for Caite. The men stood by, bemused, watching as the two women embraced.

"Thanks for coming when I called," Caite said.

"I would've been pissed if you'd called anyone else," Sidney returned.

"You'll let me know how Hannah's doing?"

"Of course. We should go to lunch sometime." Sidney pulled back and looked Caite in the eyes, keeping her arms around her waist.

"I'd like that. I want to hear more about the animals you've rescued."

"And I want to know more about Bahrain and NCIS."

"I also want to introduce you to the other SEAL wives," Caite said.

"The ones you said you didn't feel like you fit in with?" Sidney questioned.

"Well, yeah. But they're still awesome. Super nice. I just don't fit in because they're already a family. But now *we're* going to make our own family. So we can hang with them because they have each other and we have us."

Gumby raised an eyebrow at Rocco at their women's conversation. He shrugged his shoulders, but smiled in return.

"That's right. We have us. I'd invite you over, but I just have a trailer," Sidney told her new best friend.

"What's wrong with a trailer?" Caite asked. "A home is a home is a home."

"True. It's cozy. I like it. Oh! And I have to introduce you to Nora. She's addicted to sex, so her conversations are a bit off-the-wall, but she's nice."

"And I want to introduce you to Brenae. She's the rear admiral's wife. Remember? I told you all about how that crazy bitch held us hostage in the mail room in our building."

"Isn't a rear admiral, like, crazy high? Should I even be talking to her?" Sidney asked.

"Of course you should!" Caite exclaimed. "A rear admiral *is* pretty high-ranking, but you'd never know it by talking to her. She's so *normal*—"

"Okay, you two," Gumby interrupted. "It's time to go. You can talk to each other later."

"I'm gonna miss you," Sidney said, slurring slightly and hugging Caite once more.

Gumby could only stand there, surprised. He'd never seen Sidney so...touchy-feely with anyone before. She'd definitely let her guard down. Whatever had happened to Hannah—and the alcohol—had obviously allowed Caite and Sidney to bond. He couldn't say he wasn't happy about it. He just hoped they'd both feel the same way tomorrow when they didn't have the rum coursing through their veins.

"Go on upstairs, Sid," Gumby said, and watched as she slowly made her way toward the stairs, weaving and stumbling as she went.

Grinning, he turned to Rocco to see the same indulgent smile on his friend's face as he said, "Come on, Caite. Time to go home."

"I like this house," Caite informed Rocco. "Did you know the beach is like...right *there?*" She threw out her hand, indicating the back of the house.

"Yeah, knew that, babe," he told her.

"Blake?"

"Yeah?"

"I love you. I'm so glad you're home."

"Love you too. And me too."

Five minutes later, Gumby had locked the front door and wandered over to where Hannah was lying in front of the couch. He spent a bit of time looking her over and giving her the attention he hadn't lavished on her earlier. He saw the cut on her paw and was thankful Caite had the idea to call Sidney.

He wasn't surprised Sidney had come over to help. It wasn't in her nature to ignore any hurt animal, but especially not Hannah, who he knew she'd come to love as much as he did.

"Thank you for looking out for our girl," Gumby told the dog. He still didn't know how she'd gotten hurt, but he'd find out sooner or later.

Giving Hannah one last pat on the head, he headed up the stairs. He held his breath as he headed down the hall, hoping like hell Sidney had gone into his room and not the second bedroom. If she wasn't comfortable sleeping with him, he'd leave her alone...

But he breathed out a sigh of relief when he saw the lump in the middle of his queen-size bed.

He'd showered back at the base after they'd arrived, so he didn't waste any time in stripping off his shirt and pants and climbing into his bed next to Sidney.

She immediately cuddled into him, and Gumby swore

he felt the tension ooze out of him the second her head landed on his shoulder and her arm snaked around his stomach. Her legs tangled with his, and he had to take a deep breath because they were as bare as his own. She was still wearing one of his shirts, but she'd obviously taken off the jeans she'd been wearing downstairs.

She sighed, and her warm breath wafted across his chest, making his nipples tighten...along with his cock. Knowing nothing was going to happen right now didn't help calm his body. Gumby wasn't going to make a move on Sidney when she was drunk. Not their first time, at least. He hoped there might be a time in the future when he could make love to her after she'd had too much to drink, but for now, he was content to simply hold her.

"What happened to Hannah, Sidney?"

"She cut her paw. I guess Rocco sent Caite some flowers and they were in a vase next to the couch. Hannah must've got curious and knocked them over, breaking the vase. She got a piece of glass stuck in her paw, and those things bleed like crazy."

Gumby hated to think about poor Hannah hurt and bleeding, but he was more relieved than he could say that Sidney had taken care of her. "Thank you for fixing her up." He paused. "How do you know what blood smears look like under luminal?"

Just as he suspected, she was too relaxed and tipsy to think about her answer. "Saw the pictures of my brother's apartment. And the shed."

His mind spun. He had so many questions, but wasn't sure how many he could get away with right now. "Will you tell me about Brian?" he asked after a moment.

Sidney's head pressed harder into his shoulder, and he tightened his hold around her, trying to make her feel safe.

"You could google him," Sidney said after a minute. "I'm sure the transcripts from the trial are online."

"I want to hear it from you. Anything you want to tell me, I'm here to listen," he said softly.

"It was awful," Sidney whispered. "All of it."

"All of what, sweetheart?"

"My life," was her heartbreaking response.

"Tell me," Gumby coaxed.

"I'm three years older than Brian. And things were pretty good when we were little. I was around eight when I realized I was actually scared of him." She huffed out a breath. "He was five. *Five.* And I hated being left alone with him."

"What'd he do?"

She shrugged awkwardly against him. "He was just...*off.* He had this toy gun he got for Christmas one year and he liked to sneak up on me, hold it against my head, and pull the trigger. He'd just laugh at how scared I was. He'd hide anywhere he could around the house and jump out at me, thought it was hilarious when I freaked out.

"When I was twelve, he came into my room in the middle of the night and sat on my bed. He had one of the knives from the kitchen...and he held it against my throat. I pushed him off me, screaming for my parents. When they came in, he started crying, telling them I hurt him."

"What'd he do with the knife?" Gumby asked, doing his best to stay relaxed under her. With every word she spoke, he got more and more pissed, but being upset wasn't going to help her right now. She needed to get it all out, and he needed to hear it.

"I guess he hid it under my bed. I got in trouble because my parents didn't believe me when I'd told them what he'd done. The next day, he told me he was gonna kill me for the first time. He thought it was funny I was punished and he wasn't, but he was also pissed that I tried to get him in trouble."

She stopped talking then, and Gumby ran a hand over the back of her head soothingly. "What else?"

"Lots. He terrorized me every damn day. I joined every after-school activity I could think of, just so I wasn't at home. The weekends were the worst. And the shed." Sidney shuddered.

When she didn't continue, he asked, "What happened in the shed, Sidney?"

If Brian touched her, Gumby would find a way to make the man's life completely miserable behind bars.

"The shed was his 'workspace' when we were growing up. It's where...where he learned the best way to carve people up. How to hurt them without killing them. Where he honed his skills with a knife," Sidney whispered, as if the man was in the other room and might overhear.

"He killed people when he was a kid? When you were growing up?" Gumby asked, horrified.

She shook her head against him. "No. Animals. He killed animals."

Oh, shit.

It was suddenly *very* clear where Sidney's compassion for dogs came from.

"You know I wouldn't be tellin' you this if I wasn't drunk, right?" Sidney asked.

"Yeah. And I'm taking advantage of that fact. We both know it. But you need to get this off your chest."

"I told everything at the trial. Everyone already knows," she protested.

"I don't," Gumby said simply.

"Promise you won't hate me tomorrow if I tell you what my brother did?"

Gumby sat up a little, lifting Sidney's chin with a finger so she had to look at him. Her eyes were watery and her cheeks flushed with the alcohol still in her system. Any arousal he'd felt when he'd climbed into bed had dissipated. All he wanted to do now was comfort his woman. Reassure her that, just because she shared some DNA with her brother, she wasn't like him. Not in any way, shape, or form.

"Promise," he vowed.

She nodded, and he let her duck her head once more. If it was easier to talk when she wasn't looking at him, so be it. Gumby made a mental note to look up the transcripts she'd referenced earlier. If nothing else, he'd ask Wolf, a fellow SEAL buddy, to have his computer expert contact get him what he needed. Knowing how horrible Sidney's childhood had been, and how terrible Brian James Hale had been, even as a kid, Gumby felt a bone-deep need to know everything.

The man might already be on death row, but Gumby had a feeling after his talk with Sidney tonight, and after he'd read up on the man, he'd be figuring out a way to make Brian's life even more miserable than it hopefully already was. Being on death row in Florida wasn't a picnic, but there were always ways to make it more uncomfortable.

"One of our neighbors' cats disappeared one day. The little girl—she was about seven—was devastated. She made fliers and put them up everywhere. There was even a reward offered. Brian had been nice to me for a while, so when he said he wanted to show me something in the shed, I didn't think too much about it. I followed him out there, and after I went inside, he blocked the door and wouldn't let me leave.

"He'd either found or stolen the neighbor's cat... Scruffy...and he'd hurt it. *Bad*. I can't talk about...what he did. Can't relive it. But trust me when I say he did things to that poor kitty that no sane person could even think about doing. Then after he'd tortured the poor thing, Brian made me watch as he slit the cat's neck.

"He laughed, Decker. *Laughed*. Told me how much fun it was to watch the cat struggle."

"Jesus, Sid. I'm so sorry."

"But that wasn't even the worst of it. Not by a long shot. He captured and tortured so many animals. But the dogs... If I'd thought what he'd done to the poor kitty was bad, the things he did to the puppies were even worse. And he collected jars and jars of blood, telling me how much he enjoyed the feel of it on his hands. Once, he cut off the head of a puppy and wrapped it in a box. He gave it to me as a present when my parents weren't around, and I stupidly opened it. I'll never forget the eyes of that poor puppy looking up at me when I opened the lid."

"And your parents did *nothing*?" Gumby asked in shock. "How is that possible? They had to know what was going on in that shed."

Sidney shrugged. "I told them, and they said I needed to stop being a tattletale and to mind my own business."

"But...that makes no sense," Gumby said, not able to wrap his brain around any adult ignoring the abuse happening literally in their backyard. "Didn't they know that many serial killers abuse animals when they're kids? At the *very* least, they should've known that wasn't normal behavior and tried to get him some help."

Sidney shook her head. "I have no idea *what* they were thinking. They'd always wanted a son, and it was as if the second they had one, they forgot all about their other child. I sometimes think they both must have some sort of mental problem as well, because it's crazy that they could ignore everything he did growing up...let alone still support him after the truth came out about the women he'd killed.

"The second I graduated from high school, I was out of there. I wanted nothing to do with my brother. I didn't even go home for the holidays. After the trial, I moved out here, as far away from them as I could get. I wanted to get as far away as possible from what he'd done."

Gumby knew what Brian James Hale had done. He'd killed his first victim when he was only sixteen years old. God, that had been only a year after Sidney had left. He'd gone into downtown Miami and found a prostitute and had killed her by stabbing her in the heart.

He'd murdered another prostitute a few months later, probably feeling more secure because he hadn't been caught for the first death. Things escalated from there. By the time he'd graduated from high school, he'd killed a total of five women. Then he'd moved into a small apartment—paid for by his parents—and continued his killing spree, getting bolder and less careful.

By the time he was caught, he'd admitted to murdering twenty-five women. He could describe how he'd murdered every single one too. Right down to the little details about what their last words were. He'd gotten more sadistic in his methods as time went by, keeping the last two women alive in his apartment for more than a week as he tortured them with his knives. He hadn't sexually assaulted them, that wasn't his kink. He simply enjoyed their terror and watching them bleed.

Yeah, Brian James Hale was one sick bastard...and Gumby *hated* that Sidney was related to him. Hated that she'd had to grow up witnessing his cruelty. But more relieved than he could say that she'd escaped.

"How'd you get involved in his trial?" Gumby asked after a minute or two had passed.

"My parents asked me to come testify on his behalf. I couldn't believe they'd even asked me that! I mean, he'd murdered over two dozen people! And I truly think the number is way more than that, he's just not admitting it. There was no way I was going to go into a courtroom and try to convince people that he wasn't that bad of a dude, like he was merely misunderstood or something.

"I called the prosecuting attorney right after I hung up with my parents and made sure he knew that Brian was as sane as I was. That he'd had a good childhood. There wasn't any abuse or anything like that. I wanted him to know that I was normal, and that our upbringing wasn't to blame. He asked if I would tell the jurors and the judge in person what I'd told him. And I said yes.

"I sat through the entire trial. Saw all the pictures the investigative people took of his blood-soaked apartment. They'd even gone to my parents' house and taken pictures of the shed after I'd told the prosecutor what Brian had done in there. That's how I know about the luminal thing."

"I am so proud of you, Sid. You have no idea," Gumby told her.

She sniffed against him.

He hated that she was crying, but didn't try to stop her. It seemed maybe his Sidney got sad when she drank. Or maybe it was just the conversation. Either way, he'd have to watch that. He liked this mellower side of her, but didn't like that she might seriously be hurting.

"I feel *so* guilty that I didn't do more when I was a teenager."

"What could you have done differently? I think you know as well as I do that your brother was born the way he was. Nothing you could've done would've fixed him."

"Not about Brian. About the animals," Sidney said softly. Then she looked up at him. "I could've done more to help those poor animals he tortured."

Gumby's heart broke, and it *all* made sense now. Why she was so adamant about confronting abusers. Why she put herself at risk to rescue dogs. Why she put their well-being above her own.

Guilt was a powerful thing, and it was driving her to put herself in danger. She obviously needed professional help to assist her in getting over something that wasn't her fault in the first place. To appease the guilt she was feeling. This wasn't the time to bring it up or try to convince her. But now that he knew what was driving her, he could do his best to help.

"Oh, Sidney. He would've found a way to get his hands on animals no matter what you did."

She shook her head.

Knowing there was nothing he could say right now

that would change her mind, Gumby settled for tightening his arms around her and kissing her forehead.

Ten minutes later, Gumby whispered, "Sid?"

"Hmmm?"

"Just checking to see if you were asleep."

She lifted her head. "I'm awake. The room is spinning pretty fast so it's hard to fall asleep. How was your mission? Did you win? Was anyone hurt? I didn't even ask."

He smiled. "It was fine. No one was hurt."

"Good. I'm glad."

"Me too. And for the record, I was going to get a few hours' sleep, then call you first thing in the morning. Imagine my surprise when I walked in my house and there you were. Snuggled up to my dog like a fantasy come to life."

She chuckled. "Oh, yeah, complete with me snoring, your dog bleeding, and me blotto after drinking too much to deal with cleaning up all that blood."

"Yeah, Sid. Complete with you wearing my clothes, cuddled up with my dog, safe and sound in my house. It was the perfect end to a very long mission."

"Is that the normal length of time you're usually gone?" she asked.

Gumby didn't respond, and she continued.

"Because I can handle that. I mean, I can handle it if you're gone longer too, but knowing that your normal 'gone time' is only like a week or two, that's different from thinking you'll be gone for months."

He understood. He'd left without being able to give her any kind of time frame for when he'd be back. "What would you have done if I *had* been gone for months?" he asked, genuinely interested in her answer.

"Cried. Probably a lot. Been sad that we hadn't taken any pictures together. Gotten on with my life."

"Meaning?" Gumby didn't like that last part. Did she mean she would find someone else to date? Decide they were done as a couple?

"Called Max to see if he was serious about hiring me. Started saving up money. Rented an apartment. Tried not to think of how much I missed Hannah. Things like that."

Gumby relaxed. "I can't say for sure that there won't be times when I won't be gone for a month or more, but generally we're sent in for shorter periods of time. Once all the intel is gathered, we go in to do the dirty work." He couldn't really say more than that, but he hoped it was enough.

"Good," she breathed. "Because I missed you. I didn't like not being able to text you. To call when I wanted to tell you something. I've never had that before, you know."

He definitely liked that. "Me neither," he told her. "There were so many things that made me think about you while I was gone."

"Like?" she asked.

He thought about what he could safely tell her, and settled for a heartwarming scene they'd come across on the outskirts of the town they were infiltrating in Afghanistan. "One day, we were on top of a building doing recon and something caught my eye below us. A little boy was walking a puppy. He had a piece of string around the puppy's neck, and he was trying to get him to follow him. But, being a puppy, every little thing that caught his eye made him want to play. It took about five minutes for the two to go even one block. But every time the puppy got distracted, the little boy didn't get upset or impatient. He simply waited until the little guy was ready to go again. He reminded me of you...or what you might've been like as a child."

"Are you serious? You didn't just make that up to make me feel better?" Sidney asked.

"Swear it's true. In the past, I wouldn't even have noticed that kid and dog. I would've seen them, of course, but not thought twice about them. Having you in my life has made me open my eyes to the little things. That kid and dog don't have even half the things kids here in the States do, but they seemed content."

"Decker?"

"Right here, Sid."

"Are you mad that I'm wearing your clothes?"

He shook his head at how her brain, in its inebriated state, went from one topic to another.

"No. In fact, I think it's pretty hot."

"Even though I totally rifled through your stuff? I had to open a bunch of drawers to find your T-shirts and even once I did, I couldn't stop snooping."

"Find anything interesting?" he asked, more amused than anything else. He had nothing to hide, especially not from her.

"A stack of dirty magazines from the nineties, some lube, an old Rubik's Cube, and a drawer full of socks with no matches."

Gumby chuckled. "Sounds about right."

"Deck?"

"Yeah?"

"I was a little upset that you didn't ask me to dog-sit Hannah, but I understand now."

"You do?"

"Uh-huh. Caite told me how Rocco was worried about her being by herself in that apartment complex after what happened there, and he felt safer with her here. And I can take care of myself, so I get it."

"You think I wasn't worried about you?" he asked.

"Well... We haven't been dating that long, and I'm not the kind of person who people worry about."

"I called Jude and asked him to keep his eye on you. He said he would. I also called Faith and told her that you promised not to go after any dogs by yourself until I got back. She also promised to keep her eye on you."

She went up on an elbow at his words. "You did?"

"I did," he confirmed. "You're right about Rocco and Caite. I wanted to ask you, but I knew Rocco would feel better with Caite here. And I knew you could definitely take care of yourself. I still worried about you, but more because I didn't want you to put yourself in a dangerous situation with the animals than anything else. I hated that you wouldn't get to see Hannah while I was gone, and her you. I'm glad Caite called you. I told her a million times if anything went wrong with Hannah, to get in touch with you. That you'd know how to help."

"Oh."

"And...you should know. Now that I know you and Caite get along, if Rocco hasn't found a new place for him and Caite to live by the time we're sent on another mission, I'm going to ask you *both* to stay here with Hannah." He hoped he could convince her to move in with him way before his next mission, so it would just be Caite who was the guest, but he left that part out.

"I like Caite," Sidney said, lowering herself back down onto his chest.

He merely shook his head at how she ignored everything else he'd said. It boded well that she hadn't freaked out on him for going behind her back to talk to Jude and Faith though. Hopefully she'd figured out that he'd done it out of worry for her, not because he was trying to be controlling.

"And it seems as if she likes you too," Gumby reassured her.

Several more minutes went by before Sidney said, "I'm tired."

"Me too."

"We should sleep."

Gumby chuckled. "Okay."

And just like that, Sidney was out. Her breaths against his naked chest felt good. Right.

Closing his own eyes, Gumby tightened his hold around Sidney. He hadn't ever had a homecoming like the one he'd had today. In the past, he'd always come home to an empty house and a headful of the people he'd killed, all in the name of fulfilling his duty to his country.

But tonight, he'd come home to not only his dog, but to his woman as well. A sleepy, tipsy, talkative, snuggly Sidney, who let him know in no uncertain terms that she'd missed him. Who let him in about her past. Who freely admitted to snooping in his stuff, and not being all that apologetic about it either.

Yeah, life was good—and he was the luckiest son of a bitch ever.

CHAPTER FOURTEEN

Sidney woke up and realized she was the luckiest woman ever. She took stock of her surroundings and her body. She remembered everything about the day before. Getting the call from Caite, rushing over to Decker's house, being shocked by the state of the house, cleaning, drinking, Rocco and Decker arriving home unexpectedly, cuddling up to him in his bed...and their conversations.

She probably wouldn't have shared what she had about her brother if it hadn't been for the alcohol, but in the light of day, she was glad she'd told him. It felt as if a weight had been lifted from her shoulders. Talking about Brian was never fun, but Decker had been the perfect blend of compassionate and outraged on her behalf.

She wasn't hungover in the least. She never was. Thank God.

And now she was lying next to an almost-naked Decker in nothing but one of his oversized T-shirts. The covers had been pushed off them in the middle of the night, and he still slept, so she had free rein to check out his body without worrying about being caught.

She'd seen him when they'd gone swimming, but that was different. Now she could look her fill without trying to be sneaky about it.

Decker didn't look like he had an ounce of extra fat on his body. His abs were amazing. Sidney didn't think she'd ever seen a six-pack on a man in real life other than on him. She moved her hand down and placed it on his stomach gently. He shifted, but didn't wake.

Smiling, Sidney's eyes roamed from his neatly trimmed beard, to the tattoos on his muscular arms, to the bulge between his legs. All he had on was a pair of boxer briefs, and they clung to him in all the right places.

His thighs were also muscular, and she could see them flexing in her mind as she imagined him up on his knees between her legs, pounding into her. Blushing, Sidney tried to get control of her libido. She wasn't like Nora. Didn't lust over every good-looking man she saw. But there was something about Decker that pushed all her buttons.

It wasn't only that he was a fine specimen of manhood, there was no doubt he was gorgeous. It was more that she knew the kind of man he was inside. Brave. Considerate. Protective. It all blended together to make him absolutely irresistible.

Rubbing her legs together, Sidney realized she was wet. She might've been embarrassed in any other situation, but not with Decker.

"Like what you see?"

Sidney jumped and her gaze whipped up to Decker's face. His eyes were open and he was smiling at her.

"Oh. Hi." She tried to play it off. No such luck.

One of his hands covered hers on his stomach, holding it in place. "Because I'll tell you that I'm *loving* what I'm seeing right now." His eyes went from her face, to her chest, and down to her bare legs. "That shirt never looked so good on me."

Sidney propped herself up on an elbow and licked her lips nervously. "You really aren't mad that I raided your drawers?"

"Anytime you want to raid my drawers, go right ahead."

The sexual innuendo in his reply was impossible to ignore. Sidney knew she was blushing, but didn't pull away. She just stared down at him.

"How do you feel?" he asked.

"Fine."

"No headache?"

"No."

"Your stomach isn't queasy?"

"No, I'm good. I never get hungover for some reason."

"Good." Then, without warning, Decker pounced.

Sidney found herself on her back with Decker hovering over her before she could even blink. She gripped his biceps and opened her legs when he settled over her. Her shirt had ridden up slightly, and his cock came to rest between her thighs.

She swallowed hard and stared up at him.

"You remember last night?" he asked.

Sidney nodded.

"All of it?"

"Yeah."

"You gonna freak out? Back off?"

She shook her head.

"Good. Because as far as I'm concerned, we crossed a

line last night. You opened up to me and told me shit that you haven't told hardly anyone else. Am I right?"

"Yes."

"I can't do anything without thinking about you. I see someone walking their dog and it makes me wonder what you're doing. I hear Rocco talking about Caite, and it reminds me that I haven't texted you in a while. I look around this bedroom and see how far it has to go before it's done, and I think about how you'd probably have it completed in a heartbeat. You've somehow made your way so deep into my subconscious, there doesn't seem to be a minute that goes by when I'm not thinking about talking to you or wishing you were with me."

"Decker..." Sidney protested.

"Last night, I was disappointed that I would have to wait an additional five or six hours to see you, but when I pulled up to my house and saw your car here, everything inside me breathed a sigh of relief. I slept better than I have in ages because you were by my side. I don't care that our relationship has been fast. I don't care what anyone else says or thinks. I need you, Sid."

With every word out of his mouth, Sidney's heart melted further. He could just be saying these things to get her to sleep with him, but she didn't think so. And she felt the exact same way. She hadn't ever really noticed military guys before. She knew they were there, but they didn't register. Now, every time she saw a navy bumper sticker, she thought about Decker. When she saw a guy in a store in his navy uniform, she thought about Decker. Hell, when she saw a cute guy with a beard, she thought about Decker.

He was always on her mind, as much as he claimed she was on his.

And she couldn't deny that she felt safer in his arms. But when she woke up and saw him kneeling beside her last night, everything in her relaxed. He was home. Safe and unhurt. It felt as if she could take a full breath for the first time in eight days.

"I need you too," she told him, meeting his gaze as she said it.

"Thank God," he breathed before dropping his head.

Sidney didn't worry about morning breath or anything else. All she could think about was getting Decker inside her.

His head slanted, and he took her mouth as if he couldn't stand one more second without her. They went from lazy morning to fiery inferno in seconds. Sidney lifted one leg and wrapped it around his hip as he devoured her mouth. His cock hardened against her core, and she felt herself dampen even more.

His hands went to her waist, and Sidney arched her back to help him remove the shirt she was wearing. He pulled back from her mouth just long enough to rip the material over her head, then he was back. Nipping at her lips and plunging his tongue inside.

Groaning, Sidney could only hang on for dear life as his every action ramped up her libido. When his hands closed on her breasts and his fingers zeroed in on her nipples, pinching lightly, she grabbed hold of his ass cheeks and squeezed...hard.

His head lifted and he stared down at her. They were both breathing raggedly, and Sidney noticed his pupils were dilated and his cheeks were flushed.

"I'm not sure I can go slow," he warned.

"Then it's a good thing I don't want slow," she returned, licking her lips and tasting him on them.

And with that, Decker shifted over her, crawling down her body.

Sidney tried to tug him back up, but he was relentless. He stopped to worship her nipples for just a moment, and the feel of his lips, tongue, and teeth on her sensitive buds made her back arch and a growl of impatience escape from between her lips. His beard scratching against her skin made the moment all the more erotic.

She felt him smile against her, then he was settling between her legs.

For a second, Sidney was embarrassed. It had been a very long time since anyone had gone down on her, and she couldn't remember when she'd last trimmed herself down there. But then his mouth was on her, and she ignored everything but the feel of his tongue lapping at her.

"God, Decker!"

"You taste amazing," he murmured. "I want more."

Then he attacked her.

There was no other word for it. His hands gripped her thighs, pushing them as far apart as he could get them, and he buried his face between her legs. He alternated licking between her folds and sucking her labia into his mouth. Sidney had never experienced anything like Decker going down on her, and knew she'd never be the same after this morning.

He hiked one of her legs over his shoulder and pressed the other to the mattress. She was splayed open and could actually feel her excitement leaking from her body.

"So fucking beautiful," he murmured, looking up at her.

Sidney could see her juices shining on his beard. It was carnal and obscene at the same time, but she couldn't look away from him. He licked his lips and smiled at her. "Hold on, Sid."

She opened her mouth to reply but didn't get the chance as he lowered his mouth and suckled on her clit.

Screeching in ecstasy, Sidney couldn't think. His tongue lashed against her sensitive bud as one finger slid inside her soaking-wet body. The hair from his beard brushed against her folds and her thighs, making her aware of him in a whole new way. Sidney couldn't control her hips, thrusting upward as he finger-fucked her.

She had no idea how he was able to keep his mouth on her clit with all the squirming and bucking she was doing, but somehow he managed it. His tongue was like a motor against her clit, flicking and rubbing, never stopping, like the freaking Energizer bunny.

"Decker!" she exclaimed as she felt herself getting closer and closer to losing it.

As if he knew, he increased the speed of his finger inside her, adding another. Sidney's thighs shook and her stomach muscles tightened in preparation for an orgasm.

Then he twisted his hand, changing the angle of his fingers inside her, and his middle finger brushed over something that made Sidney freeze.

"Oh, God," she breathed as he did it again. Was that her G-spot? She had no idea, but nothing in her life had ever felt as good as whatever he was doing to her at that moment. He latched onto her clit and sucked the same time he caressed that special spot inside her, and Sidney exploded into a million pieces.

She had no idea what she said or did in that moment, all she knew was that the orgasm he'd pulled from her was almost painful in its intensity. She was breathing hard, as if she'd run a marathon, and was having a difficult time getting her muscles to obey the messages her brain was sending them.

The next thing she knew, Decker was hovering over her, a condom already on, holding her hips in his hands as he prepared to take her.

The look on his face was as intense as she'd ever seen it. Generally, Decker was a pretty easygoing man. Quick to smile and with a joke. But at the moment, she imagined this was what he'd look like on the job. Intense and with a single-minded focused. Every muscle in his body was tight, and between her thighs, she felt the tip of his cock brush against her absolutely soaked folds.

"Sid?" he bit out between clenched teeth. "Say yes."

Looking up at him, Sidney realized he was serious. That if she pushed him away, or wasn't sure about this, he would absolutely back off and not fuck her.

And that was unacceptable. After that monster orgasm, she seemed to need him even more.

"Yes," she breathed.

The same time she lifted her hips, he slammed inside her.

They both inhaled sharply and Sidney couldn't take her gaze from his. Without breaking eye contact, Decker pulled out of her body, then thrust back in. Hard.

He took her that way, pounding into her fast. And Sidney loved every second. She was the first one to break eye contact, her eyes roaming down his body, marveling that this amazing, beautiful man was making love to her.

Her.

Suddenly needing to touch him, Sidney moved her hands to his chest and caressed his skin. When he inhaled sharply as her fingers brushed his nipples, she did it again. Then she pinched them lightly as he continued to pound into her.

"Holy fuck," he breathed as he took her.

Sidney smiled. She'd never had a sexual encounter like this. Decker was almost desperate, and she loved it. She clenched her inner muscles when he pulled out the next time and reveled in the way he groaned.

"So tight," he muttered. "So wet."

That was definitely true. The sounds his cock was making as he hammered in and out of her were carnal and almost obscene, but she couldn't make herself care.

When one of his hands moved between their bodies and began to rub her clit once more, she jolted in his grasp.

"Oh, yeah...you like that," Decker said with a smile in his eyes.

"Duh," she breathed.

"I'm close," he informed her. "But I'd love it if you came around my cock."

She wanted that too. She'd never been the kind of woman who had multiple orgasms, but Decker seemed to know exactly what she needed in order to get her there. His thumb gathered some of the wetness between them and he aggressively rubbed her clit.

Throwing her head back, Sidney gasped at the pleasure that coursed through her body. He wasn't being gentle.

Wasn't trying to patiently coax a response from her. He was demanding it. Forcing it. She'd never felt anything like it, and couldn't stop her body from doing exactly what Decker wanted it to.

Her legs once more began to shake, and she tried to pull away from his touch. "Too much," she managed to say, but Decker ignored her.

He pressed harder against her clit, his hips slapping loudly against her flesh as he fucked her. "Come, Sid. For God's sake, come!"

And she did.

Her inner muscles fluttered and gripped his cock as he powered in and out of her while she spasmed. Groaning, he shoved himself as far inside her as he could get and threw his head back.

Even in the midst of her own orgasm, Sidney reveled in the beauty of the man above her as he exploded. The cords of muscles in his neck stood out, and he went as still as a statue above her as he lost it.

He stayed like that for a heartbeat, before letting out a long, loud groan. Then he collapsed, making sure he didn't crush her, landing on his side and pulling her close. He turned until she was lying on top of him, still connected. They were both breathing fast and were damp with sweat.

Sex with Decker had been messy and intense. He'd done just as he'd said and taken her hard and fast. And it had been glorious.

Every muscle in her body hurt, but in a good way.

Good God, if he made love to her that way every time, she'd never survive.

Neither said anything for a long moment, reveling in the closeness their lovemaking had forged.

"Did I hurt you?" Decker eventually whispered.

"Took me apart piece by piece then sent me flying, yes. Hurt me? No."

She felt more than heard his chuckle, with her cheek lying on his chest.

"That was the most beautiful experience of my life," he said softly. "Thank you."

"I think that's my line," Sidney quipped.

She felt him hug her, then his cock slipped out of her body. They both moaned. Sidney lifted her head. "Thank you for putting on a condom. I was too out of it to even ask."

Decker shook his head. "I'd never put you at risk. I know we should've had the birth control conversation before things went this far, but honestly, the second I tasted you, I was a goner. I'm clean, Sid. It's been a long time since I've been with anyone, and I get tested regularly for my job."

She appreciated him letting her know, but a part of her, deep inside, already suspected that. "I am too. Clean, that is. I haven't been tested, but it's been at least a year since I've been with a guy. I can go down to the free clinic and do it to make sure though."

Decker shook his head. "Not necessary. Birth control?"

It was her turn to shake her head. "I tried the pills for a while, but they made me really sick."

He nodded. "Condoms it is then. If you want to try out another form of birth control, we can, but I'm not willing to let you do anything that hurts you."

Sidney's heart melted once again. "Condoms aren't foolproof," she felt obligated to say.

Decker shrugged. "We'll be careful."

She lifted her head and rested her chin on his chest and eyed him. "That's it?"

He smiled at her. "Yeah. I've always wanted kids. I hadn't planned on having them anytime soon, but then again, I hadn't met you yet either."

Sidney wasn't all that fired up about having children. Period. She'd had an up-close-and-personal experience with nature versus nurture. She and Brian hadn't been raised any differently, but he'd turned out to be a serial killer. With her luck, and DNA, she'd have a child who turned out the same as her brother.

"Stop worrying," Decker scolded. "I just had the most memorable orgasm I've ever experienced in my life, got to eat out my girl, and I'm exhausted."

Shaking her head, Sidney rolled her eyes. "You are such a guy."

"Yup," he agreed. Then belying his claims of being exhausted, he sat up with Sidney still in his arms.

She screeched and straddled him. The wetness between her thighs was almost embarrassing, but she clung to him and didn't let go, even when he stood up and headed for the bathroom.

"Until the bathroom gets remodeled, sharing a shower won't be too exciting, but we need to check on Hannah, let her out, make some breakfast, and get on with our day."

Loving how easily he carried her around, Sidney asked, "What are your plans?"

"To spend time with you," he said immediately. "After we get back from a mission, we typically have a day or two of downtime." He placed her ass on the counter next to the sink in the bathroom. Resting his hands on either side of her hips, he trapped her in place as he asked, "That okay?"

Sidney immediately nodded. She ran her hands up his sides and looked at him, getting the full picture of a naked Decker for the first time. His cock was semi-hard and still encased in the used condom. As she stared at him, his dick flexed and began to grow.

"Seriously?" she asked.

Shrugging, Decker smiled and reached down and removed the condom. He opened the cabinet beneath the sink and threw it in the trash before resuming his earlier position. "I think I'm pretty much hard around you all the time."

"How did this happen?" she asked, more to herself than to Decker. But he answered her anyway.

"Fate," he said without an ounce of self-consciousness.

She couldn't really argue with that.

"Ready to shower?" Decker asked.

"With you? Definitely."

He helped her down off the counter and pointed to a drawer. "There's a new toothbrush in there. Got it the last time I went to the dentist and never switched my old one out." Then he faced the shower/tub combo and leaned over to turn on the water.

Sidney couldn't take her eyes off his ass. It was whiter than the rest of his body and the sight made her grin.

"Stop ogling me, woman," Decker complained without turning around.

The smile still in place, Sidney pulled open the drawer and pulled out the toothbrush and got to work brushing her teeth. Decker came up beside her and did the same. They shared the single sink and when they were done, he took her face in his hands and leaned close.

The kiss they shared was slow and sweet. But it felt very different, since they were both naked as the days they were born.

Groaning, Decker pulled back. "Hannah's probably crossing her legs trying to hold it. We don't have time to make love again right now."

"But later?" Sidney asked.

"Definitely later," Decker agreed. Then he took her hand and led her over to the shower.

Afterward, as they ate the breakfast Decker had made for them, Sidney admitted to herself she was happier than she'd been in a very long time. Not only that, she was content.

And with that thought, she shivered. Generally, when things were going well in her life, it was only a matter of time before the shit hit the fan. She hoped like hell this time would be different.

"So where's this bitch you were so sure was gonna show up?" Miguel asked as he leaned against the fence behind Victor's house.

"Yeah, it's been like two weeks and she still hasn't shown her face," Kyle added.

Victor spat a loogie on the ground and glared at the two men. "She'll come by, she won't be able to resist."

"See, you're saying that, but even with those ads you've been puttin' online, she's still not here," Miguel skeptically.

Victor was secretly afraid he'd been wrong about the stupid bitch.

He'd run his mouth to his friends, and they'd told others, and now everyone in their circle was expecting a big shindig with the cunt when she finally showed up.

The new ad he'd put online a day ago should have sent her running straight into his trap...but so far she hadn't taken the bait.

"She'll show," he insisted.

"She better," Kyle said. "Dallas liked your idea so much, he spread the word. There are quite a few people who're waiting on the big fight. There's huge money to be made on this shit, so if she doesn't show soon, heads are gonna roll."

"Shut the fuck up," Victor mumbled, pushing off the fence. He headed for the two puppies he'd recently acquired and kicked at them. Neither would be a good fighter, they didn't have the temperament, but they'd be decent bait dogs when they got a little bigger.

The two brown-and-white puppies yelped and ran, their tails between their legs. Victor felt better, calmer, after seeing the dogs run scared.

He couldn't believe how naïve some people were. They had no problem giving away dogs to anyone who asked for them online. They didn't bother to check into anyone at all, they were just happy they didn't have to worry about the animals anymore. They'd rather believe they were going to nice, happy homes than put in a bit of effort to make sure. Morons.

"She'll show up," he said, more to himself than his friends. "And when she does, you both need to be ready to spread the word about the fight."

"It's still gonna be at Dallas's place, right?"

"Of course," Victor said with an eye roll. "He's got the setup. We just need to get our fighters and the bitch there, and we'll make money hand over fist. We'll be set—and will finally be respected in this crap town."

Kyle and Miguel gave each other a high-five as Victor cornered the frightened puppies. He picked them up by the scruffs of their necks and threw them back into the plastic crate they'd been living in since they'd been dropped off. He'd learned his lesson about leaving the dogs outside. Nosey neighbors and the incident with the bitch stealing his last trainee had taught him it was better to keep them all downstairs in his basement, only letting them outside for short periods of time.

As the three men headed back into the house, Victor couldn't stop fantasizing about how awesome their next fight would be. People were planning on coming from all corners of the city, and Dallas had even said he had a contact from Mexico who was planning on crossing the border for the one-of-a-kind event.

He just needed his prize fighter to show up.

CHAPTER FIFTEEN

Five days later, Gumby drank a cup of coffee and eyed Sidney over the rim. She was on edge today, and he wasn't sure why.

Things between them had been good. Really good. She was an easy person to live with. They'd spent most of their time at his house. Though he'd also spent a night at her trailer when Jude had called with an emergency repair late one evening, and after she'd finished, they were both too tired to go back to his place.

She'd seemed uneasy to have him in her trailer, and when he'd pushed her about it, she'd admitted that she was afraid he was going to judge her because of where she lived. He'd told her she was completely wrong, that he didn't give the smallest shit where she lived as long as she was safe—then proceeded to make love to her until she forgot everything except for how he felt inside her.

Gumby had never felt for anyone the way he felt about Sidney. She was perfect for him, and he couldn't wait to see her every evening after work.

But this morning, something seemed to be bothering her. But he didn't know what. And that was frustrating the hell out of him.

"You okay?" he asked for the third time when she finally sat down next to him with her toasted bagel.

Sidney shrugged.

"Talk to me," he begged. "Something's wrong, and even if I can't do anything about it, at least I can be an ear to listen. Did you talk to Jude? Did he change his mind about you taking the job with Max?"

"No. He's cool with it," Sidney said. "The new guy'll start shadowing me next week to meet the residents and to see what I do."

"That's good, right?"

"I guess."

"Did you talk to Max again?" Gumby asked.

"Yeah."

"And?"

Sidney sighed. "Everything's fine there. In about two weeks, I'll go over to his office and fill out papers and shit and get on the schedule."

Gumby frowned. "You don't sound too excited about it."

"I am," she insisted. "It's an amazing opportunity, and I'm more grateful than I can say that you introduced us."

He racked his brain trying to figure out what else could be bothering her then. "You haven't heard from Brian or your parents, have you?"

"What? No!" she exclaimed. "Although they would definitely put me in a bad mood," she muttered.

At least she was admitting that something was wrong.

"How's Nora and Faith?" If it wasn't her job bothering her, maybe something was up with one of her friends.

"They're fine. Look, I'm just in a bad mood. I get this way sometimes. It's a girl thing."

Decker wasn't so sure about that. "Did *I* do something?" he asked straight up. "Because if I did, you need to tell me. Don't pretend everything's fine when it isn't, Sid. That's the quickest way to fuck up our relationship."

She froze with a piece of bagel halfway to her mouth. "Are you being serious right now?"

He shrugged and lifted an eyebrow.

"It's not you. If you have to know, I'm just feeling antsy to get back to Victor's house and check things out."

Gumby stared at her in irritation. "I think *you're* the one who can't be serious right now." He knew he was being kind of a dick, but he'd done his best to reason with her on this subject. To make her understand the danger of confronting suspected animal abusers. And after everything they'd talked about, she still wanted to go to Victor's house? It was crazy.

"Don't start with me, Decker. I'm really not in the mood."

"I can see that. I'm trying to figure out why but you won't talk to me. You can't *really* be thinking about going back to that asshole's house, can you?"

She sat up straighter in her chair. "Yes. I looked online last night, and he's put up another ad about wanting a dog. It's disgusting! This time he said the dog he has wants a brother or sister. I hate thinking about *one* poor dog already in his clutches, and now he wants another? It's been almost two weeks since I've rescued any abused animals, and I feel as if I'm letting them down. I promised not to do anything while you were gone, but you're back now, and I've been so busy with you and Jude that I haven't had time to do anything else."

Gumby tried to hold his temper and be reasonable. "So, you're saying spending time with me is cramping your style when it comes to putting your life in danger for a dog?"

She glared at him. "You make it sound as if a dog isn't worth it," she accused.

"That's not what I said, and you know it."

Sidney took a deep breath. "I can't help the way I feel, Decker. You know what happened, and why I need to do this. I just feel as if I'm letting Faith and the dogs down."

"Have you talked to her about this?" Gumby asked.

Sidney shook her head. "No, because she'd just say I wasn't letting her down, and that she appreciates anything I can do to help."

"You say that as if you think she'd lie about being appreciative of whatever you do for her and the rescue group."

"She would," Sidney said with conviction. "She's as invested in saving animals as I am. And I know the fact that I haven't brought her any dogs is concerning her."

Gumby seriously doubted that. He'd met Faith, and he hadn't sensed anything other than concern for Sidney when they'd talked about her methods of rescuing dogs for the group. "Actually, no, you're only half right. Faith *is* invested—but in a safe, healthy way. She's not slinking around people's houses stealing dogs. She's using her connections and working with the authorities to try to shut down the assholes who abuse animals."

He saw Sidney clench her fists, but she didn't respond. Simply glared at him.

Gumby did his best to rein in his temper, but now that they'd opened these floodgates, he couldn't stop. Doing his best to gentle his tone, yet still keep it firm enough to get his point across, he said, "You saw some horrible things when you were a kid. You lived in terror for a lot of years. Scared about what your brother was doing to animals and what he might make you watch next, or whether he might hurt *you*. I'm worried about you, Sid. I think you have a kind of survivor's guilt thing going on. I've seen it in some of my fellow SEALs when missions go wrong, and they come back alive when their friends and teammates didn't. I really think you need to talk to someone about everything that happened, someone who can help you try to deal with it."

"I did talk to someone. I talked to *you*," Sidney said stiffly.

"I know you did, and that means the world to me that you opened up. But I'm not a psychologist. I don't have the knowledge or tools to help you like someone who's trained would," Gumby told her.

"I'm not ready," Sidney said stubbornly.

Frustration welled inside Gumby once more. She *knew* her need to save animals and her willingness to put herself in danger were a direct result of what had happened to her as a child. "I can't go with you today, so you're just going to have to wait another day to put yourself in danger over a dog."

"So now you're rescinding your offer to go with me? To keep me safe? *Your* words, not mine."

Gumby nodded. "Yeah, I am."

"Well, that's just great. So all your talk of not wanting me to get hurt, of understanding how I need to help the dogs, was just crap?"

"You know that's not true," Gumby said. "I've just got a lot of stuff I have to do at work today, and I can't drop everything when you get a little overactive on the Internet and decide to go tromping around Riverton on a one-woman crusade to steal dogs."

"It's not stealing dogs," Sidney insisted in a hiss.

"Then what do you call sneaking around a house, climbing over fences, and taking people's dogs?"

"Gumby, Victor's *abusing* those dogs!" she practically yelled.

"Right. I know that. But I was there, Sid. I saw him *hitting* you. If I wasn't driving by, he would've hurt you a lot worse than he did."

"Thanks for the vote of confidence," she said sarcastically.

"Don't do that," Gumby said, pissed now on top of his frustration. "You know as well as I do that if push came to shove, he'd *really* hurt you. He's done it twice! And you aren't thinking about this clearly. You're thinking like the scared ten-year-old you used to be. News flash, Sidney, you aren't ten. Victor isn't Brian, and I'm not the kind of man who will be okay just watching you throw your life away over a dog."

The second the words were out of his mouth, he knew he'd gone too far.

"I know I'm not ten, Decker. But you don't get to stand there and tell me what I should and shouldn't feel! You didn't see what Brian did to those poor animals! You didn't have to stand in a courtroom and have people judge you and wonder if you weren't the same as your little brother since you share DNA! You don't have to live your life wondering if there was anything you could've done to help just *one* of those defenseless animals. You don't want to go with me? Great! I don't need you. I've been just fine on my own up until now, and I'll continue to be just fine. Your condescending, holier-than-thou attitude is getting a bit old anyway!"

"I don't want you going back to his place, Sidney," Gumby responded, a lot louder than he'd intended.

She sat up straighter in her chair and glared at him. "Just because you're fucking me doesn't mean you get to tell me what I can and can't do."

"Seriously?" he asked.

"Seriously!"

Sighing, Gumby rubbed his face and tried to rein in his temper. "Sidney, you can't be serious about this. That guy *hurt* you. You can't go back out there by yourself!"

"If you won't go with me, I'm going to have to, aren't I?" she argued, the bagel she'd been eating forgotten on the table in front of her.

Realizing he was getting nowhere, and if he continued to antagonize her, Sidney would leave his house and go straight to Victor's, damn the consequences, Gumby didn't reply immediately. He knew she wasn't thinking straight right now. She was too emotional about the subject and was feeling guilty she hadn't done anything recently to help any of the abused animals she felt obligated to assist.

So he did his best to smooth things over. "How about a compromise?"

"How about you go fuck yourself?" Sidney flung back, obviously not willing to be placated. She pushed her chair back from the table and stomped into the kitchen. She threw the rest of her uneaten bagel away.

Gumby followed, and by the time she turned around, he was right in her face. He backed her up until she was caged in by the counter and his body. "Listen to me," he ordered.

"Why should I?" she threw back, trying to push him away, but he didn't budge.

"Because I'm *worried* about you!" Gumby said. "Because I know where this obsession of yours comes from, and I think there are healthier and *safer* ways to deal with it. And because I love you!"

Gumby hadn't meant to blurt the words, but once they were out there, he wasn't sorry.

Sidney's eyes widened. She stared up at him in disbelief, the hands that were pushing him away now resting limp on his chest.

"Yeah, Sid. I *love* you. You mean everything to me. I'm worried about you. I want you to do what you need to do to help abused animals, but not if it means you're putting yourself in danger. Don't you understand? If you get killed, you won't be able to help *any* animals. Dog-fighting rings are nothing to mess with. The men and women who run them and attend the fights have no compassion whatsoever. That's obvious in the way they can hurt and kill the very dogs that are making them money. They won't hesitate to mow down anyone who stands in their way."

"So what am I supposed to do then?" she asked in a more reasonable voice than she'd used a minute ago.

Gumby wasn't surprised she was ignoring his declaration of love. He didn't mind...for now. They could deal with that later. Right now, he had to convince his woman not to run headlong into a danger she wasn't equipped to deal with. And for as gung-ho and street-smart as she was, she was in over her head when it came to the hard-core dog fighters.

"I'm not saying you should stop working with and for abused animals. Not at all. I'm just suggesting that maybe you don't need to be on the front lines anymore. Maybe you could do what you've been doing all along...work behind the scenes, checking out social media and passing along tips to the cops. Or you could do what Faith does and be an intake coordinator. Hannah took to you right away. Hell, she put herself between you and Max when he came over that first time, remember? The dogs need someone with your kind nature to help them when they're brought in."

Sidney didn't say anything, just continued to look at him with an unreadable expression.

"I don't want you to quit altogether. I know your soul needs to help. I'm just begging you not to put yourself in direct danger. I don't know what I'd do if something happened to you."

"He's hurting them, Decker," she said, the agony clear in her voice. "If I don't do something, who will? No one helped the poor animals my brother tortured, and they died horrible deaths. I can't stand by and do nothing!"

"I'm not asking you to," Gumby insisted. "We can talk to animal control and the cops and make sure they're aware of this guy and what he's doing."

"It'll take too long! By the time they do anything, how many more Hannahs will he have hurt?"

Upon hearing her name, Hannah whined. She was sitting just outside the kitchen, staring at them.

Gumby sighed. "I really do have to go into work today. I'm sorry I said I wouldn't go with you. I was frustrated and worried. I'll go, Sid, but it'll have to be tomorrow. We'll go together to check out his place, okay?"

He knew she wanted to protest. Wanted to argue that tomorrow would be too late. But eventually, she just sighed and nodded.

Gumby put his hand on the side of her face and waited until she looked up at him. "At least think about what I said," he implored. "I like seeing your face and body without bruises and scrapes. We can figure out a way for you to help the animals like you need to without putting your life at risk."

"I think you're exaggerating. I can handle some cuts and scrapes…but fine."

Gumby pulled her into his embrace and closed his eyes. He couldn't imagine not having her around. She was his everything. His world. Intellectually, he understood her need to put herself in danger to help abused animals. She felt as if she were atoning for something she wasn't at fault for in the first place. He really wanted to get her to agree to talk to a therapist about everything she'd been through, to try to understand the part of herself that needed to be there for abused animals. But that was something he knew she wasn't quite ready for.

He stepped back and said, "We good?"

"Yeah, Deck. We're good."

"What's on your agenda for today?"

"Heading over to the trailer park to work for a bit. Then me and Caite are having lunch with Caroline."

"Caroline Steel?" Gumby asked in surprise.

"Yeah."

He was as pleased as could be. Caroline was married to Wolf, a fellow SEAL. One he respected a hell of a lot. "Sounds awesome."

Sidney shrugged. "I'm more looking forward to seeing Caite. I've talked to her a few times since that night here at your place, but we haven't been able to connect in person."

"Cool."

"Yeah. I like her a lot."

"I should get off around three-thirty or so. You want to come back here again tonight?"

"I'm thinking I need to do some stuff around my trailer. It's been a while since I've been there."

Gumby frowned. He didn't like that she was trying to pull away from him. "I'll come over and bring dinner then."

She didn't say anything.

"Sid, we had an argument. We talked it out. I know things haven't been great this morning, but I love you. I want to see you. I *need* to see you. We can even just sit in the same room and do our own thing if you want, but just because I don't agree with you about something, it doesn't mean that I don't want to hang out with you."

"Okay."

"Okay? I can come over?"

"Yeah. But...I can't say it back. Not yet."

Gumby knew exactly what she was talking about. "That's okay, Sid. Take your time. I didn't tell you that I loved you to force you to say it back. I just needed you to know how much you mean to me. That everything I do, I do with your best interests at heart."

"You're too perfect," she whispered.

Gumby huffed out a laugh. "I'm not perfect. I screw things up all the time. I suck at cooking, I hate housekeeping. I'm selfish, and would prefer to hang out here in my house with you and my dog than do anything with my friends. Most of the time I have no clue what I'm doing with Hannah, and I know for a fact that I'm gonna continue to piss you off in the future. I'm not perfect, Sidney, and I don't want you to think I am. I can't live up to that kind of pressure."

She smiled.

"I *am* good at a lot of things though. Working out, swimming, making omelets, driving, shooting, and making you orgasm. I can work on everything else."

That got him a small chuckle. He'd take it.

"Thanks, Decker."

"Feel better?"

She nodded. "Yeah."

"Good. Call me after lunch and let me know how it went?" he asked.

"Are you sure? I don't want to interrupt you."

"I've told you over and over again that you aren't interrupting when you call. If I'm in the middle of something and can't talk, I just won't answer, and I'll call you back when I can. I *like* talking to you, Sid."

"Okay."

"You want me to pick up something specific for dinner?"

"Chinese?"

"Perfect. Think about what you want and you can tell me when you call after lunch."

"Cashew chicken," she told him. "With crab rangoon and pot stickers for appetizers."

Gumby chuckled. He loved that his girl always knew what she liked. "You got it." He leaned forward and kissed her forehead. "I know you're worried about the dogs. I promise we'll figure something out to hopefully stop this guy for good. Okay?"

Sidney nodded. "Okay. Decker?"

"Yeah, sweetheart?"

"I'm sorry I'm a pain in the ass."

He smiled. "I wouldn't want you any other way than exactly how you are. I love your big heart. If you weren't compassionate, you wouldn't have followed me to the vet that day we met because you were concerned about Hannah. We wouldn't be where we are now. How could I want to change that part of you?"

"You should probably know that we're probably going to end up with more pets."

Gumby's smile widened. The fact that she was thinking that far into the future, and was including him in her vision, was encouraging and exciting as hell. "I figured as much," he told her. "Eventually we'll outgrow this house, but I don't think I ever want to sell it. It'll be a perfect weekend getaway house."

Sidney blinked in surprise.

Not wanting to push too hard, too soon—he'd already pushed her way further than he'd planned—Gumby said, "It's getting late. I need to get to the base, and I'm sure Jude is waiting impatiently for you to arrive. Have fun at lunch." Then he lowered his head. When Sidney came up on her toes to meet him halfway, he finally relaxed completely, and kissed her.

It was a long, slow kiss, and Gumby did his best to show Sidney how much he loved her without words. He knew she was probably still irritated with him, and definitely worried about the dogs Victor might be abusing, but he appreciated that she had calmed enough to at least talk to him.

When he pulled back, Sidney slowly brought a hand up and palmed the side of his face. She ran her hand down his beard and smiled slightly. "I wasn't a beard kind of girl until I met you," she told him.

He couldn't help the sexy thoughts that raced through his mind at her words. How much she liked the feel of his facial hair against her inner thighs as he ate her out. How she squirmed against him when he kissed his way up her belly because his hair tickled. It was safe to say he was probably not going to shave it off anytime soon. Not if his woman liked it.

"Glad to hear it," he said after a moment.

Sidney rolled her eyes as if she knew he was thinking something sexual. "You're such a horndog," she said, smiling and playfully pushing at his chest.

Glad they were back on a lighter footing, Gumby said, "Only when it comes to you, Sid."

"Good answer," she quipped. Then ducked under his arm and headed for her shoes, which were sitting against the wall.

He watched as she tied the laces of her Chucks and spent a minute or two petting and praising Hannah for "being the best dog in the whole wide world." Then she stood and grabbed her purse and phone.

"Drive safe," Gumby said as she headed for the door.

"You too. Talk to you later," she called back, then disappeared out the front door.

Hannah whimpered.

"I feel the same way, girl," Gumby told his dog, then shook his head and got ready to head to work himself.

———

Sidney stared down at the phone in her hand as she sat outside the restaurant where she was meeting Caite and Caroline for lunch.

Victor had posted another message...on Facebook this time. He'd included a picture of two puppies sitting in the dirt next to a fence. They were cowering and looked scared to death. His post read,

Just got these 2 pups and I think they need an older dog to make them more comfortable. Their really skared. If you have an older girl dog that you need to get rid of Ill take her and give her a gd hme.

Sidney wanted to scream. There were already a ton of responses, asking where he was located. One person even said she'd found a stray dog and couldn't keep her, and if Victor wanted her, she could meet him somewhere.

Furious at Victor, and scared to death for the puppies he currently had in his clutches, Sidney marked the post as offensive in the hopes Facebook would take it down. Putting a hand on her chest, Sidney realized her heart actually hurt for the puppies. She closed her eyes—and a memory from her past flashed through her mind as if it had happened yesterday, rather than years and years ago.

Brian had been nice to her for almost a full month. He hadn't done anything that had made her nervous or wary, and Sidney had let her guard down a little. Despite that, when he told her he wanted to show her something out back, she refused. She remembered vividly what she'd seen the *last* time she'd gone into the shed with him.

But even though he was younger than her, Brian was a big kid. Taller and stronger. He dragged her, kicking and screaming, to the backyard...and the dreaded shed.

The second he opened the door, dread filled her at the thought of whatever Brian might want to show her. He shoved her inside and stood in front of the door, not letting her escape.

"They were strays," Brian told her, pointing at something on the floor in the corner of the shed. "No one wanted them. Probably sick too."

There, in the corner, were two puppies...at least, that's what she thought they'd been. She had no idea what Brian had done to them, as she'd turned her head and squeezed her eyes shut—but not before the image of the blood, the flies, and the poor mutilated bodies had been burned into her memory.

She'd known Brian had been spending more time out back in his shed of horrors, but she'd stayed inside the house, as far away from him as she could get. Out of fear.

And while she'd been sitting around doing nothing, those poor puppies had died a horrible death.

Sidney threw up right then and there in the shed.

Brian was furious with her for "fucking up his work

station." He grabbed her by the hair and dragged her out of the shed, throwing her to the ground and kicking her hard in the stomach before heading back inside and slamming the door.

Sidney opened her eyes and did her best to shake off the flashback. Brian was in jail, and he couldn't hurt any other puppies or kittens—or women—again.

But Victor could.

Sidney had saved the picture of the puppies before she'd reported the post, and she stared down at it now. She hadn't saved those poor dogs all those years ago...but she'd be damned if she just sat around and did nothing this time.

She *had* to save them.

Plans whirled in her head. She'd have lunch with Caite and Caroline, then go check out the situation. Maybe Victor didn't have any puppies. Maybe he'd taken the picture from the Internet or something. She'd just peek in his backyard and leave if they weren't there. If they were, then maybe she could sneak them out. If she was careful, if she stayed away from Victor, Decker didn't have to know. She'd be in and out. Ten minutes, tops.

She knew Decker would be pissed at her if he found out. And she reconsidered what she was planning...for just a second. She knew she was fucked up. Knew her brother and everything he'd done had messed with her head. She'd do anything not to feel so damn guilty about what Brian had done. Maybe she *would* talk to Decker about seeing a psychologist. If that would lessen the intense and overwhelming need to save animals, it might be worth it.

But then she looked again at the picture Victor had posted.

She couldn't live with herself if she didn't do something to help those dogs.

Going over her plan in her head once more, Sidney climbed out of her car. She was looking forward to lunch and seeing Caite again, but she hoped it didn't last too long. She had puppies to save.

CHAPTER SIXTEEN

"I had the worst headache the next morning, but Sidney said she wasn't hung over at all. That amazes me, because we drank a *lot* of rum." Caite was smiling and laughing as she recounted the story of how she and Sidney met to Caroline.

The other woman chuckled and leaned her elbows on the table. "Sounds like you guys hit it off pretty well."

Caite nodded. "I know I could've called you, but Gumby swore that Sidney was a dog expert, and I figured she'd know what to do."

"Good call. I probably would've freaked if I'd walked in and seen all that blood," Caroline said.

Sidney doubted that. The other woman looked as put together and levelheaded as anyone she'd ever met.

Before Caroline arrived, Caite had told Sidney a bit about the her, including how she'd saved an entire plane full of people from crashing, and how she'd been targeted by terrorists, but managed to outsmart them and get a secret message to her now-husband and his SEAL team about where she was being held, so they could get to her and save her.

It was almost unbelievable, but now that she'd met Caroline, Sidney knew Caite hadn't been exaggerating. She was feeling completely out of place between the two women. She wasn't intimidated by a lot of people, but Caroline definitely made her feel inadequate. Not only was she down-to-earth and married to a well-respected and decorated Navy SEAL, she was a chemist. A freaking *chemist*, for God's sake.

Between that, and Caite being fluent in French and helping the navy with criminal cases involving French-speaking bad guys, Sidney felt like the frumpy black-sheep family member next to these two.

It wasn't until Caite started talking about how protective Rocco was that Sidney perked up and showed a bit more interest in the conversation.

"I swear, after all the shit that happened with me, Rocco is completely paranoid. That's why he wanted me to stay at Gumby's house while the team was on their latest mission. He doesn't trust anyone in the apartment complex anymore, even though he was perfectly fine with them before that thing with the rear admiral's wife happened."

"It's just how they're wired," Caroline commiserated. "Wolf is the same way, and we've been together for years. They just can't stand for anything to happen to us."

"But it drives me crazy, and I feel bad that I get annoyed with him about it," Caite said. "I mean, I'm a grown adult. I'm perfectly able to drive myself to lunch if I want to. But he insisted on coming over to NCIS, picking me up, and driving me here. He said he'd come and get me when we were done, but I told him Sidney could take me back to work. Is that okay?"

Sidney tried to hide her frustration. She wanted to get to those puppies as soon as possible. But she couldn't begrudge Caite a favor. She nodded. "Of course. I could've come and picked you up too."

"I know. But the fact of the matter is, I feel like I'm constantly putting Rocco out...and now my friends. If he'd have just let me drive myself, no one would have to go out of their way to take me to *or* from work."

Caroline put her hand over Caite's. "I admit that their protectiveness can get overwhelming, but you have to remember that they see the worst of humanity. They get sent to poor countries where people are literally starving in the streets. Or to rich countries where men and women with money sometimes enslave those who can't afford to buy food, so they willingly indenture themselves just to eat. They kill, and are constantly targeted to *be* killed, when they're out of the country. Then there are people in *this* country who think that our SEALs are brainless drones, who do whatever they're told without thinking about whether it's right or wrong.

"Our men just want us safe. They want to protect us from the evils of the world that they see on a regular basis. And really, is that so bad? Think about the alternative. That Rocco doesn't care. That he isn't concerned about you working late and driving home at night. That he sits on his ass and lets you answer the door late in the evening when someone rings the doorbell."

"Hmmm," Caite hummed. "It *is* nice to know when I get in late from visiting my mom that Rocco will always be there to meet me at the airport. I don't have to worry about walking through the big parking lot alone to get to my car."

"Exactly," Caroline said. "And if he can't be there, he'll make sure someone else he knows and trusts is, right?"

"Right."

"But what about when he orders you to do something, or stop doing something, that you love to do?" Sidney asked.

Both women turned to her.

Sidney looked curious as hell, but Caroline merely nodded as if the question didn't surprise her in the least.

"Right. So, I'm assuming this isn't exactly a rhetorical question, and without knowing the details, it's hard to answer. But I'll give it a try. What I've learned from being married to a SEAL is that they tend to be super blunt. Matthew isn't very good at being subtle or trying to work his way around a topic. He just plows full-steam ahead and lays his thoughts about things right out there, without really thinking about how I'll react. It's only when I react in a way he doesn't *expect* that he stops to think about what he just said. Usually, we talk things out and I realize he's not really demanding that I stop doing something. He's just concerned about how I'll be affected by my actions."

"Example?" Sidney asked.

Caroline thought for a long moment before saying, "Okay, so there was this time when I thought it would be a great idea to find our friend Tex's adopted daughter's family, over in Iraq. I had myself all worked up about it too. I imagined in my head how happy everyone in Iraq would be to see Akilah, and how thrilled she would be to see her family again. I told Matthew about it one night, and he flat-out told me it was an awful idea. I got pissed.

Super pissed. How could meeting up with your family be bad?

"After I told him off and stormed away, he came to find me. I didn't want to talk to him, but he forced me to listen. And he explained that when Akilah was hurt, none of her relatives had done anything to get her the help she needed. It had been a soldier who'd come across her, screaming in pain in the middle of her bombed-out home. Apparently the Red Cross had tried to find the people responsible for her, but no one claimed to know her. Fast-forward to now. She's acclimated to life here in the States, happy with her family, complete with a little sister. I can imagine that she doesn't have the best memories of her time in Iraq, and if someone told her they were bringing her back to meet family who'd abandoned her, she probably wouldn't have been happy about it.

"Matthew and I talked it out for at least an hour, pros and cons, and I finally decided that my idea wasn't exactly the best. He agreed that maybe I could see what information I could gather, and if, later in her life, when she was an adult, she wanted to reach out to her family, that would be *her* decision, and not something I'd forced on her. If Matthew had approached the topic calmly and rationally when I'd brought it up, I probably wouldn't have reacted so badly. But because he was worried for *me*, and how the whole thing could blow up in my face, he initially just vetoed my idea straight-out. It annoyed me, but now I understand."

Sidney remained silent, thinking over everything Caroline had said.

"Rocco forbade me to get a tattoo," Caite blurted.

Sidney stared at her in disbelief. "You wanted a tattoo?"

"Why are you acting so surprised?" the other woman asked.

"You just don't seem the type," Sidney soothed. And she didn't. Caite was too...cautious...to want to mark her skin with something as permanent as a tattoo.

"Yeah, well, I got pissed at Rocco and told him he wasn't the boss of me and he didn't get a say."

"I bet that went over well," Caroline teased.

Surprisingly, Caite blushed. "He refused to let me give him the cold shoulder and seduced me. Then, once he had me relaxed and sated, he told me that he liked my body as it was. And while ultimately it was my decision if I wanted to get a tattoo or not, he wanted me to really think about it for a while before I did something I might regret."

"And?" Sidney asked.

"He was right. I was feeling insecure because it seemed I'd noticed more and more hot, tattooed female sailors on base, women I figured he saw and interacted with on a regular basis, and I didn't want Rocco to regret picking me when he could have someone cooler and more hip."

Sidney didn't want to admit that both women had a point. Decker was extremely blunt. Then again, so was she. They'd both said some things that morning that, had they thought about them first, maybe they wouldn't have said quite so candidly. He spoke his mind, but when she recalled their conversation, she admitted he hadn't said he wanted her to quit working with abused animals altogether, just that he wanted her to stop with the front-line stuff.

But then she thought about the picture Victor had posted earlier, and mentally shook her head. Even if she reported it to the cops or animal control, it would take them forever to investigate, and Victor could just move the puppies somewhere else and continue to abuse them.

"You want to tell us what you're thinking about so hard over there?" Caite asked.

Sidney forced herself to pay attention. "It's nothing."

"You and Gumby okay?" Caroline asked gently.

Sidney nodded. "Yeah. We're great. We just had a little disagreement this morning. But everything's okay."

"Good. You guys haven't been dating that long, right?" Caroline asked.

"Right."

"Just remember, when these guys fall, they fall hard. And when they do, they'll do whatever it takes to make you happy. Not all military guys are the same way. Some will sleep with anyone who spreads their legs, simply because they can. But Matthew's team is different...and I think Rocco's team is the same way. When they commit, they *commit*. They won't cheat. They won't give up when things get hard. They don't always communicate the right or best way, but deep down, they mean well and would kill anyone who dares hurt you."

Caite nodded vigorously. "I saw that firsthand. Rocco was *pissed* at that commander guy who wanted me dead, and the only reason he didn't jump in the ocean to save me himself was because he wanted to make *sure* the threat to me was gone."

Caroline looked at Sidney then. "Make no mistake, if Gumby has decided you're it for him, you could hurt him deeply by putting yourself in a situation where he has to kill to protect you. He's a SEAL, but that doesn't mean he can't go to prison."

Sidney was a little freaked out that Caroline seemed to

sense she was thinking about doing something she shouldn't. Something she promised she wouldn't. "I know, and I wouldn't do anything to hurt him."

For a second, she thought Caroline was going to call her on what she'd just said, but eventually she simply nodded. "Good. But I'll tell you one thing, if it was Matthew in danger, I'd sure as hell do whatever it took to help him."

"Me too," Caite piped in.

Sidney was amused. "We know. You already did, and you hadn't even had a first date yet when you did it."

All three laughed.

"True," Caite said. "I guess I did throw myself headfirst into a situation I didn't think all the way through when I went after Rocco, Gumby, and Ace in Bahrain, did I?"

"It all turned out okay, though," Sidney soothed.

The three women talked for a while longer, and even though she liked Caroline a lot, Sidney knew she clicked a lot more with Caite. She was new to a relationship with a SEAL, just like Sidney, and they were closer in age. And Caite was just as funny today as she'd been the other night when they'd been three sheets to the wind.

"This lunch is on me," Caroline said when things were winding down.

"No way," Caite protested. "I invited you, I got this."

"I can pay for myself," Sidney added.

The waitress came over then and, instead of putting a bill on the table, said, "It's your lucky day, ladies. A Matthew Steel called in and paid for all three of your meals with a credit card...including tip. So you're good to go whenever. No rush though, I just wanted you to know."

Sidney stared at the waitress in disbelief.

After the woman left, Caite huffed out a frustrated breath. "Well, that was sneaky."

Caroline simply smiled. "Rocco and Gumby are off their game. They'll learn soon enough."

Sidney had to admit it was a nice thing to do. If Decker had done that for her, she would've been extremely flattered.

But then, when she thought about it, she realized he *had* done the same sort of thing for her time and time again. He was considerate and attentive, and she'd soaked in every single thing he'd done for her almost without thought. Opening doors, getting up and refilling her drink when she was comfortable on the couch. Letting her have the last piece of pizza. Setting the alarm on his watch instead of his clock so when it went off, he didn't wake her up. Washing her dishes. The list went on and on.

Feeling guilty about what she was planning on doing after lunch, she almost changed her mind. But then she remembered the frightened faces of the puppies...and she couldn't walk away.

She'd have a heart-to-heart with Decker tonight and explain why she'd done it. He'd understand. He had to.

"Thanks for inviting me," Caroline said as she stood.

"Thank you for coming," Caite told her, and gave her a quick hug.

Sidney wasn't expecting Caroline to turn to her for a hug, so she felt good when she was included as well.

They all walked to the door, and Caroline waved as she headed for her car.

"Thanks for coming too," Caite told Sidney as they walked toward her Accord. "I didn't want to admit it, but Caroline intimidates me. It's silly, but she's been a military wife for so much longer than me that I'm scared I'm going to say something stupid when I'm around her."

Sidney understood that for sure. She felt the same way. "And she already has a group of friends. So I know what you mean."

Caite smiled. "I guess we're making our own group now, aren't we?"

"Yes! So, groupie, shall we hit the road?"

"Lead on," Caite said.

Once settled in the car, Sidney felt the slight antsy-ness she'd endured throughout lunch come back full force. She didn't mind helping Caite, but every minute she spent driving her back to work, then coming back to this side of town to Victor's house, could be one more minute the puppies were being abused. Victor might kill them before she could get a chance to save them...and that would be like Brian and his damn shed all over again.

Knowing what she was about to do was shitty, and a betrayal to Rocco for putting his girlfriend in possible danger, but not able to stop herself, Sidney turned to Caite and asked, "Do you mind if we make a quick stop before I drop you off?"

"Of course not. What's up?"

Sidney's stomach clenched. She'd done it now. She had to keep going. "Nothing much. I just need to stop and check something out. We're close, and it should only take a few minutes."

"No problem. I've still got like twenty minutes before I'm supposed to be back. But that's totally fluid, so if it takes a bit longer, it's okay. I've got a great boss, and he knows that I work a lot of overtime I don't claim, so he's pretty lenient about my start time and me getting back late if I take an outside lunch."

Sidney started the engine, relieved her friend wasn't asking for more details—and feeling guilty as hell at the same time. Might as well throw one more pile of guilt on top of the ones she already had.

Taking a deep breath, she did her best to smile over at Caite and pulled out of the restaurant parking lot. She had puppies to rescue—and no matter what Decker said, there wasn't anyone else who could do it, and those precious pups didn't have any time left. She'd left them there long enough.

CHAPTER SEVENTEEN

"I'm not sure about this," Caite said ten minutes later.

"It'll be fine. I'm just going to go and look," Sidney tried to reassure her. That wasn't exactly a lie. She *was* going to look...and if she saw the puppies in Victor's back-yard, she was going to sneak in and grab them. "You stay here."

"Maybe I should go with you," Caite said uneasily.

"No!" The word came out louder than Sidney meant it to.

She felt bad about lying to Caite about what could happen. But she'd had enough run-ins with Victor to know that he could get violent, and the last thing she wanted was Caite getting hurt. She had to convince her to stay in the car. Sidney could handle it if *she* got roughed up, but if something happened to Caite because of her, she'd never forgive herself. Hell, Rocco would never forgive her, and Decker would probably dump her ass in a heartbeat.

Taking a deep breath, she thought fast. She didn't want to scare Caite, but she needed to make sure she stayed put.

"This isn't a big deal. I just want to peek over the fence and see if the puppies this asshole posted about are there. We'll be more conspicuous if there are two of us lurking around. You need to stay here. No matter what. Do not come looking for me and don't follow me. All right?"

Caite studied her for a moment. "Okay...but for the record, I don't like this."

"It's seriously not a big deal," Sidney said, hating that the more Caite protested, the more uneasy she felt. "I'm gonna leave the keys in the car so you can keep the air conditioner on. I'll take my phone and if I need your help, I'll call or text. Okay?"

"Okay. But why are we parked three houses down if this isn't a big deal?"

Caite was asking all the right questions, and she clearly had a pretty good sense that what Sidney was about to do wasn't exactly safe. She decided to tell her just a little bit about Victor. Enough that she wouldn't freak out, but so she'd stay away from his house. "Fine. The guy who has the puppies is an asshole, and he wouldn't be happy if he saw me. But trust me when I say that this has to be done *now*." She clicked on her phone and brought up the picture she'd saved from Victor's post. "Look. These are the precious pups I'm trying to rescue."

Caite bit her lip as she looked at the picture. "They're really cute."

"Yup. And scared to death." Sidney knew Caite couldn't deny that. They looked terrified in the picture.

"Fine. But I'm only giving you ten minutes. If you're not back, I'm coming after you."

"Great," Sidney said with enthusiasm. She didn't need ten minutes. Five tops. She smiled at Caite. "I'll be back before you know it," she said brightly as she opened her door and climbed out. She put her phone in her back pocket, gave Caite a thumbs-up, and shut her door.

The smile left her face as she headed for Victor's house. The area was quiet this time of day, as most of the neighbors were probably at work. Deciding to work her way to Victor's house via the nearby backyards, to be less obvious, Sidney took a look around and, not seeing anyone, slunk around a house two doors down from Victor's.

There was about a four-foot space between the fences surrounding each backyard on this side of the street, and the ones that backed up to them, creating a narrow, unkempt alleyway. Glad she was wearing jeans, since the weeds were knee high in places, Sidney cautiously approached Victor's yard.

She heard the puppies before she saw them. The privacy fence kept her from seeing in, just as it kept any nosey neighbors from doing the same.

Testing the wood on the fence, Sidney was thrilled to discover it was old and rotting. It took a minute or so she didn't have, and all her strength, but she was able to break off one of the planks at the bottom in one of the corners. Lying down on the grass, Sidney peered into the yard and saw the puppies were indeed there.

One of the pit-mix puppies was sleeping, but the other was pulling at the huge chain around its neck and yipping pathetically. They were covered in dirt and feces, and Sidney's resolve strengthened. She was doing the right thing.

Tugging on the boards, she managed to make a hole big

enough that she could shimmy under into the yard. Once inside, Sidney realized that all her fears were warranted.

There was a stack of metal crates against the house that hadn't been there two weeks ago, and blood was splattered on one part of the fence. There were also several stakes in the ground with empty chains discarded next to them.

The most heartbreaking sight was the carcass in the corner of the yard. It had obviously been there for quite a while, as Sidney could see bones amongst the fur.

Trying to block out the sight, she hurried over to the puppies, and the brown guy woke when she picked him up. He immediately began to shiver in fright, and Sidney's heart broke even more.

Because she was concentrating on figuring out how to remove the chain from around the puppies' necks and get them out of the yard, she didn't hear Victor until it was too late.

The second he wrapped something around her throat from behind, she dropped the puppy and reached for whatever it was around her neck. She felt bad when the puppy let out a pained yip, but she wasn't able to worry about him—she was concentrating too hard on breathing.

"Gotcha, bitch," Victor said into her ear. "Think you can steal my dogs again? Wrong. But if you wanna take care of the assets so much, I'll help you."

Sidney knew she was in trouble when Victor began walking toward his house. She tried to get her fingers under whatever was around her throat but couldn't. Her body was bent backward, and she couldn't even figure out how to kick or otherwise hurt him so he'd let her go.

The second they were inside, her hopes crashed even further when she saw another man was there.

"She actually showed up?"

"Of course she did. I told you she would," Victor said.

Sidney could barely breathe, but was still relieved he wasn't strangling her to death...yet.

"Well, fuck me! I'll call Dallas," the other man said.

"You do that. Tell him the fight is on. Tonight. I'm not wasting any time. We've waited long enough for this."

Sidney began to scream, but Victor tightened whatever was around her neck, enough that it finally cut off all her air. She tried to suck in oxygen, but nothing happened. Despite fighting with all her strength, the tightness around her neck didn't relent. Her legs gave out, and Victor lowered her to the floor.

"Don't kill her," Sidney heard the other man call out.

"I won't. She's our main moneymaker and entertainment tonight," Victor said.

It was the last thing Sidney remembered hearing before she lost consciousness.

Caite chewed on a fingernail as she waited for Sidney to reappear. Ten minutes had gone by, and she still hadn't returned to the car.

As she was debating on what she should do, Caite blinked in surprise when she saw movement at the house Sidney had been headed toward.

Two men came out of the house carrying a large metal dog crate between them. They headed for the small pickup parked in the driveway. The cage was covered with a tarp, and they set it on the ground as one of the men lowered the tailgate.

When they picked up the cage once more, the tarp slid off—and Caite was shocked to see a body lying inside.

Sidney.

It was easy to recognize the long black hair hanging through the holes in the bottom of cage, not to mention the light blue blouse she was wearing.

Instinctively, Caite hunkered down in the passenger seat of the car and watched with horrified eyes as the men placed the crate in the back of the pickup. They quickly recovered it with the tarp, hopped into the cab, and backed out of the driveway.

Caite lifted her phone and took a picture of the truck, then squinted to try to read the license plate. She jotted it down on a piece of scrap paper in Sidney's car, feeling sick as the truck disappeared down the street.

She quickly clicked on Rocco's name in her contacts and held her breath as she waited for him to answer.

Gumby was shooting the shit with his teammates, waiting on their commander to return from his lunch break, when Rocco's phone rang.

Wondering if Sidney was done with her lunch yet, Gumby wasn't paying much attention to his friend's phone conversation. He was anxious to talk to her. He had a feeling she still wasn't thrilled with him, but he knew that messing with the urban dog fighters would end up badly for her in the long run.

He'd been doing some research on dogfighting, and

what he'd read didn't exactly surprise him, but it made him more determined than ever to get Sidney off the front lines. The men who participated in dogfights were almost always violent criminals, often gang members, who used the fights as a forum for drug trafficking and gambling. The fights were also used to intimidate younger members, and as a way to gain supremacy and respect in the dogfighting and gang worlds.

The last place he wanted Sidney was anywhere near that shit.

"Gumby!" Rocco yelled from across the room.

Gumby's head whipped up from where he was looking at his phone, and he met his friend's gaze.

"Caite's on the line, and she said Sid's in trouble."

Shit.

Gumby knew immediately his talk with Sidney that morning hadn't sunk in. If anything, it might've made her more determined to put herself in danger. He was at his friend's side in seconds.

Rocco put the phone on speaker and the six SEALs hovered around it, listening as Caite told them what she knew.

"...was waiting here in the car for her. She said she was only going to look. Too much time had passed, and I was trying to decide what to do when I saw these two guys come out of the house. They were carrying a dog cage between them, and when the tarp fell off, I saw her inside it!"

"Was she conscious?" Gumby asked urgently.

"No. I mean, I don't think so. She was lying on the bottom, not moving."

"Did you see any blood or anything?" Ace asked.

Gumby's heart almost stopped beating as he waited for the answer.

"No, but I was kinda far away. Sidney parked three houses down," Caite said, her voice breaking.

"What did the truck look like?" Phantom asked.

"I took a picture of it," Caite told them. "I didn't know what else to do," she said, the worry and sorrow easy to hear in her reply. "The keys were in the ignition, but I didn't want them to see me if I ran around to get into the driver's side or crawled over the console."

"Send me the picture," Rocco said gently.

"Okay. I also wrote down the license plate number."

"Good job," Rocco told her. "Send that too."

Gumby's hands clenched in anger and fear. Victor had taken Sidney. God knew what he and his friends had planned for her.

He felt a hand on his arm and looked over at Ace.

"Easy, man. We'll find her."

Gumby wasn't sure about that. He knew they'd do everything they could to get to her, but what shape would she be in when they did?

The things Victor and his buddies could do to Sidney wouldn't stop running through his head like a bad movie on repeat.

"What's the address there?" Rocco asked Caite.

She rattled it off. "Oh, and she had her phone with her. At least, she had it when she left the car."

"That's good news. We'll see if we can get a trace on it," Rex said.

"Snap out of it, Gumby," Bubba barked. "We need you on this one."

Gumby blinked and straightened. His teammate was

right. He had to stop thinking about what could be happening to Sid and concentrate on finding her. The sooner the better.

As Rocco did his best to reassure Caite, telling her to stay put, that he'd be there as soon as possible, Gumby clicked on Faith's number in his phone. He waited impatiently for her to pick up.

"Hi, Decker," she said in greeting.

"Sid's been taken," he clipped out. "She went back to Victor's house and they knocked her unconscious and drove off with her. We need to find her."

"Oh my God!" the older woman exclaimed. "What can I do to help?"

"I need the name and number of the contacts you've got in the Riverton Police Department. The detectives who investigate dogfights. They could have an idea of where these guys might've taken her."

"Of course! I'll text them to you in just a second."

"Thank you."

"I told her to back off," Faith said. "Told her that those guys were dangerous."

"I know," Gumby said sadly. "I did too."

"She was just too determined to do whatever it took to save the dogs."

"Right...the names and numbers?" Gumby reminded her. He knew Faith was shocked about what he'd just told her, but he didn't have time to talk about why Sidney did the things she did.

"Sorry. I'll reach out to my contacts in rescue circles too. Maybe we can think of somewhere they might've taken her or something that will help."

"Appreciate it. I'll let you know if we hear anything."

"Okay. I'm sending the text now."

"Thanks. I'll talk to you later."

"I'll be praying for her," Faith said, then hung up.

Seconds later, his phone vibrated with her text with the names and numbers of the officers who would know the most about the dogfighting ring Victor was involved in.

Commander Storm North entered the meeting room just then—and every muscle in his body instantly tightened. "What's going on?" he asked, obviously reading the tension in the room.

Bubba went over to explain the situation, even as Gumby was lifting his phone to his ear. He needed to get the cops on this immediately. Every second Sidney was in the clutches of the vicious dog fighters was one second too long.

Sidney came awake slowly. At first she was confused about where she was and what had happened...but she quickly realized she was in deep shit.

First of all, she was lying almost naked inside a dog crate. She had on her bra and panties, but that was it. They'd even stripped her watch and necklace from her. The latch was locked shut with a padlock and no matter how hard she tried, she couldn't bend the metal bars around her. She couldn't even sit up straight, all she could do was hunch over while sitting on her ass—or stand on all fours, which she refused to do. They might have her in a cage, but she wasn't a fucking dog.

Her neck hurt, and Sidney realized how lucky she'd been. Victor could've easily strangled her. *Had* strangled her. But he'd obviously only wanted to make her pass out, not kill her...thank God.

Her thoughts turned to Caite. Where was she? Had she gotten impatient and come to check on her and gotten caught up in whatever was going on? Sidney would never forgive herself if that happened.

Looking around her, she had no idea where she was. She couldn't see much, as there was a tarp covering most of the crate, but there was a small corner in the front that had been dislodged, and she could see a high ceiling overhead. At least thirty feet high. It didn't look like she was still at Victor's, the place was too big to be a house or garage.

Shivering, even though the air was actually somewhat warm, Sidney had never been so scared in her life...until she heard a few men begin talking nearby.

"I still can't believe she actually showed up."

"I told you she would."

The latter was Victor. Sidney recognized his voice, but not that of the other man he was talking to. She could only listen in horror as they discussed the evening's activities.

"So we're set for the fight tonight?"

"Yeah. Dallas said we'd start at eight sharp. Bets start at seven."

"How many are we expecting?"

"Full house."

"Fuck yeah! This is gonna be epic! Those assholes are gonna have to give us mad respect for this shit."

"'Bout time. Now come on, help me get this fencing up. Can't have our bitch escaping the fun, can we?"

Sidney tried not to cry. She wasn't stupid. She knew

whatever they had in store for her wasn't good, especially if it involved bets and fences.

Then shame threatened to drown out her fear. She'd done exactly what Caroline had told her not to do. She was putting Decker in a position where he might get in trouble. He might have to seriously hurt or, God forbid, kill someone to rescue her.

She'd fucked up. Royally. She'd not only put Caite in extreme danger, but her own psychological issues had finally put her in a situation that she had no idea how to get out of.

Even knowing all that, despite knowing she was putting Decker in extreme danger, she whispered, "Please find me, Decker." She lay back down and curled into a small ball at the bottom of the cage, and whispered those same words over and over, hoping the more she said them, the faster she'd be rescued.

Officially, the Riverton Police Department was in charge of the case. Unofficially, Gumby knew they were relying on the team's strength and experience to assist them.

Sidney's phone had been tracked...back to Victor's house. So that had been no help. With Caite's statement about what she'd seen, the cops had probable cause to search Victor's house to try to find Sidney.

They'd found a lot of evidence of dogfighting, but not Sidney. Her jeans had been left in the middle of the kitchen floor, along with her phone still in the back pocket, but she was nowhere to be found.

The basement was a horror show, however—and

Gumby understood why Sidney felt so strongly about rescuing animals after seeing it.

There were only two dogs in the basement, but they were in bad shape. They had scars all over their heads and chests, and were shackled with heavy chains around their necks. They were separated by a flimsy curtain, but the detectives who were experts in dogfighting explained it was enough. The animals were somewhat loyal to humans, but had been trained to go berserk when around another dog.

The officers were a treasure trove of information about dogfighting in general, and what everything they'd found in the basement was used for.

There was evidence of blood around the entire room, indicating that fights had been held there in the past. Blood-spattered wooden boards were stacked in a corner, having obviously been used as barriers for the ring the dogs fought in. There was a treadmill in another corner, used to run the dogs to increase cardiovascular fitness and endurance. Heavy chains were lying in a heap off to the side, and the cops explained the heavier chains helped build neck and upper-body strength in the dogs as they constantly bore the immense weight.

There were weights attached to some chains, and Gumby was told sometimes owners ran their dogs with the chains and weights attached to their collars, to help build strength as well.

But the most damning evidence in the basement was the vast amount of drugs, vitamins, and supplements. There were anti-inflammatories, epinephrine, speed, painkillers, antibiotics, testosterone hormones, vitamin K to promote blood clotting, Canine Red Cell vitamins, and a ton of first-aid supplies, including super glue.

It was all overwhelming and horrifying to the team, but even more so to Gumby.

This was what they'd had planned for Hannah. The idea of his sweet, docile dog living in this house of horrors was almost too much for him.

No wonder Sidney felt such a calling to help animals like Hannah. After seeing what she had while growing up, and knowing this was what people like Victor did to defenseless dogs, he understood her a lot better now. He still didn't want her on the front lines of this madness, but at least he grasped why she was so vehement about doing *something*.

Though he wasn't happy that she'd involved Caite in her obsession. Yes, she'd told Caite to stay in the car. No, she hadn't told Caite everything she'd planned to do, but the fact remained that there had been the possibility of Rocco's woman getting hurt.

And...she'd lied to him.

Gumby *hated* that. He'd said he'd go with her tomorrow to check out Victor's place, and she'd agreed, when she'd probably known all along she was going to go without him. It hurt, and it rankled.

But at the moment, he needed to concentrate on finding her. On getting her back. He'd deal with the other stuff later.

"This isn't helping," Gumby said in frustration. "Yeah, it shows that Victor's involved in dogfighting, but it doesn't tell us where they took Sidney."

"True. But now that we know definitively that he's neck-deep in this shit, it gives us probable cause to search known dogfighting venues," Detective Francisco Garnham said.

Gumby understood why the detective was being sure to follow every procedure to the letter, but it was frustrating as hell. Going the legal route always took time. And if Victor had known the cops were investigating him, he would've moved the dogs and hidden the evidence of his participation in the fights. Something Sidney had pointed out.

But just because going through proper channels took time—time the dogs maybe didn't have—he still couldn't condone her stealing the animals from under the dog fighters' noses and putting herself in danger.

Still, Gumby was beginning to realize there was no easy solution.

"I'm going to take Caite home," Rocco said. "She's extremely upset and feeling guilty that she didn't do anything."

"This wasn't her fault," Gumby told his friend.

"I know, and I'm very glad you feel that way."

"Did you think I would blame her?" he asked, upset.

"No."

Gumby felt better at his friend's immediate answer, but frowned when he continued.

"But I know you, Gumby, because we're cut from the same cloth. I know you've already gone over what happened a hundred times in your head and have come up with a hundred different things that might've gone down differently to prevent your woman from being taken."

Rocco wasn't wrong.

"That doesn't mean that I blame Caite for any of it," Gumby said. "I love her like a sister, and pretty much every alternative scenario I've thought of ends with Caite being hurt or taken right along with Sidney."

"The fault lies with Victor," Ace interjected. "And we're gonna find that asshole and his buddies and stop this shit once and for all."

"If only it was that easy," Detective Garnham said.

All six SEALs turned to look at him. "What do you mean?" Bubba asked.

"Dogfighting's been around a very long time...since ancient Roman times, when they fought against each other in the Coliseum. In the early eighteen hundreds, the American Kennel Club actually formulated rules and had sanctioned referees because the 'sport' was so popular here in the US. It was outlawed by all states in nineteen seventy-six, but it continues to thrive, in part because the legal system is somewhat apathetic toward the practice.

"The street fights are out of control, and when one ringleader is taken down, two more pop up to take his place. Just about every child who lives in an urban environment is exposed to dogfighting in their neighborhood, and a lot of parents purposely expose their kids to it to 'harden them up' to life's realities. Like violent crimes, it continues to fester throughout the country, and even worldwide."

"Well, isn't he a ray of sunshine," Phantom muttered under his breath.

Gumby had to agree. But now wasn't the time or place to discuss the social problems that gave rise to dogfighting. They needed to concentrate on finding Victor and his cronies and making sure Sidney was safe. "I get that your job is almost impossible, but at the moment, all I care about is my woman and making sure she doesn't end up a statistic. What's the next step?"

The detective nodded. "You're right. My guys will continue to wrap things up here, including confiscating the dogs and all the equipment we found. There's an informant I'm fairly close to that I'm going to see if I can find. He's been very useful in the past in letting me know when and where impromptu fights will be taking place. He can be hard to find, though."

"Can I come with you to look for him?" Gumby asked.

Francisco eyed him for a long moment. Then asked, "You going to control yourself if I find him and he tells me something you don't like?"

Gumby nodded. "Yes."

"I'm coming too. I can make sure Gumby behaves," Ace said.

Gumby wanted to argue, but he knew he'd feel better with one of his team members at his back. The truth of the matter was, while he *said* he'd control himself...he wasn't at all sure he could.

"Fine. Let's head out then. We don't have any time to spare. These fights usually spring up with very little lead time, to try to throw us off," the detective said.

Gumby's stomach clenched at hearing that. On one hand, it was good. If they could figure out where the fight was taking place, they could get in there and rescue Sidney that much sooner. But on the other hand, if they couldn't find this informant, the fight could begin and end without them ever figuring out where it was. And Gumby didn't want to think about what Victor and all the other bloodthirsty assholes had in mind for Sidney.

They were going to force her to watch, that much was certain. And seeing dogs tear each other to pieces was going to break her. Especially if they had some sort of bait animal, like a puppy or cat, that they used to incite the fighters.

But he knew it was more than that. These weren't good men, and there was no telling what they'd do to Sidney after—or during—the fight. He needed to get to her. To make sure she was safe. His gut was screaming at him that the shit was about to hit the fan, and his gut had never been wrong.

"Keep me up-to-date," Rocco ordered as Gumby headed out of the basement with Ace and Detective Garnham.

"Will do," Ace said.

Rocco stopped Gumby with a hand on his shoulder. "Don't do this on your own. She's important to all of us."

Gumby nodded. He knew there wasn't a chance in hell he'd be able to get Sidney back on his own. The cops were involved, and it wasn't like they'd simply stand back and let a SEAL team rush into an active dogfight and kick ass. He and his friends were a unit. They were only as good as their weakest member, and Gumby knew in this case, *he* would be the weak link. All he could think about was Sidney. Not the bad guys. Not any dogs that might be set loose. He needed his team, and he didn't feel even the least bit ashamed about that.

"If we find anything here that will be useful, we'll call," Rex called out from the bottom of the stairs.

Gumby nodded once more. He knew the other cops still on scene would get in touch with Francisco as well. There was no way information wouldn't be flowing back and forth, but ultimately none of that made Gumby feel any better at the moment. While they were running around trying to track her down, Sidney could already be hurt. Or dying. And that was what haunted him the most.

"Come on," Francisco said. "It's almost three-thirty, and my informant is probably coming down from a high and will be looking to score. I know where his usual haunts are, and I want to see if I can find him before he's too high to be any good to us."

As they headed through the house toward the detective's undercover car, Ace asked, "Why do you keep him as an informant if he's constantly jacked up?"

"Because he delivers," was Francisco's immediate reply. "Look, these guys aren't all bad. This guy is addicted to drugs and has done some pretty fucked-up things to score a hit. But I've gotten to know him over the last year, and he's had a hell of a life. He's got a wife and a little girl who live up in Los Angeles, but he left. It's fucked up, but he was selling anything he could get his hands on, which he knew was hurting his family. So he left them. Came down here to keep them out of his reach."

"That *is* fucked up," Ace said. "Why doesn't he just get clean?"

"He's tried. Several times. And failed each and every time. The addiction is just too strong. He knows he's gonna die on the streets and doesn't want his little girl to remember him as the asshole who sold her brand-new iPad to get some drugs. Believe it or not, he left to protect them."

"And you think he'll help us find Sidney?" Gumby asked as he climbed into the passenger seat.

"If he knows anything, he'll help," Francisco confirmed.

As they drove away from Victor's house, Gumby had never prayed so hard in his life that they'd be able to find this informant quickly. Given his current desperation, he'd even buy the man a hundred bucks of his drug of choice if he told them anything useful.

Sidney didn't bring any attention to the fact that she was conscious. The last thing she wanted was to give the assholes who'd kidnapped her a chance to do anything else. But as time went on, and Decker and his teammates didn't burst through the doors to rescue her, she got more and more worried.

The activity around the warehouse steadily increased. Most horrifying was when several crates holding snarling, pissed-off dogs were placed around her. She kept her eyes closed as the men who'd brought them in talked about the upcoming fight.

"My money's on Thor tonight."

"No way, Kujo's gonna kick some ass."

"Dallas says there's six-to-one odds on the girl."

"There's no way she's beating Thor and Kujo."

"Maybe, maybe not. But that fight is last on the docket. They'll be tired by the time they get around to the last fight."

"Hmmm, true."

"And he's gonna make a killing selling that shit he got from his Mexican contact tonight anyway. The fight's just a bonus."

"Come on. Those assholes are having a hard time with the fence. They wouldn't be able to put together a cardboard box."

When the voices faded away, Sidney shivered in terror.

Had she heard them right? They were planning on pitting her against two dogs named Thor and Kujo?

She was so fucked. This wasn't how the night was supposed to go. She was supposed to be hanging out with Decker and eventually making love. Not lying in a locked cage scared out of her mind.

The more time that went by, and the more people that showed up, the more depressed Sidney got. Decker wasn't going to find her in time. But she didn't blame him. Her actions had put her in this position. He'd been right the whole time. She should've left the amateur sleuthing to the experts. As a result of her carelessness and obsession with rescuing the puppies, she'd most likely gotten them, and herself, killed instead.

Sending up a prayer that Decker would eventually forgive her and move on with his life, she wrapped her arms around her knees as much as she could while on her side, and finally cried.

Gumby stood behind Detective Garnham as he questioned the informant, Martin Bierman. At one time, the man had probably been fairly good-looking, but now he was a walking skeleton. His body was so frail and skinny, he looked like he could be blown over by a swift wind.

He also smelled horrible. Like body odor, piss, and rotting trash. He was wearing a pair of torn jeans, sneakers with holes in the tips, and several layers of shirts. His brown hair was greasy and hanging in his eyes, and his teeth were yellow and rotted.

This was a man at the end of his rope, and any sane

person would steer well clear of him if they passed him on the streets.

But Detective Garnham didn't give any indication that he had a problem with the man. For a couple minutes they shot the shit as if they were old buddies who hadn't seen each other in several months.

It had taken hours to track down the guy. Gumby was about to crawl out of his mind with impatience when Francisco finally got down to the reason why they were there.

"Heard about any dogfights going down soon?"

Martin shrugged. "There's always dogfights going down," was his response.

Gumby clenched his teeth and felt Ace put a hand on his arm. It was obvious his friend could read his mind and knew he was two seconds away from putting some of the interrogation techniques they'd learned to good use.

"This one would be new, just sprung up tonight. There's probably a lot of buzz about it. Excitement."

"Yeah." Martin nodded. "I've heard some rumblings." His eyes seemed to light up. "Heard there'll be a lot of good shit there."

"What time?"

"Eight."

"Where?" Francisco asked.

Gumby was impressed. Instead of seeming too eager for the information, the detective remained nonchalant. As if he didn't care whether Martin told him or not. Gumby knew he wouldn't have been able to remain that calm if he'd been the one asking the questions. Not when Sidney's safety depended on the answers.

"I can't remember."

Martin's reply was bullshit, and they all knew it. But it

seemed as if it was all part of a game Detective Garnham had played with the man more than once.

"I stopped at that fast food place you like so much, couldn't finish my dinner," Francisco told him. "I could let you have my leftovers if you want."

That was also bullshit. The officer had stopped to get a bribe meal not too long after they'd left Victor's house. It was probably cold by now, but they all knew Martin wouldn't care.

"I could eat," the homeless man said.

"I'll grab it," Ace volunteered, and headed for the car they'd left parked down the road while they'd searched for Martin.

"What else have you heard about the fight?" Francisco asked.

Martin shrugged. "Heard there was gonna be some excitement, some new bitch who'd be fighting. Apparently it's this big thing between Dallas and some other guy who wants to move up the ranks."

"Victor?"

"Don't know. Don't care. You know what I care about."

Francisco nodded. "I do. But you know what *I* care about, Martin?" Without waiting for the other man to respond, the detective went on. "I care that there's an innocent woman who was in the wrong place at the wrong time. You know what she wanted to do? Rescue two innocent puppies from being sucked into the world of dogfighting."

"And I care about that because?" Martin asked.

Gumby almost lost it then, but Francisco held out an arm as if he knew Gumby was about to flat-out tackle

Martin. He went on, cool as a cucumber, as he rocked Martin's world. "Because if I'm right, the 'new bitch' they'll be fighting tonight *is* this innocent woman. Because Sidney Hale could be your daughter. You told me how much she likes puppies and kittens. What if it was her, and she wanted to rescue those dogs? What if *she* was the one Dallas and his friend had their hands on? Would you care then?"

Gumby saw Martin flinch before he looked down at the ground.

"I know how much you love your family. I *know*, Martin. Take a look at the man behind me. He loves his woman just as much, and she's missing. We're pretty sure the fight tonight is gonna involve her somehow. If it was *your* wife or daughter, wouldn't you want someone to help you find them?"

Gumby held his breath. He had no idea if Francisco had just pissed Martin off so badly he would refuse to tell them anything else, or if he'd just tipped the scales in their favor.

After several seconds, Martin mumbled, "Washington Avenue. That big warehouse at the end of the street."

Gumby exhaled loudly. He had no idea where Washington Avenue was, but the detective obviously did. "Thank you," he said softly.

Martin didn't acknowledge Gumby's presence in the least, just stared up at Francisco and asked belligerently, "What do I get for that?"

The detective started to take his wallet out but Gumby stopped him. He pulled five twenties out of his own wallet and handed them to Martin without a word. The man snatched them out of his grip and hid them on his person so quickly, he wouldn't have believed it possible if he hadn't seen it firsthand.

Ace returned with the bag of fast-food hamburgers and handed it to Martin. Francisco nodded at the homeless man and turned around.

Gumby and Ace followed him, and Ace whispered, "What did I miss?"

"We know when and where the fight's going down tonight."

"Thank God," Ace said.

Thank God indeed. Looking at his watch, Gumby saw that it was already seven. They didn't have a lot of time to get the team together and for Francisco to notify SWAT. Every minute that went by was a minute that Sidney could be hurt or killed.

He pulled out his phone and shot off a text to Rocco and Phantom at the same time Detective Garnham started speaking into his own phone. The troops were being rallied, but Gumby had no idea if they'd be in time or not.

CHAPTER EIGHTEEN

Sidney struggled against the hands that held her as fiercely as she could, to no avail. All she got was a bunch of men leering at her as her breasts jiggled in her bra. She couldn't believe she was standing in front of at least a hundred men in nothing but her underwear. But, honestly, that was the least of her worries at the moment.

More concerning was the dogfighting ring in front of her.

She'd listened as the thing had been constructed and as the room slowly filled with eager spectators for the night's fight. She'd heard what sounded like several vicious rounds of fighting, and the gunshots that had killed the losing dogs of each fight. The snarling and barking scared the shit out of her.

It was meaner than anything she'd ever heard in her life. These weren't dogs who were protective of their property. They weren't like Hannah, who had barked and growled at Max when he'd arrived at Decker's house. No, these were the sounds of dogs fighting to the death.

Willing to do whatever it took to take down their opponents.

And standing there, looking at the fencing that had been erected around the fighting ring, her worst fears were confirmed. Victor and his buddies were going to put *her* in the ring with two of the biggest, meanest dogs she'd ever seen. Thor and Kujo. They'd been victorious in the two fights they'd each participated in tonight, and for the finale of the evening, they'd fight each other...and Sidney.

"Please don't," she begged as the two men holding her walked forward, hauling her toward the ring.

"Shut up, bitch, or we'll put a muzzle on you."

The other men around them laughed as if that was the funniest thing they'd ever heard.

Victor opened the gate to the ring, and she was roughly shoved through the open door.

Sidney fell to her hands and knees and the crowd around her went wild—cheering, yelling, and laughing at her expense.

Feeling dizzy, Sidney leapt to her feet and lunged for the door she'd just been shoved through. But she was too late. Three men were holding it shut, and they snickered in her face as she grabbed hold of the fence and tugged.

Horrified by her predicament, Sidney looked around her. The temporary fence was around ten feet high, and included a chain-link cover over the top, as well. She couldn't simply climb over the fence to the other side of the ring and escape. Not to mention there were wall-to-wall men gathered around the square fenced-in area, watching the action.

There were drug deals going on in plain view, money

changing hands for little baggies. The smoke in the room was thick and made Sidney feel nauseous.

She didn't see one friendly face.

Blinking suddenly, Sidney looked again—and couldn't believe what she was seeing. There were kids there too. They couldn't be more than nine or ten years old. They were laughing and holding stacks of money right along with the adults around them.

Shocked, Sidney could only back away from the door in revulsion. The floor beneath her bare feet was covered in blood, and she slipped once as she tried to figure out what in the hell she could do to get out of this situation. On one side of the circle was the dead carcass of a loser from an earlier match. The poor dog was bleeding everywhere on its body, but it was easy to see the cause of its death was from its throat being torn out.

Sidney couldn't breathe. This was a nightmare, and she couldn't believe she was in the middle of it.

Victor stood up on a box and tried to address the crowd. It took a while for everyone to quiet down enough for him to be heard, but eventually she was able to hear what he was saying.

"And for tonight's last match, Thor and Kujo will finally meet! There are three possible outcomes to this fight. Kujo kills Thor..."

Half the men in the room let up a huge cheer that made Sidney wince at the volume.

"...Thor kills Kujo..."

Again, the room exploded in cheers and taunting from the men.

"...or both dogs turn on the bitch and kill *her*."

The walls seemed to vibrate from the level of cheering after Victor's statement.

Sidney was crying now. There didn't seem to be any reason to keep her tears locked inside. Was this how victims felt back in Roman times when they were in the Coliseum? Helpless and terrified out of their minds?

She backed away from the area where Victor was standing, but when she got too close to the fence, the men on the other side pulled out knives, along with sticks they'd probably collected from outside, and thrust them through the links, forcing her to step away from the edge of the ring.

Through her tears and the ringing in her ears, she heard Victor continuing his inflammatory speech to the spectators.

"As you all know, Thor is undefeated and has proven time and time again that he's the superior fighter here."

With that, amongst boos from the crowd, another man pushed Victor off the box he was standing on and stood up. "You're wrong, asshole! Kujo is gonna tear your fighter up *and* take down the bitch as well!"

Sidney heard people calling out things like, "You tell 'im, Dallas!" and "Fuck yeah," but all she could think about was how in a few minutes, she was going to be in the middle of this ring with two pissed-off, out-for-blood dogs.

Victor looked irritated that the Dallas guy had stolen his spotlight. He pushed him off the box and reclaimed his throne, so to speak. He stood up and began shouting once more. "This bout has been a long time coming, but I know many of you are wondering why this bitch is here."

After some murmurs of agreement from the crowd, Victor went on. "She fancies herself a *do-gooder*. Saving the animals from lives as championship dogfighters." More boos and cat-calls sounded around the room. "She doesn't understand that these dogs were *born* to fight. That they love it! But after tonight, she'll finally get it, won't she?"

When the room exploded in cheers once again, Victor stepped off the box and crooked a finger at her. Sidney didn't want to get anywhere near the heartless animal abuser, but if there was a chance he was going to let her out of the ring, she had to take it. She shuffled forward, not getting close enough to him that he could hurt her, but near enough that if he opened the door, she could make a break for it.

"Can you hear me?" Victor asked when she got close.

Sidney nodded.

He grinned. It was an evil smirk that made the hair on the back of her neck stand up. "You're gonna die in this ring tonight," he said with no emotion in his voice. "You shouldn't've stolen my dogs, bitch." And with that, he turned his back on her and motioned to someone nearby.

Sidney heard the growls before she saw the dogs. The crowd behind Victor and Dallas parted as four men carried two cages toward the ring. The noise level in the warehouse went from deafening to so quiet, the only sound heard was the dogs' toenails scrabbling on the bottoms of their cages.

Looking around, Sidney confirmed the only entrance to the fighting ring was the door she'd been shoved through. From what she'd researched of dogfighting matches, the owners normally stood on opposite sides of the ring, holding their dogs until it was time for them to fight. There were complicated rules for when the dogs could be collected and taken back to the side of the ring, until the match resumed.

But it was clear these street fights didn't operate in the same way as those she'd researched. No, the dogs in these fights were set loose from their cages and the fight began. No rules. No timeouts. Only a fight to the death.

And she was going to be right in the middle of it.

Swallowing hard, she watched as Victor and Dallas set up the cages, one on top of the other, in front of the door. It was obvious they were going to open the cages, let their dogs out, then slam the fence door, locking them inside.

Looking up, she considered climbing the fence once more, but one look at the men standing at the fence with their sticks and knives made her realize there was no way she'd make it to the top without being seriously injured.

Then she looked back at Kujo and Thor.

She was going to be seriously injured one way or another, and she'd have to decide if it would be at the hands of the men leering at her and practically drooling to see her torn to pieces, or by the very animals she'd spent her life trying to protect and save.

She had a momentary thought about Decker, how she regretted not having more time with him. Not having told him she loved him. Because she did. More than anything. But then she had no time to think about anything other than staying alive.

"One, two, *three!*" Victor shouted loudly, and the doors to the cages were opened and the two snarling, pissed-off dogs leaped into the ring and immediately turned to each other and started to fight.

Gumby knew he should be grateful for how quickly the dozens of law enforcement personnel gathered and situated themselves around the warehouse on Washington Avenue...but it wasn't nearly fast enough for his peace of mind. They'd been hearing cheering and yelling coming from inside the warehouse for a while now, and the thought that Sidney was inside, in the middle of the mayhem, was unacceptable.

If it was up to him, he and his team would've been inside and broken up the gathering and saved Sidney by now. But this wasn't their mission. They had to follow the cops' rules—and it was tearing him apart.

"Easy, man," Ace said, putting his hand on Gumby's shoulder. "We're gonna get her out of there."

Gumby knew that. But what he didn't know was what kind of shape she'd be in when they got to her. He didn't voice that thought. He didn't have to. He knew without a doubt that each of his friends was thinking the same thing.

Rocco looked sick. He was the only one of the team who could really empathize with how Gumby was feeling. When Caite's life was in danger, Gumby had felt bad, but he hadn't really understood the emotions that Rocco had been feeling. He did now.

The officers around him were all wearing bulletproof vests and had their riot gear at the ready. They all knew the second they burst into the warehouse, mayhem would ensue. The occupants would try to escape through any door possible, and by the sounds of things, there were a ton of people stuffed inside the warehouse. There was no way the police officers would be able to contain them all, but they wanted to catch as many as possible.

But all Gumby cared about was Sidney. She was his

only objective. He had to get to her before Victor did something stupid, like try to take her out because he was pissed.

"You holding it together?" Phantom asked.

Gumby nodded. He couldn't talk, his teeth were clenched together so he didn't scream out in frustration that the perimeter was taking so long to set up.

"It's almost time," Rex said quietly.

"She's gonna be in your arms in a few minutes," Bubba assured him.

Gumby knew his friends were trying to help, but all they were doing was making him more nervous. Glancing to the side, he saw a few ambulances staging nearby, waiting for the danger to be contained before they moved in to help anyone who needed it.

Detective Garnham walked toward their group. Gumby hoped like hell this was it.

"Four minutes and we're going in," Francisco said. "As we discussed, the six of you will take up the rear. I know we already went over this, but I just want to be sure. None of you are armed, are you?"

All six men answered negatively. Gumby didn't care if they weren't allowed to carry weapons into the fray. They didn't need them. Each of the six men on the team knew several ways to kill with their bare hands. And if Victor had harmed Sidney, he was a marked man.

He and Rocco had talked it over. They both knew it would be pandemonium inside the warehouse when the cops burst in. The confusion would give Gumby the cover he needed to make sure Victor would never be a threat to Sidney again. He didn't enjoy killing, but if it came down to Sidney or Victor, it wasn't even a question. He wouldn't feel remorse about ending Victor's life, not if it meant Sidney could live hers in peace.

"Be careful," Francisco said. "In raids like this, the owners have been known to let their dogs loose, to give them time to escape."

The SEAL murmured their assent. They were ready for just about anything.

The detective eyed them all one more time, then nodded, turned and walked away.

Gumby took a deep breath.

"Ready?" Rocco asked.

Pressing his lips together, Gumby nodded. As did the rest of his team. They were as focused and ready as they'd ever been. This wasn't a rescue mission for some unknown target. This was one of their own. None of the six men would leave without Sidney. A SEAL didn't leave a SEAL behind. Ever. And Sidney Hale might not be a Navy SEAL, but she was still a part of their team.

Gumby and the others moved behind the SWAT officers. Every one of Gumby's senses was attuned to the job at hand. Everything else fell away.

One moment they were standing there, muscles tense in anticipation, and the next they were moving. The door to the warehouse was flung open and the officers streamed inside, yelling orders, telling everyone to freeze.

Just as expected, the inhabitants of the warehouse immediately scattered. They headed for the other two exits as fast as they could, ignoring the orders from the officers.

As the crowd thinned, Gumby desperately searched the space for a familiar petite, raven-haired woman. The noise was so loud he couldn't talk to his team, but without needing to be told, they fanned out, searching for Sidney.

Then he heard it. Screams and growls coming from the center of the room.

Looking up, Gumby saw a fenced-in area in the middle of a warehouse. And when more people in front of him fled, he realized exactly what he was seeing.

A fifteen-foot diameter ring, enclosed by a tall chain-link fence. And inside was the reason he was here. Sidney.

As was a large, powerful, pissed-off pit bull who was doing his best to get to her.

Gumby literally pushed two men and a child out of his way as he headed for the cage, eyes locked on Sidney. "Hold on, Sid," he murmured. "For God's sake, hold on."

When Kujo and Thor were let into the ring, Sidney froze in terror for a moment as the dogs immediately turned on each other. Their teeth gnashed together as they snapped and lunged. She backed away as far as she could while still staying out of reach of the spectators and their knives.

For a moment, the two dogs were more interested in tearing each other apart than turning on her. Blood spattered in every direction when one of the dogs shook his head, sprinkling Sidney in the process, but she ignored the way her skin crawled, her eyes glued to the fight in front of her.

But way too soon, Kujo managed to get his jaws around Thor's throat. It was vicious and brutal, and like every single one of the spectators, Sidney couldn't tear her gaze from the sight. Tears filled her eyes once more as Thor's struggles got weaker and weaker.

When it was obvious Thor wasn't going to win the fight, the crowd went absolutely berserk. They hooted and hollered, and Sidney saw a ton of money changing hands as those who bet on Thor had to hand over their hard-earned cash to those who'd bet on Kujo.

She vaguely heard Victor yell, "The fight's not over! Time for some incentive!"

Flinching when something hit her leg, Sidney turned her head to see a man holding a gun, aimed right at her. Her eyes got wide—then something stung her in the back.

Spinning, she saw someone else holding a gun. Suddenly, there seemed to be guns in just about everyone's hands around her. Were they *shooting* her?

Then she heard Kujo yelp. Her eyes went back to him, and she realized the spectators weren't shooting them with bullets, but BBs or something similar.

As another projectile hit Kujo, he turned toward her and snarled.

"Oh, shit," she said under her breath, before letting out a scream when the pit bull started stalking toward her.

"No!" she yelled. "Kujo, sit!" she said desperately, but the dog just snarled and continued his slow, measured steps toward her.

Before she was ready, Kujo leaped at her.

Instinctively, she turned to the side and kicked out, catching the dog in the hindquarter. He veered off course, but wasn't deterred. He lunged at her again, this time catching her calf with his teeth.

Screaming in pain, all Sidney could think about was getting away.

She pummeled the dog's head with her fists, trying to get him to let go. The pain in her leg so intense, she felt blackness threatening to take her under. Knowing if she went down, Kujo would tear out her throat, she fought to stay upright.

Then the crowd began pelting Kujo with their BBs again. The dog shook his head and yelped, letting go of her leg in the process.

Free from the animal's jaws, Sidney ran for the fence. The knives and sticks didn't seem nearly so bad anymore. She wasn't thinking about anything but getting away from Kujo's teeth, and since dogs couldn't climb, the only chance she had was to get to the top of the enclosure.

The dog owners had created a chain-link ceiling, of sorts, probably thinking it would keep her from escaping, but it also allowed her a way to avoid both the dog and the men surrounding the cage. If she reached the top, she could cling to the ceiling like a child might hang from the monkey bars in a playground.

As she desperately tried to climb with one leg bleeding and throbbing from Kujo's bite, the men on the other side sneered in her face. They spit at her. They laughed. And they did their best to make her let go and fall back into the ring, shaking the fence and trying to slash at her with their knives.

Ignoring the spectators, Sidney climbed for her life. If she could only get to the top, she'd be okay.

All right, that probably wasn't true. It would only be a matter of time before Victor and the others found a way to make her let go and have to face Kujo again, but anything she could do to *not* feel the dog's teeth around her flesh again, she'd do.

All of a sudden, the noise and the entire atmosphere in the room changed. Instead of cheering and laughing, there was panicked yelling and screams.

Ignoring everything but her need to get away from Kujo, now snarling and growling as he jumped against the fence again and again in an effort to get to her, Sidney clung to the chain-link. The spectators had stopped messing with her, but she was too preoccupied to try to figure out why.

She stopped climbing when she reached the top of the fence. Her fingers hurt from holding onto the chain-link and her leg was throbbing unbearably. Blood was dripping from the wound, landing on Kujo—who continued to leap up at her—and covering the floor beneath him.

Sobbing, her fingers cramping, Sidney knew she couldn't hold on long.

She was going to die. Right here. Right now. By the jaws of one of the very animals she'd spent her adult life trying to save.

Gumby took off at a dead run toward the ring. He searched for a way in as he ran and couldn't find one. His eyes finally landed on a large padlock on the opposite side of where Sidney was desperately clinging to the side of the fence. She was about ten feet high, at the very top of the enclosure. She was practically naked, but that wasn't what concerned him at the moment. It was the dog covered in blood, trying desperately to get at her, that made his adrenaline race.

Reaching the gate at the same time as Ace, Gumby lifted a leg and kicked the fence as hard as he could.

Sidney let out a screech on the other side as the entire enclosure shuddered.

"Shit," he murmured.

"Move. I got this," Ace said as he held up a pair of bolt cutters.

Gumby moved, but asked, "Where the fuck did you get those?"

Ace placed the jaws of the cutters around the lock holding the gate shut and said, "Garnham. He handed them to me right before we breached the room. Said they might come in handy."

Gumby had never been so relieved for the man's insight as he was right now. He saw Rocco run around the enclosure toward Sidney, who was still clinging to the chain-link at the top of the enclosure. His friend took a flying leap and quickly scaled the fence. He managed to carefully climb on top of the precarious rig, above where Sidney was holding on for dear life. The links were too small for him to reach through and grab hold of her, but Gumby knew he would be talking to her, telling her to hang on, that help was there.

The snarling dog was more of a problem. In order to get to Sidney, Gumby had to eliminate the threat from the dog. But without a gun, he didn't have an easy way to do it. The second the lock fell from the door, Gumby pushed his way inside the enclosure. His brain registered the almost-dead dog in the middle of the floor, but he didn't spare it a glance. He only had eyes on the one standing below Sidney.

Gumby was prepared to take the dog out with his bare

hands, but Phantom pushed him to the side and, in seconds, had swiped a blade across the dog's throat.

Realizing his friend had lied to the detective about being unarmed, and not giving a shit, Gumby headed straight for the fence. He slipped once in the blood on the floor below Sidney, and would've gone down if Ace hadn't caught his arm. Not taking the time to thank him, Gumby was climbing the fence toward his woman, desperate to get to her.

The fence swayed under his weight, but it didn't slow him down. In seconds, he was next to Sidney, trying to figure out a way to get them both down safely.

Sidney's eyes were squeezed shut as she put all her energy into hanging on to the fence. Her fingers were burning and her leg trembled, trying to hold her up. Her toes were shoved through the links of the fence, and she barely registered anything around her due to the pain. She vaguely heard someone talking to her in a low, soothing voice, but she couldn't open her eyes to see who it was.

When something touched her back, she jerked and screamed in terror.

"It's me, Sidney! I've got you. You're safe."

"Decker?" she shouted in disbelief. She had to be hallucinating. There was no way it was Decker.

"Can you let go and grab hold of me?"

Her eyes popped open finally—and she blinked at seeing Rocco crouched above her on the outside of the enclosure. She looked around and didn't see any of the spectators. No one was poking at her anymore, laughing and cheering.

Turning her head, she then saw Decker. He was there!

"Decker!" she croaked.

"Shhhh. Can you move your arm and put it around my neck? I won't let you fall. Grab hold of me."

"No! Kujo!"

"Who?"

"The dog! He'll get us!"

"He's dead, Sid. We need to get you down and get that leg looked at."

Peering down, Sidney saw Phantom standing below Decker. Ace was also there. She didn't see Bubba or Rex, but knew they had to be in the warehouse somewhere.

Not only that, but the bloody body of Kujo was lying on his side on the concrete floor, not moving.

Everything hit her at once. Decker had found her. Just in the nick of time.

Her body moved without her even consciously telling it to. She let go of the fence with one hand and wrapped it around Decker's neck. She immediately turned and looped her other arm around him, and did her best to hitch her good leg around his hips too. She had no doubt he'd be able to hold her. No way would he let her fall.

Ever so slowly, Decker began to inch his way back down the fence. She had no idea how his large feet fit in the small holes of the chain-link, but at the moment, she didn't care. She felt hands touch her sides as they got near the floor, and she gripped Decker tighter. She felt the second his feet touched the ground, and then they were headed for the door to the ring.

"Put her down, Gumby," a voice ordered.

"Not here," he said, his voice rumbling through her as she clung even harder.

A shout to her right made Sidney pick her head up and look in that direction.

Victor was standing in front of Rocco, who'd climbed down after Decker had reached her—and was pointing a gun at the SEAL's head.

She saw everything unfold as if watching through a long, dark tunnel. She opened her mouth to scream, to say something, but she needn't have worried.

One second Victor was threatening Rocco, and the next he was lying on the floor, motionless.

Bubba had come up from behind and quickly disarmed him, then Phantom had spun him around and punched him with one strong blow to the face.

Even as Decker carried her out of the ring, toward the door of the warehouse, she looked back and saw Rocco leaning over, checking Victor's pulse.

"Fuck, no heartbeat," Rocco said as he knelt down and immediately started doing CPR.

Feeling out of it and dizzy, Sidney noticed the cops had many of the spectators lined up or lying on the ground with their hands behind their backs. The thing that struck her the hardest was how many kids there were. She remembered seeing them from inside the ring. They hadn't been cowering, scared to be there. They'd been cheering and yelling just as loudly as the adults.

"Hang on, Sid. You're okay," Decker murmured.

She didn't feel okay. She felt heartsick and depressed. Her leg throbbed horribly, and remembering how close she'd come to being mauled by Kujo made her breathing speed up and her mouth begin to water. "I'm going to throw up," she warned Decker, mere seconds before she did just that.

Unfortunately, he didn't let go of her, and she puked all the way down his shoulder, back, and arm. She whimpered at how horrible she felt, both physically and because she'd literally just thrown up all over Decker.

When the pain and humiliation began to overwhelm her, and the dizziness crept in once more, Sidney gladly gave herself over to blackness.

Gumby felt the second Sidney passed out in his arms. He was actually relieved. Her leg looked bad, but luckily the dog hadn't been able to completely tear her apart. He quickly walked up to one of the ambulances and was grateful when the paramedics didn't try to stop him as he simply carried Sidney inside, laying her down on the gurney there. He knelt down near her head and watched as the paramedics went to work on her.

Her eyes stayed closed, and Gumby was glad. Her leg had bled a lot, and once the paramedics cleaned some of the blood away, he knew she'd need quite a few stitches. But he was still relieved it hadn't been worse.

About three minutes later, Ace stuck his head into the ambulance and gestured for Gumby to come out and talk to him. He didn't want to leave Sidney, but Gumby knew his friend wouldn't ask for privacy if it wasn't important.

"Do *not* leave without me," he growled at the paramedics. "I'll be right back."

"You've got about four minutes," one of the men said as he worked to get an IV started in her arm.

"I'll be back," Gumby repeated, then eased out behind the men and jumped to the ground. The second he turned to Ace, the other man began speaking.

"Victor's dead. Phantom's punch likely ruptured some veins to his brain and led to internal bleeding."

Gumby was glad the piece of shit was dead. He wished he'd suffered more, but at the moment could only be relieved Sidney wouldn't have to ever come face-to-face with the man again. "Will Phantom be in trouble as a result?"

Ace shook his head. "He didn't use the knife he obviously had on him, and Garnham saw the entire thing go down. Saw Victor point the gun at Rocco. He knows it was self-defense."

Gumby nodded.

"The other main guy, Dallas, was caught as he ran out and was identified by several of the other men in attendance."

"Any other dogs found?"

"None alive," Ace told him.

"And the kids?"

Ace sighed. "Gang members and dog fighters in training. They weren't traumatized by what happened here in the least. They were more concerned about getting rid of the drugs they were passing back and forth."

"Fuck," Gumby breathed.

"It's a shame. I mean, I know raising kids isn't a walk in the park, but how do they come back from something like this? They're already desensitized from the suffering the dogs go through, and they were almost witness to a woman being torn apart right in front of their eyes. If they don't care about that, I'm not sure there's much hope that they'll turn out to be productive members of society."

Gumby agreed. But at the moment, he didn't care about them either. All his focus was on Sidney.

"So this ring's shut down? With Victor dead and Dallas in custody, that's a good thing, right?"

Ace shrugged. "Yeah, but the detective is sure someone else will pick right up where they left off."

"Fucking dogfights," Gumby said.

"How's Sidney?" Ace asked.

"It's not too bad, but it's not good either," Gumby told his friend. "If she hadn't managed to climb that fence, that dog would've torn her to pieces."

"Shit..."

"Yeah."

"I'll go and grab you some clean clothes," Ace said. "And I'll make sure Hannah's taken care of. You need anything else?"

Gumby breathed out a sigh of relief. Honestly, he hadn't been thinking about anything but Sidney. He felt guilty for not sparing a thought for Hannah. "No, I'm good. There's no rush, I can find a pair of scrubs at the hospital for the short term."

"Fuck you," Ace said. "As if we're all gonna go home and take a nap when your woman is hurt."

Gumby nodded. It was a good feeling to have friends. "I don't know how long it'll take to hear anything from a doctor," he warned Ace.

"Doesn't matter. We'll be there."

"Sir? We're ready to go," one of the paramedics said from inside the ambulance.

"Go," Ace ordered. "We'll catch up with you at the hospital."

Gumby nodded and turned to climb back into the back of the ambulance. He took a seat this time next to Sidney's head and did his best to keep his shit together. She had two IVs, one in each arm, and a C-collar had been put around her neck for precaution. Her bra was lying on the floor and a blanket had been wrapped around her torso. Her leg had been covered in gauze and she was hooked up to all sorts of beeping machines.

She was still unconscious, and Gumby was grateful yet again. He gently took hold of her hand, wincing at the bruises he could see on her fingers and palm.

Ignoring the man sitting next to him, he leaned over and put his lips near Sidney's ear. "Hang on, Sid. I love you."

At his words, her fingers tightened in his grasp for a moment before relaxing once more.

It was enough. She'd heard him, and Gumby knew she'd eventually be okay.

CHAPTER NINETEEN

Sidney smiled at Decker. The last couple of weeks hadn't been great, there was no doubt about it, but having Decker at her side had made every bandage change, every setback, easier to deal with.

And it hadn't only been Decker. It had been all of his friends too. During her stay in the hospital, Ace had visited almost as much as Decker. Phantom, Bubba, Rex, and Rocco had also been in and out, entertaining her and keeping her spirits up.

She'd had to have over a hundred stitches in her leg to properly close the bite. Then it had gotten infected almost immediately, and the pain of the wound having to be cleaned regularly was extremely difficult to endure. What started as a short hospital stay had stretched into two weeks as doctors battled and watched the injection closely. Sidney knew she was lucky. Knew it could've been a lot worse, but it was hard to stay positive when she'd been in so much pain.

Nora had visited, and Sidney had never laughed so hard

when her friend ended up going home with one of her nurses. Apparently they'd hit it off out in the hallway, and Nora had done what Nora did best...seduced him.

Faith had come by as well, telling her how sorry she was about everything that happened, but things were a little weird between them. Sidney felt horrible for her role in the whole mess, and because she'd ignored her friend's warnings about getting too personally involved in rescuing the dogs.

There had also been visits from another SEAL team on the base, and their families. Caroline had started it by stopping by with her husband, Wolf, and every day after, she'd met another family on that team. Abe and Alabama, Cookie and Fiona, Mozart and Summer, Benny and Jessyka, Dude and Cheyenne. Even their commander and his wife, Julie, had stopped by.

It should've been awkward, but instead, it made her feel even more cared for.

But it was Caite who Sidney was most excited to see. She visited every other day or so, keeping her up-to-date on what was happening with Dallas and the other participants of the dogfights. Decker hadn't wanted to talk about it much, feeling as if she was better off not knowing, so Sidney was grateful when Caite was willing to give her details.

Dallas was still in jail, but the cops hadn't been able to make charges stick to most of the other men at the fight. There was no way to prove who the drugs belonged to that were found discarded on the floor of the warehouse. While Sidney had identified the men who'd pushed her into the ring, and who'd kidnapped her in the first place, the other men had been let go without charges.

Luckily, Phantom hadn't been charged with the death of Victor, since Detective Garnham had vouched for the fact that he'd hit him in self-defense. Sidney barely remembered what had happened as she'd been too traumatized.

But the best part of the last couple weeks was Decker.

Twenty minutes earlier, he'd wheeled her out of the hospital after one last assessment of her stitches. She'd be back for more checkups, but she'd been officially discharged. Decker's truck had been waiting at the entrance to the hospital, and he'd gently picked her up and placed her in the passenger side. Now, they were almost to his beach house.

"You okay?" he asked, glancing over at her.

"Yeah." And she was. Her leg still hurt but she was feeling better every day.

Sidney wanted to tell him something important, but hadn't had a chance while she'd been recovering. Either someone was visiting or the time just wasn't right. But the more she thought about it, the more she felt now was the right time and place. It wasn't romantic, but not having his intense concentration on her while she spoke was a good thing.

"I need to tell you something," Sidney said softly as Decker drove out of the hospital parking lot.

"Okay," he said. "Can it wait until I get you home and comfortable?"

"No." The word came out louder than she'd intended.

"All right. Shoot."

This was harder than she'd imagined it would be. "When I was in that cage, waiting for whatever they had in store for me, I couldn't think about anything other than how pissed you were going to be at me."

"Sid, no, I—"

"Please, let me get through this," Sidney begged.

Decker nodded.

"I know I screwed up. You begged me not to go there by myself, and I did it anyway. Of course, I didn't know Victor was waiting for me, or that he'd baited me with those puppies, but still. As I was sitting in that crate, listening to them building the fighting ring, knowing there was a good chance I'd be raped or killed, I could only think about one thing I regretted most of all. Something I hadn't told you."

Decker reached over and grabbed hold of her hand, but didn't speak, for which she was thankful.

"Then, when I needed you most, you were there. It was a miracle, and I still can't believe how everything came together for you to find me so fast. I thought for sure there was no way it would happen." She took a deep breath and got out the words she'd been thinking about for weeks. "I love you, Decker. I hadn't planned on falling in love, but before I knew it, you'd become the most important thing in my life."

He squeezed her hand, tightly.

"I'm sorry I went behind your back and checked out the puppies by myself. I'm sorry I almost got Caite dragged into that horrible shit as well. I wish I'd listened to you...and I was so wrong."

Decker pulled the truck off to the side of the road into a big box store's parking lot. There were people all around them, but somehow it still seemed as if they were the only two people on Earth.

He put the truck in park and turned in his seat. The console between them kept him from getting too close, but he leaned over and took her face in his hands. His gaze was intense, and Sidney was nervous about what he might say.

"I think I've loved you from the first moment I saw you. And one of the things I love most is your loyalty and tenacity. I love how much you care about the animals and how you feel so deeply. I'm sorry you didn't wait for me as well, but that doesn't diminish my love or respect for you. I think you might benefit from talking to someone about what you went through as a child, and how it all manifested itself in the person you are today, but no matter what you choose, I'll always be here for you."

Sidney breathed a sigh of relief. And the thought of talking to a psychologist wasn't something she was opposed to. Maybe talking to someone who didn't know her personally would be easier.

Decker fumbled in his pocket for a moment before turning back to her.

In his hand was a princess-cut solitaire diamond ring.

Sidney gasped in shock.

"I love you, Sid. You're more important to me than anything else in my life. I'd do anything to keep you safe. Give you anything your heart desires. Be by your side in whatever you want to do. Will you marry me? I know being the wife of a Navy SEAL isn't the easiest job in the world, but I swear I'll do whatever it takes to ease the burden. I'll never cheat, and I'll do whatever I can to make sure I come home to you after every mission. I can't promise but—"

"Yes," Sidney said breathlessly, interrupting him.

"Yes?"

"Yes!" she confirmed.

The smile that crossed Decker's face was beautiful, and something Sidney knew she'd never forget. He took ahold of her hand and slipped the ring on her finger. It fit perfectly, and she couldn't believe how right it felt.

"Fuck, I love you," Decker breathed before he kissed the ring, then took her face in his hands once again. He leaned forward and kissed her, a long, passionate kiss that took her breath away.

When he pulled back, they were both breathing hard. He'd kissed her many times since she'd been injured, but this one felt different. It was a promise. A beginning.

"I hadn't planned on doing this here," Decker mumbled as he adjusted his cock in his pants and settled back in his seat.

Sidney chuckled. She stared down at her ring. She couldn't take her eyes off it. It was probably around a carat, and it seemed huge to her. It was perfect.

"I'm not going to want to wait that long to get married," Decker told her as he drove out of the parking lot. "But my dad and stepmom are going to want to be there. As is my brother. I'm thinking maybe we can have a small ceremony on our beach with the team and my family and anyone you want to invite. Faith and Nora for sure. Maybe Jude?"

Sidney smiled. She hadn't ever really thought about getting married. Certainly didn't have an image in her head for what she wanted the actual ceremony to be like. But a beach wedding seemed perfect. "Maybe Wolf and his team can come too?"

Decker smiled as if she'd just made his day. "Anyone you want, sweetheart."

"I don't deserve you," she told him.

"Wrong. We deserve each other," he said with a smile.

Sidney grabbed hold of his hand and held on tightly the rest of the way home.

Gumby felt on top of the world. The last two weeks had been hard, but Commander North had been very understanding, and he'd given Gumby a lot of time off to be with Sidney while she was recuperating. He'd also made sure the team hadn't been slated for any missions while she was still recovering. Gumby knew the reprieve would soon be over, now that Sidney was home, but he'd deal with having to leave her when the time came.

They hadn't talked about her moving into the beach house with him, but since she'd agreed to marry him, it was a moot point anyway. They had plenty of time to figure out their living arrangements.

The guy who was going to take over the maintenance for Sidney at the trailer park had started sooner than everyone had planned, since Sidney had been in the hospital, and so far he seemed to be working out.

Gumby had gotten Max to finish remodeling the top floor of his beach house just as he and Sidney had discussed. He'd wanted the house to be completely done by the time Sidney got out of the hospital, so she'd be as comfortable as possible. The work required a full crew working night and day, but the master was just as she'd envisioned, including the bathroom, complete with a huge shower that would easily fit them both.

Max still wanted to hire Sidney, and had even brought over the paperwork for her to fill out while she was in the hospital. As soon as she was ready, she could start shadowing one of Max's teams. She'd need to take it easy for a while, not climb any ladders or anything, but the doctor reassured them both she'd be fully cleared for work soon.

Gumby pulled his truck into the driveway and said, "Stay put until I come around."

"I can walk, Decker," she complained.

"Shuffle forward, yes. Walk? Not so much."

"Whatever," she muttered.

"Humor me," Gumby pleaded.

After she nodded, he climbed out of the truck and went around to her side. He felt his heart grow in his chest at seeing the ring he'd picked out on her finger.

He lifted her in his arms bride style, and she wrapped her arms around his neck. He shut the truck door with his hip and headed for his front porch. Once there, he eased her down and made sure she was steady on her feet before opening the door.

In the weeks that Sidney had been in the hospital, Hannah had healed almost miraculously. The wound on her back was light pink, and no longer painful to the touch. The pads of her feet had also healed enough that the vet said she was cleared to go out on the beach. She absolutely loved scampering in the surf, chasing waves, and running up and down the sand, barking joyously. She was a completely different dog from the battered and beaten, scared-to-death animal he'd taken in all those weeks ago.

Gumby couldn't wait for Sidney to see how well

Hannah was doing, and for Hannah to see one of her favorite humans again.

He unlocked the door and opened it for Sidney to precede him inside.

Hannah barked enthusiastically and danced in place in the foyer, turning in circles in her excitement.

Unfortunately, instead of Sidney being overjoyed to see the ecstatic pit bull, she was clearly scared. She backed against him then scooted around his body so he was between her and Hannah.

Gumby immediately turned and hauled Sidney against him. He felt her legs give out and he carefully lowered them both to the floor. She was in his lap, burying her face against his chest. He could feel her trembling, and was confused for a second as to what was happening.

When he finally clued in that it was *Hannah* who terrified her so badly, his heart broke for Sidney.

Confused as to why her humans weren't greeting her, Hannah whimpered and lay down on her belly. She crawled toward them, pathetic sounds coming from her throat. She nudged Gumby's elbow.

"Sid?" he asked quietly

"For a second, I...I was back there," she whispered. "In the ring. I saw Hannah and thought she was going to bite me."

"She won't. She loves you."

"But I saw her, and the only thing I could think about was how much it hurt when that dog had ahold of my leg."

"Give me your hand," Gumby ordered gently. She immediately put her hand in his, her trust making him feel so much better. Moving slowly, he placed it on Hannah's head. As if the pit bull could tell Sidney was frightened, she didn't move.

Sidney still shook in his lap, but she let him pet Hannah, her hand under his. "See? It's just Hannah. She isn't going to bite you."

When Sidney took a deep breath, Gumby knew she was going to be all right.

He'd never met anyone braver than she was. He'd thought so the first time he'd seen her, taking on a man twice her size, but he knew it even more now. She began to pet Hannah on her own, so he put his arm back around her waist.

"She looks good," Sidney said after a few minutes. She was no longer shaking, but was still being cautious.

"Yeah. The doctor says she's healing remarkably well."

As they talked, Hannah's tail wagged, and she crawled even closer to them.

Gumby chuckled when the dog rested her head on his knee and looked up at Sidney as if she were the sun to her moon.

"I can't go back to doing what I was before this happened," Sidney said quietly, her eyes on Hannah.

"What do you mean?" Gumby asked.

"You were right. Chasing after the hard-core abusers by myself was stupid. Obviously. I thought if I was careful, I'd be okay. But I was just being naïve. I could've gotten Caite hurt, and you and the others. But it's more than that." Sidney looked up at him. "I was scared, Decker. Scared to death. The dogs in that ring weren't salvageable. They were too far gone. I couldn't have saved them no matter what I did."

"I know," Gumby said softly, feeling sad, but relieved that she now realized it.

"I thought you were just being bossy. I was so upset with you that day, and I think that fueled my stupidity. You even *said* you would go with me, and I just plowed ahead like I always did. I'm so sorry."

Gumby kissed her temple. "You made a mistake. You don't have to apologize."

"I do. I should've realized you just wanted what was best for me."

"Apology accepted," Gumby said, wanting to move on.

She looked back at Hannah. "I want to keep working with abused animals, but not on the front line anymore. I'll talk to Faith, see if she still wants me to help her out. I can help with adoptions or something."

"I think that's a great idea," Gumby told her.

Still focused on Hannah, she asked, "What if I can't even do that? What if I'm scared to death of every dog now?"

"You aren't."

"How do you know?" Sidney asked, staring up at him, her eyes wide and full of tears. "Look how I reacted to Hannah. And I *know* her."

"Cut yourself some slack, sweetheart. She's the first dog you've come into contact with since you were attacked. And she's the same breed. It'll take some time, but I know you'll beat this. You won't ever be the same person you were before, but that's not all bad. Having a bit of caution when it comes to abused dogs, and animals in general, is probably a good thing. But I know you. You'll bounce back. Promise."

"What'd I do to deserve you?" Sidney asked quietly after several moments had gone by.

Deciding not to answer, Gumby said instead, "Come on, let's get you to the couch. I'll make you some lunch and you can take a nap."

"I'm not tired," she complained, but a huge yawn belied her words.

Smiling, but knowing better than to contradict her, Gumby slid out from under her and stood. Then he helped her to her feet. "Easy, Hannah," he scolded when the pit bull jumped to her feet in anticipation of playtime.

He saw Sidney wince, but she bravely held out her hand to the dog and smiled when Hannah licked her.

He kept one arm around Sidney as he walked her to the couch and got her settled, propping her feet up on a pillow on the coffee table. Hannah jumped up on the cushion next to her, and he was about to pull her off when Sidney said, "She's okay."

"If she starts bothering you, let me know."

"I will. Decker?"

"Yeah?"

"I love you."

Gumby sighed. He'd never get tired of hearing those words. "Love you too, Sid. Close your eyes and relax while I get us something to eat."

"God, I can't wait. Hospital food sucks."

Gumby grinned. She was right, it did, but he knew for a fact that his friends, and hers, had all been bringing her meals on a regular basis. It wasn't like she had starved during her stay.

By the time he'd finished cooking a protein-laden omelet and brought it into the other room, Sidney was asleep. Her head was resting against the back of the couch, and Hannah's head lay on her thigh. Sidney's hand was on the dog's back, and she was clearly out cold.

Turning, he went right back to the kitchen and put the eggs into the fridge. He'd heat them up later. Then he couldn't help himself; he went back into the living room and sat on the other side of Sidney. She stirred only briefly when he put his arm around her, moving so her head rested on his shoulder rather than the couch, then she settled again.

It was the middle of the afternoon, and Gumby knew he should be heading back to the base as the commander had warned him a mission was on the horizon, but he couldn't make himself move.

All was right in his world, and he'd never been happier.

All six Navy SEALs studied the maps in front of them as if they were a matter of life or death, which they were. Theirs, and the woman they were being sent into East Timor—otherwise known as Timor-Leste—to rescue.

Ace had only vaguely heard of the Southeast Asian country before this mission. It was an island just north of Australia, and was last colonized by Indonesia. Up until nineteen ninety-nine, there had been widespread turmoil between the guerilla forces of the small country and Indonesian forces.

It was now a part of the United Nations, and despite a few assassination attempts on the prime ministers over the years, things had been relatively peaceful. Until now.

Factional fighting had broken out again recently,

causing unrest in the region. Australian reinforcements had once more been sent into the country to try to restore order, but there were still skirmishes forcing thousands of civilians to flee their homes, especially outside the larger cities.

None of this would normally concern the United States government or be a reason for the Navy SEALs to get involved, but there had been over fifty Peace Corp volunteers in the country when the most recent fighting broke out, and the government had only been able to safely evacuate about half of them.

That still wouldn't have been enough to send the SEALs, but apparently one of the missing volunteers was the daughter of a very influential local businessman, with ties to Washington, DC. And when he hadn't been able to contact his daughter for seven days, he'd called in as many favors as he could...hence the team getting ready to fly across the world to Timor-Leste to see if they could find the missing Peace Corp volunteer.

They'd pinpointed the location of the house she'd lived in, the school where she'd taught English, and had concluded that it should be a fairly straightforward mission. The location was in a mountainous region, which was one of the rebels' strongholds. The SEALS weren't going to the country to engage in any combat—although they were prepared to defend themselves. They were under strict orders to grab Kalee Solberg and get the hell out.

"There's been a complication," Commander Storm North told the team, frowning.

Ace sighed. There always seemed to be complications. It was annoying, but not entirely unexpected.

"Kalee had a visitor arrive in the country right before the shit hit the fan. One of her best friends from college decided to go out and visit her."

"Shit," Rocco mumbled under his breath.

Ace privately echoed the sentiment but kept his mouth shut. Rescuing one person was tricky enough; add in a second and everything just got way more complicated.

"Piper Johnson is thirty-two years old, average height and weight, blonde hair, blue eyes. She's a cartoonist who's had her comics featured in the *New York Times*, *Wall Street Journal*, and has had several go viral on social media as well." The commander passed out info sheets to the team and continued.

Ace flipped the paper over, immediately recognizing the cartoon at the top of the page. It was political in nature, and funny without being cruel. His eyes wandered to the picture near the bottom of the page—and he blinked.

In the image, Piper Johnson was laughing at something, and her eyes were closed with her head thrown back.

The pure joy and happiness on her face was absolutely beautiful.

Ace had the sudden urge to know what had been so funny, so he could share in the joy with her.

It was a crazy reaction to a photo, and he immediately felt uneasy about it. He was a professional. A soldier. And Piper was a job. He'd never had such a visceral reaction to a job before.

He focused on what their commander was saying.

"...also not been heard from in over a week. Your main mission is to find Kalee and get her out of the country, but be on the lookout for Piper Johnson as well. Any questions?"

As the rest of the team asked their commander questions, Ace stared at the picture of the blonde. He hoped like hell she'd somehow made her way out of the country to safety. Being in the middle of a possible civil war wasn't a place for anyone, but especially not someone who had as much happiness and joy inside her as Piper Johnson.

Piper Johnson held her breath as the rebels stomped on the boards feet above her hiding place. She was hungry, dirty, and scared out of her mind. But she didn't dare make a sound. If the rebels knew she was here, she had no doubt they wouldn't hesitate to kill her—just like they'd probably killed Kalee.

Thinking about her friend made her want to cry, but she bit her cracked lip and forced back the tears. She was lucky to be alive, and she knew it. And it was *because* of Kalee. She had to keep her shit together.

Not just for her, but for the children.

Taking a silent breath, Piper looked over and saw three pairs of dark brown eyes staring at her. Four-year-old Rani appeared scared to death, seven-year-old Sinta looked at Piper as if she would somehow magically make everything all right, and thirteen-year-old Kemala seemed heartbreakingly resigned.

Piper brought her finger up to her lips and reminded the girls to be as quiet as they could. All three nodded solemnly.

When the rebels above their heads began laughing and

shouting, she closed her eyes and tried to figure out how in the world she'd gotten here. She was a single woman in her thirties who drew funny pictures for a living. Now she was somehow smack-dab in the middle of some sort of civil war...and responsible for three orphaned children.

She wasn't a soldier, didn't even know how to shoot a gun.

She didn't know Portuguese and couldn't understand what was being said by the soldiers above them.

And she was definitely not mother material.

They were all screwed.

*

Find out what happens with Piper and the children in *Securing Piper,* book 3 in the SEAL of Protection: Legacy series!

JOIN my Newsletter and find out about sales, free books, contests and new releases before anyone else!!
Click HERE

Want to know when my books go on sale? Follow me on Bookbub HERE!
Would you like Susan's Book Protecting Caroline for FREE?
Click HERE

AUTHOR NOTE

Not everything I write is based on fact. I'm sure you guys can figure that out. But I do incorporate things I've seen or read into my stories here and there. Hannah is one of these instances.

Hannah is real. She exists. And the things that I described happening to her in this book, happened to the real Hannah. She was found dumped on the side of a busy road like a piece of trash. She was taken to the vet, and they determined her injuries were exactly as I described them in this book.

And, like the fictional Hannah, the real Hannah healed up beautifully and is now living a wonderful, safe, happy life with my friend Amy and her new "brother," a pit bull named George.

Dogfighting is a horrendous, awful thing that exists in almost every country today. Dogs like Hannah, dogs who just want to be loved, are out there being abused by the thousands. Am I saying every pit bull is sweet and docile?

No. I think I proved that in this story. But they are also not all the killers they've been portrayed as in the media.

I just wanted to reassure you that the real Hannah is alive and well and thriving in her new home, just like the fictional Hannah in this story.

Also by Susan Stoker

SEAL of Protection: Legacy Series

Securing Caite
Securing Brenae (novella)
Securing Sidney
Securing Piper (Sept 2019)
Securing Zoey (Jan 2020)
Securing Avery (TBA)
Securing Kalee (TBA)

Delta Force Heroes Series

Rescuing Rayne
Rescuing Aimee (novella)
Rescuing Emily
Rescuing Harley
Marrying Emily
Rescuing Kassie
Rescuing Bryn
Rescuing Casey
Rescuing Sadie (novella)
Rescuing Wendy
Rescuing Mary
Rescuing Macie (novella)

Badge of Honor: Texas Heroes Series

Justice for Mackenzie
Justice for Mickie
Justice for Corrie
Justice for Laine (novella)
Shelter for Elizabeth

Justice for Boone
Shelter for Adeline
Shelter for Sophie
Justice for Erin
Justice for Milena
Shelter for Blythe
Justice for Hope
Shelter for Quinn
Shelter for Koren (June 2019)
Shelter for Penelope (Oct 2019)

Ace Security Series

Claiming Grace
Claiming Alexis
Claiming Bailey
Claiming Felicity
Claiming Sarah (Sept 2019)

Mountain Mercenaries Series

Defending Allye
Defending Chloe
Defending Morgan (Mar 2019)
Defending Harlow (July 2019)
Defending Everly (TBA)
Defending Zara (TBA)
Defending Raven (TBA)

SEAL of Protection Series

Protecting Caroline
Protecting Alabama
Protecting Fiona
Marrying Caroline (novella)

Protecting Summer
Protecting Cheyenne
Protecting Jessyka
Protecting Julie (novella)
Protecting Melody
Protecting the Future
Protecting Kiera (novella)
Protecting Alabama's Kids (novella)
Protecting Dakota

Stand Alone

The Guardian Mist
Nature's Rift
A Princess for Cale
A Moment in Time- A Collection of Short Stories
Lambert's Lady

Special Operations Fan Fiction

http://www.AcesPress.com

Beyond Reality Series

Outback Hearts
Flaming Hearts
Frozen Hearts

Writing as Annie George:

Stepbrother Virgin (erotic novella)

ABOUT THE AUTHOR

New York Times, *USA Today* and *Wall Street Journal* Best-selling Author Susan Stoker has a heart as big as the state of Tennessee where she lives, but this all American girl has also spent the last fourteen years living in Missouri, California, Colorado, Indiana, and Texas. She's married to a retired Army man who now gets to follow *her* around the country.

She debuted her first series in 2014 and quickly followed that up with the SEAL of Protection Series, which solidified her love of writing and creating stories readers can get lost in.

If you enjoyed this book, or any book, please consider leaving a review. It's appreciated by authors more than you'll know.

www.stokeraces.com
www.AcesPress.com
susan@stokeraces.com

facebook.com/authorsusanstoker

twitter.com/Susan_Stoker

instagram.com/authorsusanstoker

goodreads.com/SusanStoker

bookbub.com/authors/susan-stoker

amazon.com/author/susanstoker

CPSIA information can be obtained
at www.ICGtesting.com
Printed in the USA
FSHW010503140819
61033FS